SEX
DRUGS
& OPERA

ROLAND ORZABAL

Published by Acorn Digital Press Ltd, 2014 in partnership
with Crucial 7th Publishing.

Most of the events and characters in this novel are fictitious,
the rest is not.

ISBN 978-1-909122-71-0

Acorn Independent Press

SEX
DRUGS
& OPERA

ROLAND ORZABAL

THERE'S LIFE AFTER ROCK 'N' ROLL

Special thanks to Tom Bromley, Eve and Jack
at Eve White Literary Agency, Leila, Ali and Harry at
Acorn Digital.

For C, my ghost in the machine.

CHAPTER 1

I'm standing at the window of the Savoy Hotel's river deluxe room 720 watching the London Eye revolve incrementally. Stare too hard and you wonder if it's moving at all. The Eye's pods are lit up and occupied by tiny human shapes, all except one, which is dark and resting at an odd angle; it fails to right itself against the horizon. That's the one to watch, I decide. I mark its progress against the roof of County Hall till the gap between the two no longer exists.

This is a cool room. If you open the window and crane your neck to the right, you can see Big Ben and the Houses of Parliament, smoky tan buildings, edges blunted by the western haze; hold a mirror to the east and you'll glimpse the crisp, reflective glass of The Gherkin, No. 30 St Mary Axe. If the Wizard of Oz lived in London, he would live right there, right at the very top.

It's four twenty-five; the sky is already beginning to darken and the electric lights in the windows of the opposite buildings, the headlights of passing traffic, and the lights of the Eye are slowly turning the city into a fairground. Switch focus and I see, reflected in the window, Jenny, my wife, sitting on the bed, book in one hand, minibar snack in the other. Her blonde hair is pulled back into a short ponytail; she's cosy in her self-knitted wrap and wearing reading glasses that make her look slightly bug-eyed.

'I can't believe the last time we stayed here was twenty-eight years ago,' I say, unsure whether she's listening. 'What a change in the London skyline – not that I can picture what it looked like. We didn't have a view of the river back then, did we?'

'No,' says Jenny, surprisingly attentive, 'but we got bumped up to the honeymoon suite, remember? There was seaweed from the Thames coming out the bath taps in the first room; we had the maid, the head of housekeeping, and the duty manager huddled

1

in the bathroom like a scene from Fawlty Towers, all staring at it, wondering what the hell to do.'

I remember alright. It was April, 1983. My band, Fortune Favours The Brave, were playing at the Hammersmith Odeon at the beginning of a career in pop music that scaled the heights almost immediately, but went into decline following the death of our guitarist, Fran. The rest of the band were staying at The Columbia, a dingy, music biz hotel on the Cromwell Road, but it was Jenny's eighteenth birthday and I really wanted to treat her, wanted her to taste the lifestyle I was beginning to afford.

'Yeah, the seaweed,' I say, 'bright green strings of it, same colour as your hair, wasn't it?'

Jenny puts down her book and reflects for a moment. 'No. Red, or pink, perhaps?'

'I'm sure it was green. What were we wearing at the time?' I ask, turning to face her.

'Katherine Hamnett, Chinese Laundry, Doctor Marten boots. Remember the looks we got in reception?'

'Very clearly. Maybe that's why we never came back?'

There's a flash of anger across Jenny's face. Her frown, her intense bug eyes are telling me I've said the wrong thing. 'Or maybe it's because we split up a week later?' she reminds me. 'What were those Dutch girls called who were always at the front of every gig? Anki and Panki?'

'Anke and Petra,' I correct her, 'you're never gonna let me forget that are you?'

'Nope. I suppose you keep in touch with them on Facebook?'

'I'm not on Facebook. I was twenty-one,' I protest, 'I was a pop star; women were throwing themselves at me. Besides, that year apart made me realise how much I loved you.'

'Loved?' repeats Jenny. She removes her glasses, blows on the lenses and starts polishing them with the corner of a bed sheet.

I'm not sure if she's hurt or simply annoyed that we're here in the first place.

'Love…still do…alright, don't wind me up any more, I'm nervous enough as it is.'

We were in Puglia on one of my Italian-relative-searching missions when I received the email, forwarded to me by my London agent at CAA, a small, chubby ex-stockbroker called Simon Ferris. The email came from a celebrity producer at ITV, a woman called Sylvania Angelopoulos.

Dear Simon,

I am currently working on Series 2 of the ITV hit show Popstar to Operastar. We would love to talk to Solomon Capri about this amazing opportunity. Initially we are looking to start seeing people who are interested in Jan/Feb so they can spend half an hour with our vocal coach to get a feel of their range/vocal tone. This initial meeting is totally non-committal and a chance for us to meet people, to talk about the show and give them a feel for what is involved and what they can achieve. And vice versa for the singers to question us and see if it's something that would interest them. We will then be into casting which we hope to complete in March with the idea of starting training in April. With Solomon's vocal talent, we'd be really keen to see him for the show. We will once again be joined by some of the world's greatest opera stars and there is also talk that The Arts Council would also like to support the 2nd series as they see it as a great way to get to raise the public's interest in classical music. The show is going to be on air in summer on ITV1 with a new day and time slot in the pipeline to make it more 'family' viewing. Look forward to hearing your thoughts,

Kind regards,
Sylvania

I'd seen snippets of the previous series of Popstar to Operastar, but found it at times a little cringeworthy, especially watching some well known faces struggling with the arias and having to face the indignity of an X-Factor style vote-off. In normal circumstances I would have turned this opportunity down, regardless of the fact that I have, in the past, sung a little opera. But it was another ego-sapping argument with Jenny that convinced me I had to start putting myself back in the spotlight again; I had to rediscover some of the rock star swagger that attracted her to me in the first place. Hard to believe, looking at her now that she used to worship me in that fan/idol way. But I guess it's very different gazing adoringly up at someone on stage when they're twenty, to listening to them at forty-nine complain about their piles.

It was at the White Heat Club in Acton, 1982, when I first set eyes on Jenny, when she was just another cute, trendy girl in the audience. FFTB were opening for some second rate, second tier Two-Tone act – God knows why – and the audience was divided between Mods who were hanging on to the past, and New Romantics who were embracing the current trend.

A couple of months before, we'd started picking up a few plays a week on the John Peel show and were gaining a small, mainly female following. That night, however, Fran chose to go on a bender; he'd scored some coke off one of the crew and was already halfway through a bottle of vodka an hour before we were due to go on stage. When we finally did, he just started jumping around like an idiot. I think he was riled or scared by all the Mods and Skinheads who kept calling us pansies, poofs, throwing the odd empty beer can – aimed mainly at him. He wouldn't look at me; he certainly didn't do that flirty eye contact that used to wind me up. To make matters worse, he came on for the encore – yes, we had an encore – in a dress.

The gig was appalling as far as I was concerned, a complete disaster. But one girl seemed to be enjoying it immensely. She was about ten feet from the stage: blonde, backcombed hair, short at the back and sides, wearing a furry, purple sweater and a very short skirt. Somehow she'd created a space for herself. No one was pushing into her; everyone seemed to leave her alone. And she danced not in a frenetic, angular way, but smoothly, sexily, as though she was listening to a different style of music entirely. And she wouldn't take her eyes off me. After the show, I went looking for her while the Two-Tone band were skanking away on stage, but she was nowhere to be seen. It wasn't until the next gig, when she showed up again, this time right down the front, that I managed to talk to her, that I found out her name was Jennifer Whittaker, and that, rather embarrassingly, she was still at school.

And then we started dating: lunch in the Wimpy Bar and long walks on Clapham Common. She wouldn't have sex with me for the first two months, but she'd sometimes stay the night, cuddle up, frustrate the hell out of me in cheap hotel rooms that always smelled of smoke, with Fran pretending to be asleep, secretly wanking in the other twin bed. Then, when the gigs and the crowds got bigger, she liked to stand side-stage, kiss me and wish me luck as I walked on to whoops and cheers. 'You don't need luck when you're Solomon Capri,' I used to say. And then she'd smile that besotted smile. We've come a long way since then, Jenny and I. We have a son, a daughter, and a huge country pile just outside Wells, Somerset. But because of her business, and the money it brings in, music is now just a glorified hobby for me; I don't really have to work at all. Yet I miss it, miss those unpredictable visits from the muse; miss the connection I had with Fran as well. Maybe it's wrong to want more than you have, maybe I'm being foolish, but I'd swap a great chunk of my life as it is now just to have her look at me the way she used to, just to regain the spark we felt when we first fell in love.

The idea of Popstar to Operastar is to take eight pop singers with little or no experience in the world of opera, coach them, then have them compete against each other for the public's vote. There are two professional classical singers who guide the celebrities: Rolando Villazón, a Mexican-born tenor, and Katherine Jenkins, a mezzo-soprano from Wales: "mentors" who explain the subtleties of the arias, the meaning behind the Italian or French lyrics, and also co-judge the result. One of my problems with the first show was that the additional judges seemed a random choice: Meat Loaf, that beefy cartoon of a rock singer, and a man called Laurence Llewelyn-Bowen, who, unless I'm mistaken, is an interior designer. Regardless, I told Simon, my agent, I was definitely up for an initial meeting, then started communicating with Sylvania directly.

> *Hi Solomon,*
> *Just to let you know the format of the meeting. A chat with our Exec producers will be followed by an informal 20 min session with our vocal coach to establish your range, so we will be doing some vocal exercises. This is really good for you to get an idea of what to expect if you took part, as we have a go at an operatic verse of a song. It's really laid back and fun!*
> *Thank you,*
> *Sylvania x*

Well, at least she signed off with a kiss; it's more than my agent got. I imagined what Sylvania looked like. Obviously Greek like her name suggested, I saw a short, dark young woman, glamorous and formal like a stewardess on Olympic Air, with thick, ink-black hair, heavy eyebrows, a soft, sexy vellum moustache, perhaps. Yet when we spoke on the phone, there was no trace of a Greek accent; she was polite, well educated, flirty even.

'Hi, Solomon, thanks for letting me have your mobile number, promise I won't start sexting you.'

I wasn't entirely sure if she'd said, 'sexting' or 'texting.'

'Are you still OK with the five o'clock slot?'

'Is there a choice?'

'Not really.'

'Then I'm fine with it. Will you be there?'

'Wouldn't miss it for the world.'

It's four-thirty and almost time for me to leave, however, Jenny fancies a glass of white wine and is too comfortable to move. I grab a bottle of Chablis from the minibar, try to open it, but all I manage to do is snap the handle off the corkscrew and leave the screw in the cork, and the cork in the bottle.

'Sorry,' I say, 'it must be the nerves.'

Jenny sighs and starts leafing through the drinks menu for an alternative. While she's on the phone to room service, I head into the bathroom for one last look in the mirror. I add a little wax to my curls, a little concealer under my eyes. All the time I'm preening, I'm doing my vocal warm-ups, the same ones I would do before a show, and the same ones I was taught by an opera coach at the age of seventeen. Scales, up and down, quiet at first, solemn, controlled, then building in volume to a vibrato-rich, operatic roar. It fills the bright, mirrored room, makes my chest vibrate and my sinuses itch. It's loud as hell and Jenny is complaining; something about the people in the next room, so I shift to a quiet falsetto.

There's a car waiting for me downstairs: a Mercedes S-class, the same one that drove us up from Somerset. The driver's name is Mo. It's four thirty-five and by now he'll be outside.

'Good luck with the audition!' I hear Jenny shout as I head out the door.

'It's not an audition,' I yell back, 'it's an initial meeting!'

Besides, you don't need luck when you're Solomon Capri.

CHAPTER 2

I stride down the hall and into a twenties-style elevator, the walls of which are lined with a deep red velvet. I press 'G' and it begins to whirr like Doctor Who's Tardis, before descending and landing with a clunk. On the ground floor, I walk past a function room with the word *Iolanthe* painted on its beige door, past another bearing the name *Gondoliers*. Strange, but I didn't make the connection between the show and the hotel when I booked the room. I'd forgotten, completely forgotten about the history of the Savoy: the Savoy Theatre, Gilbert and Sullivan, the D'Oyly Carte. Along with Joy Division, the music of Gilbert and Sullivan was part of my youth: seventeen years old, local comprehensive, press-ganged into playing the Pirate King, headhunted by the local operatic society, headhunted further by a local opera coach. "Amazing Bass," the Evening Post had written following a performance of Handel's *The Trumpet Shall Sound*. No one believes me when I tell them, they just see some middle-aged, long-haired rock star type. They can't quite place my name, yet they recognise the face and with a little jog of the memory they'll start humming *Dust in the Attic* or any one of Fortune Favours' greatest hits.

It's not far across the river to the south bank of the Thames, just a short ride down Victoria Embankment, and then across Westminster Bridge. With Mo at the wheel, we sweep past the London Eye and I get a superb view of its underbelly from the back of the Merc. I wind down the window and take a snap with my iPhone. Mo drops me off just outside the ITV studios reception. I walk through the glass doors and approach one of the female receptionists.

'Hi, I have a meeting with Sylvania at five o'clock. I'm a little early. Solomon Capri?'

The young woman has strikingly clear turquoise eyes, which suddenly glaze over. 'Mmm, Sylvania,' she says as though she were about to tuck into a cream cake. 'Look into the camera, please,' she says, 'it's for your security pass.'

Security pass in hand, I retreat to what appears to be a café-style area and sit down in front of four suspended plasma screens airing the four ITV channels. On the back wall are two giant display boards: one, featuring the X-Factor judges, the other, Ant and Dec on a rope bridge in the Australian jungle. I'm fifteen minutes early and reality is kicking in. These images, larger than life, are making me feel small. Those last minute nerves really start to kick in and I'm thinking that even with the best will in the world, I could still get chewed up by the big ITV machine and spat out the other side…a loser.

Bang on five o'clock, a slip of a girl wheels through the security turnstile. She heads straight for me. 'Solomon Capri?'

I stand, somewhat relieved, and say, 'Yes.'

'Follow me.'

It's not obvious when you walk in, but the ITV studios are a vast labyrinth of internal and external corridors weaving through interconnecting buildings, past offices, sound booths, control rooms, theatres and rehearsal spaces. We've been walking for five minutes and I have no idea where I am. We pass only one other person along the way: a tall, heavy-jawed woman in a red leather jacket. Could that be Sylvania? No, she would have said something. I'm beginning to feel increasingly uncomfortable and have to mentally step outside of who I am and where I am. I picture myself, not as an eighties pop star, but as Pavarotti. My gait becomes slower, heavier; I suddenly feel bloated. I see plates of pasta piled high on a table in front of me, a serviette tucked into my collar, spaghetti spilling from my mouth. I'm sitting across from Bono and talking about the plight of the people of Sarajevo, the massacre of Srebrenica, except he can't understand a word I'm

9

saying. He doesn't speak Italian and I have spaghetti in my mouth. My ancient, Italian eyes are heavy with black make-up, which these days I don't even bother to remove. I take out my virtual handkerchief and mop the imagined sweat from my brow.

The vision evaporates when we arrive at a door, which the girl opens, inviting me inside before retreating back down the hall. The room is windowless, lit by fluorescent light, the way I imagine the War Room in No. 10 Downing Street to be. There are three people seated behind a long boardroom table: two well groomed men in their late thirties/early forties and one rather stunning young lady in her mid to late twenties; her face would not look out of place on the cover of Vogue magazine. This must be Sylvania, I think. All three rise to greet me, but stay pretty much where they are. The man in the middle holds out his hand.

'Steven Paul,' he says in a theatrical Scottish accent. His hair is short, mousey, and he's wearing, what looks like, a fashionable version of a cricketing jumper.

'Nice to meet you,' I reply, and then address the other man, 'and you are?'

'Paul…Steve and Paul.' He too has a theatrical, though south-of-the-border accent, but is decidedly more rugged with designer stubble and acne scars.

'Oh, I see. Sorry. Steve, Paul, got you.'

I get the impression that Steve and Paul are a tight unit.

'And this is Marissa,' says Steve.

Not Sylvania, after all. Marissa, I sense, has a little Asian in her background with those almond-shaped eyes. She's utterly desirable.

'Hi Melissa.'

'Marissa,' she corrects me.

'Sylvania sends her apologies,' says Steve, 'she's a little tied up at the moment.'

'No problem,' I say.

We all sit down.

'Thanks for doing this, Solomon, did you have to come far?'

'My wife and I drove up from the West Country this morning; we're staying at the Savoy, just across the river.'

'Fab. They've done a great job with that. The foyer is lovely. Sylvania loves the Savoy; you never know, you might bump into her.'

There's a smirk on everyone's face. I don't get it.

'So, you've seen the show, what did you think?'

'Well,' I reply, taking a deep breath, 'I think a lot of things. Firstly, it's a great concept, but it needs a bigger budget and better singers. I mean, in one of Sylvania's emails she mentioned the Arts Council getting involved, believing the show will raise public interest in classical music. But, I don't see how you're going to achieve that with performances like the one by that…that cheese-making bass player, who isn't a singer, and, quite frankly, made a fool of himself, or maybe the show made a fool out of him.'

Marissa is looking at me deadpan. Steve and Paul are looking bemused.

'Surely you have to decide what you're trying to achieve,' I continue undeterred, 'light entertainment, a bit of cringeworthy fun, or something a little more highbrow? Then take the show's winner: it's common knowledge he started off in Scottish Opera, then did a couple of dodgy talent shows, then made a dodgy record. But he's not a pop star, he's a professional contestant.'

'Sounds like you should be on this side of the table,' says Paul.

'Yeah, well…I feel pretty passionate about it. I sang classically when I was in my teens, I did months of intense vocal coaching; my uncle was a professional opera singer in Milan…' OK, that was a lie. '…If Fortune Favours hadn't taken off so quickly, I may well have gone into opera.'

'Wow,' says Steve, 'I didn't know that. Love your band by the way. I used to have such a crush on Fran, your guitarist.'

11

'Me too,' says Paul.

My instincts were correct.

'Lots of people had a crush on Fran,' I reply, 'male and female. He was supremely androgynous, destined to never grow old.'

'The two of you had such a strong writing partnership,' says Steve.

'Such a strong connection on stage,' adds Paul, 'all that flirty eye contact.'

Steve and Paul imitate the flirty eye contact. I know exactly what they're referring to. I've lived most of my professional life with these unfounded rumours.

'Yeah, Fran was my best friend,' I admit, trying to ignore the lump in my throat that forms whenever I start talking about him, 'I've never been closer to anyone spiritually. I was by his bedside when he passed...the last person he spoke to.'

'Must have been terrible,' suggests Paul.

'We've both lost a few friends to AIDS,' says Steve.

'Yeah,' I reply, suddenly forgetting I'm being interviewed, 'it was heart breaking.'

'But you're still playing, touring?' asks Steve, trying to lighten the conversation.

'Every once in a while,' I reply, 'we kinda have iconic status in some parts of the world – The Philippines, Ecuador...Latvia.'

'But not in England,' says Marissa. The beautiful guard dog speaks and it's a put-down.

'No,' I reply. Something tells me Marissa doesn't like me. Hopefully she's just an assistant or something.

'So, let me tell you a little about the schedule,' Steve continues. 'Voice coaching will begin mid-April, we start filming with the mentors around mid-May, and then the show airs early June.'

'Perfect,' I say, 'I'm not touring again till the autumn.'

'Any questions, any concerns?'

'Will the judges be the same?'

Steve laughs as though he knows exactly what I mean. 'The judges aren't confirmed yet,' he says tactfully. 'There are also lessons in Italian and French pronunciation, plus you'll be working with a choreographer to get you moving about on the stage.'

'Well, the Italian won't be a problem,' I reply, 'I'm fluent. And my mother was a choreographer: modern dance and ballet... should give me a head start.'

'My word,' says Steve, widening his eyes, 'you *are* the real deal.'

'Thanks. I just feel there's an element of destiny in all this; it's like my life is turning full circle.'

'Right. So are you ready to spend a little time with our vocal coach?' he asks. 'Just to warn you, you will be filmed. It's for us all to watch back later; we won't be in the room.'

'Fine by me, I've been warming up all day.'

She must be on a pager or something, because precisely at that moment, the girl who delivered me to the room, appears at the door, to escort me elsewhere. I say goodbye to the three of them, and they all wish me luck. I'm tempted to say, 'You don't need luck when you're Solomon Capri,' but I realise that, maybe on this occasion, I do.

Luckily, it's only two corridors and two flights of stairs to the next room. The girl knocks on the door, stands out the way like there's a bomb inside, and nudges me to go in without introduction. I poke my head round the door and see a handsome, motherly, large chested, middle-aged, blonde woman sitting at an upright piano, and a young cameraman standing against the back wall of a room, which is no more than ten feet square and fully soundproofed. Right in front of me is, what looks like, a chair from a junior school classroom.

'Ready for one more,' I ask the woman, 'or have you had enough for the day?'

'Oh,' she replies, feigning exhaustion, 'I think I could just about squeeze another one in. I'm Jo, by the way,' she says, standing up to offer her hand, which I take. I'm not sure she knows who I am, and I'm not sure how many people she's seen before me. She seems pure opera, pure coach, probably never listened to The Beatles, let alone Fortune Favours The Brave.

'Solomon Capri,' I say, but she doesn't reply. In fact, she seems a little wary of me, nervous, perhaps.

Jo asks me to take a seat. Now, she's not very tall and this chair must have been built for a Munchkin, but I do as I'm asked and sit with my legs splayed in front of me. Jo then stands behind me and places her hands on my shoulders. The camera has been rolling since I walked in and it's still rolling as Jo's strong hands begin to massage my deltoids.

'Just let your head drop forward,' she says, 'relax, take a deep breath.'

This is weird: I thought I was here to do some singing, not take part in an antenatal class.

'So have you sung any opera before?' she asks, her thumbs pressing into the nape of my neck. Mmm, that feels good.

'When I was a teenager,' I reply.

'Tenor?' she asks, hands moving up to my temples, shaking my head gently, physically encouraging me to loosen my neck.

'Bass-Baritone. I played the Pirate King in a school production of *The Pirates of Penzance*.'

'That's how I started,' she replies, pushing me forward a little so she can work on my back, 'Gilbert & Sullivan. Now…I want you to take another deep breath, then breathe out and sing a note, any note that feels comfortable.'

This is all very silly. Maybe it's some test to see how flexible I am, literally and metaphorically. Again, I do as I'm asked and produce a very weak note, which is more confusing than revealing. I'm a little embarrassed; this is not how I sing. Immediately, Jo leaves me half-massaged, sings the same note, and rushes to the piano. She prods away for a second, trying to locate that note, which she does eventually, and then asks me to stand.

'Let's try some scales,' she says, settling herself on the piano stool.

She hits a piano key and with the most glorious and wholesome operatic tone sings a scale for me. It's such an inspiring sound, I could marry this woman right now – the massage, the voice, I bet she even rolls her own pasta. I copy her, or the notes, at least. The scales get higher and higher; Jo has the lungs of a deep-sea diver, the rallying cry of Boudicca, but she's dragging me way out of my range. When is she going to realise that I'm not a bloody tenor?

Right now, it seems.

She drops half an octave and then I'm in my comfort zone, really singing out, loud, strong, with a practised operatic tone, nailing the scales, almost matching her for volume. I realise the nerves I've been trying to hide are adding an emotional, passionate quality to my singing. Suddenly, I'm not doing vocal exercises, I'm lamenting the death of my father, the death of Fran, pulling from some well of grief within. Jo compliments me, she seems impressed; are those tears in her eyes? I notice the cameraman is smiling and nodding.

'Do you read music?' Jo asks. Even she's smiling now, looking at me like I'm not just another pop star she hasn't heard of. There's a small pile of sheet music on the piano, which she browses before settling on something.

'Yes I do,' I reply.

She hands me a piece. I study the title, 'Caro Mio Ben,' it reads in Italian. 'My dear beloved,' I say, pretty much to myself.

'You know it?' asks Jo.

'No, I was just translating it. My father was Italian.'

'I see, that could come in very handy,' she admits.

'Very handy,' adds the cameraman.

Fifteen minutes and two arias later, Jo seems thrilled and announces that she's heard enough. She jumps up from the piano stool and hugs me like I'm a long lost member of her family. 'What a lovely way to end the day. I do hope you'll be joining us,' she gushes.

The cameraman is saying the same thing, 'So you think you'll do it?'

I'm not sure if this could have gone any better. I tell them both I'd be delighted, but something is playing on my mind.

'All that stuff earlier,' I ask Jo, 'with the massage. What was that about?'

'Oh,' she says, slightly embarrassed, 'it was to relax me, not to relax you; to put me in a dominant position, to put me in control. It's simple psychology, really. When I knew you were up next, I got all flustered, I couldn't get that video out of my mind.'

'Which one?'

'The one where you're on a bed in an attic with just a sheet draped over your groin.'

'Dust in the Attic?'

'That's the one. I used to drool whenever that came on the TV...what a body!'

CHAPTER 3

'How did it go?' asks Jenny as I close the door behind me.

'Amazing,' I say, 'my voice sounded incredible. All those warm-ups, all that practising in the studio, really paid off. The voice coach had tears in her eyes.'

'I suppose that's a good sign. Do you think they'll ask you to do it?'

'They'd be crazy not too.'

She looks as if she hasn't moved: still on the bed, reading, with a near empty glass of wine beside her on the bedside cabinet. The only evidence that she has is the rather expensive-looking stripy box on the floor.

'You weren't too opinionated?'

'I was forceful,' I protest.

'Yes, but you know what these TV people are like, they prefer people who are compliant.'

'Compliant? I can do compliant. I've been married to you for twenty-six years.'

'You know what I mean. How was Sylvania…was she as hairy as you imagined?'

I take a moment to think. 'Strange, I never met her. I think it might be some kind of code word like they use in James Bond. Anyway, have you spoken to Raffy? Is he coming to dinner?'

Jenny and I are blessed with a son and a daughter, twins, now twenty years old and both in further education. I think that when they were in the womb, they decided to swap souls. Emilia, or 'Mili,' as we call her, is a clone of Jenny, at least in looks, but with bigger biceps than me. She managed to move as far away from our home in Somerset as possible – without going abroad – by studying Sports Psychology at the University of Aberdeen. She's independent, athletic and strong willed. And then there's

17

Raphael, or Raffy. He's dark haired and maudlin, sensitive, but also strikingly carefree. He's studying fashion at St Martin's College, not too far from where we are right now.

'Yes, I spoke to him, briefly. No, he's not coming to dinner.'

'Why not?'

'He's too upset and doesn't want to darken our evening.'

'Why's he upset?'

'One of his designs got a D. His teacher accused him of plagiarism. As if there's anything original any more.'

'That's harsh. Did you mention the show? I mean, what does he think? Is it gonna make Dad look stupid, or is there some kitsch element that he and his generation might appreciate?'

'He thinks you're going through a mid-life crisis.'

'That's harsh as well. Shouldn't you be getting ready?' I say, 'Table's booked for eight o'clock. I'll phone the restaurant, tell them there's only two of us.'

'I could get used to this,' I say, as we walk past the Savoy's tea store. It's approaching eight o'clock and there are still chocolatiers and pastry chefs sculpting and placing delicacies in the shop window. 'I wonder if they'll pay for me to stay at the Savoy as part of the deal?'

This isn't just memory lane, this is time travel. The foyer is an orgy of art deco with toile de Jouy wall coverings, chinoiserie tables, and paintings invoking Edwardian splendour; portraits by John Singer Sargent, and Bertram Pegram's frieze, *An Idyll of a Golden Age*. There are doormen in top hats with futuristic, clear plastic wires spiralling out of their earpieces, and free-to-roam female receptionists, iPads tucked neatly under one arm. Everyone is smartly dressed, as are we. Jenny is wearing a light grey Chanel suit, a Bulgari blue opal and diamond necklace with matching earrings, *and* her four-carat diamond ring. If you stole her clothes and jewellery and her matching Chanel handbag right now, you'd be walking away with tens of thousands of pounds. And she'd be naked. But her transformation is remarkable: without the reading glasses, her hair twisted into blonde waves and make-up expertly done, even aged forty-four she's been turning heads ever since we got out of the lift.

'New shoes?' I ask, glancing down at Jenny's stilettos, which are making a loud clack, clack, clack sound on the black and white checked floor.

'Yes, Christian Louboutin. I bought them round the corner while you were doing your audition.'

'It wasn't an audition,' I remind her, 'it was an initial meeting… Expensive?'

Jenny looks surprised that I've asked. 'Since when did you start worrying about money?' she replies.

She's right, of course: the fact is I don't. And yet I'm in two minds about the opulence on display: one part of me is proud to have Jenny on my arm, the other resents the fact that she is by far the bigger breadwinner and is pretty much paying for everything right now. I guess my only consolation is the fact that she can't claim to have built the business herself.

Her company, Whittaker Holdings, was formed in 1934, shortly after Ronald James Whittaker registered a patent for, what Jenny likes to call, a feminine hygiene product. He died in 1993. In his will, he left all his physical assets to his son, and there were plenty of them – a large house outside Oxford, a flat in Monte Carlo, a villa in Provence. But to Jenny, his only granddaughter, he bequeathed the offshore company that handles the income stream from the patent, a stream that has been growing steadily year on year. Yes, the royalties from Fortune Favours still trickle in, and the touring income is a nice fillip, but the main reason we are swanning around this place so comfortably is because of a bloody tampon applicator. It's a sore subject, I admit, because, when I was the only breadwinner, I selfishly had Jenny sign a pre-nup; what's mine is mine and what's hers is hers.

The Savoy Grill, like the hotel, has recently been refurbished at considerable expense. The Art Deco theme continues in the light fittings, the carpet has been laid more for durability than effect, but the deep cherry wall panels, framed in chrome, are what give the place its wow factor. They are polished to perfection, or at least, they look that way. Truth is they're made from a high quality plastic, but from a distance, it couldn't matter less. We're continuing our journey back to a different time. Squint your eyes and you can see, at a table in the corner, Noel Coward or Ivor Novello spooning caviar onto a blini or sipping a Martini, cigarette left burning in an ashtray.

As is customary, I allow Jenny to sit with a view of the restaurant. We're handed menus and a wine list, which I immediately peruse, deciding on a 2009 Italian Chardonnay from Tuscany. It's one I'm familiar with: an underrated screw-top by *Isole e Elena*. I then go through the menu, where, for dietary reasons, I choose the smoked salmon as a starter and sea trout as a main.

'Know what you're having?' I ask.

'I think I might have two of the smaller dishes,' she replies, 'caviar and then omelette Arnold Bennet. How about you?'

Before I get a chance to reply, I feel the vibration of an incoming text from the phone in my jacket pocket. I pull it out to see what it says. Curiously, it's from Sylvania.

'Who's the gorgeous blonde?' it reads.

'Who's that?' asks Jenny.

'Sylvania,' I reply, confused.

While I am processing this unexpected and overly familiar message, Jenny is looking over my shoulder, her attention clearly caught. 'There's a lady waving at us,' she says. 'Look, she's on her way over.'

I turn my head and, indeed, a lady is approaching us. Her hair is dark, thick, and styled in a classic Mary Quant bob. Her jacket and skirt are also something from the sixties: a turquoise Crimplenelike material. As she nears, I notice that her eyes are large and chocolate brown, her eyeshadow is light blue and her lashes are heavily mascaraed. She's striking, exotic, with a beautifully sculpted face and a pert little Jacqueline Kennedy nose. Jenny and I stand to greet her and, for a moment, we are transfixed.

'Solomon,' she says, placing a hand on my arm and leaning forward to kiss me on one cheek, then the next. 'I saw you walk in,' she continues, 'what a coincidence. Don't mean to disturb, but I had to say hi. Sorry I couldn't be there today, they were unveiling a waxwork of Catherine Jenkins at Madame Tussauds and she wanted me to go along. So are you staying here or just eating?'

'Staying, we…we live in Somerset. Thought we'd make a day of it.'

'Oh my God, what a beautiful necklace,' she says, addressing Jenny. 'Hi, I'm Sylvania.' She holds out her hand, which Jenny shakes politely while introducing herself. 'My friend, Andreas, is staying here too.'

Jenny and I look around and see a tall, broad-shouldered man with his back to us, seated at a table for two. He's wearing a dark blue suit and has neat, short, grey-blonde hair shaved militarily at the back of the neck.

'Look, why don't we meet up in the American bar for a drink after dinner?'

'That would be great,' says Jenny.

'You look absolutely gorgeous,' says Sylvania to Jenny, reiterating what she said in the text.

'Thank you,' says Jenny blushing, 'so do you.'

Once Sylvania has returned to her table, Jenny can't express her enthusiasm enough, 'Wow, she's a stunner. I'd better keep an eye on you.'

'Hmm,' I say, 'I think you'd stand more of a chance with her than me. Did you notice the way she was looking at you?'

'No, what do you mean?'

A suspicious, 'Hmm,' is all I can muster.

'How old do you think she is?' asks Jenny.

'Mid-thirties,' I reply, 'hard to tell with so much make-up on.'

'What do you think's going on with her and Andreas?' she continues.

'No idea,' I shrug, 'maybe she does a nightshift as an escort girl?'

'I wonder how much she is?' says Jenny quietly, eyes on the menu.

An hour later and Jenny is toying with her omelette. 'So filling,' she groans. She's anxiously looking around the room between sips of wine, when suddenly her face lights up. I turn and see Sylvania and Andreas heading for the exit, Sylvania is smiling and waving at Jenny. Andreas, a rock of a man, is looking straight ahead with a stern, furrowed brow and a protracted jaw as though he's about to enter a boxing ring.

'Not boring you, am I?' I say once they're out of sight.

'No, why?'

'You seem a little distracted.'

'I'm just full. Can't eat any more. How's the sea trout?'

'Bony,' I reply.

'I don't know why you chose it. You don't even like fish.'

'No, but I'm gonna have to lose a bit of weight if I do this programme.'

Jenny's smirk seems designed to undermine my confidence; she clearly doubts my willpower and, I'm beginning to suspect, has reservations about the show. It's also clear she's in no mood for dessert or coffee or any more of my small talk, so I order the bill. While I wait, she heads off to the Ladies to touch up her make-up. I too need the loo, so agree to meet her in the bar.

It seems to take an age for the bill to arrive, but it does, eventually. I settle it with a credit card, leave a generous cash tip on the table, and, following a brief sortie to the Gents, head off in search of my wife.

The American Bar, though possessing none of the magnificence of the foyer or the Grill, manages to maintain an air of exclusivity. Early evening, you'll be lucky to get a table and it's often a case of even celebrities and rich businessmen having to queue in a line down the corridor. However, it does thin out later in the evening and I only have to wait a couple of minutes before I get to speak to the manageress manning the rostrum.

'Capriati,' I say, 'I'm a guest here, room 720. My wife and friends are already seated, I believe.'

Once inside, I spot Jenny, Sylvania and Andreas huddled around a table in the corner of the second room. Sylvania and Jenny are seated next to each other, already deep in conversation, hands occasionally touching. Andreas looks on, dwarfing them both; opposite is an empty chair.

'Don't get up,' I say, but unfortunately Andreas does, offering me a giant hand, then crushing my own within the ritual of a handshake.

'Andreas,' he says with a distinct Germanic lilt, a sharp tilt of his head and…is that a click of his heels?

'Solomon,' I reply, 'nice to meet you.'

'Ah, Solomon,' he says in a tone of recognition; he seems to know who I am, maybe Sylvania clued him in? That puts me a little more at ease. 'This is a Hebrew name,' he continues, 'son of David, first mentioned in the Book of Kings. And then we have the Judgement of Solomon as depicted in a famous painting by William Blake.'

'Right,' I reply – maybe he doesn't know who I am? – 'I did know that.'

'So how is your judgement, Solomon?' He glances at Jenny. 'Pretty good, it seems, when it comes to women.' And then he bellows with laughter. I try to laugh along.

'So are you Sephardic or Ashkenazi?' he asks, once the laughter, both self-congratulatory and fake, subsides.

'Pardon?'

'Are you a Sephardic or Ashkenazi Jew?'

'Oh…a little bit of both.'

Now, this man is serious; it's like he's standing on the balls of his feet ready to sprint off at any second. His left hand is on his left hip, keeping his jacket open enough to reveal his belt, and his shirt tucked neatly into his bulging trousers. There is no hint of a gut; his stomach is firm and absolutely flat. I notice Jenny glance at his groin. For fuck's sake Jenny! He must be around the same age as me, if not older, but there's an athleticism there, which I don't possess, perhaps from a youth filled with Alpine skiing or some genetic experiment in the Second World War. In this light, his face looks red as though he is flushed with anger or arousal; his eyes are small, piercing blue-grey rivets.

'But your wife is not a Jew,' he continues.

That really doesn't sound good with a German accent. Surely he must know that?

'No,' I reply, 'but she's very much into Jewish mysticism, Kabbalah? A bit like Madonna. In fact she's into Madonna as well…OK, maybe not so much these days, not since she did that Abba mash-up and was dancing around a gym with a fourteen-year old girl's bottom…not dancing with the bottom itself, I mean… her bottom looked like a fourteen-year old girl's…not that I know what a fourteen-year old girl's bottom looks like…it's just, that's what people were saying at the time…Anyway…Kabbalah…'

Andreas nods, clearly having lost interest, and thankfully sits back down. I too sit and exchange greetings with the ladies.

'How do you know Sylvania?' he asks, as though my knowing her is a threat to his security. Maybe he's cheating on his wife?

'Oh,' I reply, 'I don't really know her. Just a few emails and the odd conversation; a program she's working on at ITV – Popstar to Operastar?'

'Yes, yes,' says Andreas, clearly unimpressed, 'So you are an opera singer?'

'No, a pop singer.'

I think I just went down in his estimation, if there was any space left.

'It must be very difficult to make money out of the music business these days,' he suggests – snidely, in my opinion.

'Well,' I reply, putting on my best poker face, 'luckily I don't have to worry about money.'

He's staring at me like he's about to call my hand. 'Yes, your wife was telling us about her company. You're a very lucky man.'

'In more ways than one,' I say, not blinking.

I can't believe it, in less than ten minutes she's told them all about her fucking windfall of a business. Although she's probably claiming it was all her own work. I bet she never used the words, 'inheritance' or 'tampon' once. Thanks Jenny, thanks for making me look like a spent force, a kept man. No wonder all eyes are on her.

'And she is very beautiful,' Andreas continues, 'who is her surgeon?' He guffaws and slaps me with the outside of his fingers on the inside of my knee, just to test my humour and manliness.

'No surgery,' I reply, trying not to wince, 'no Botox, just Pilates and moisturiser and plenty of staff. What are we drinking?' I notice that all three have the same drink. I pick up the drinks menu but struggle to read it in the dim light.

'Millionaire's Cocktail, have you tried one?'

'No. What's in it?'

'Money,' he replies with a sneer.

With a flick of his hand, he summons the waitress and orders me a drink.

'God, this is strong,' I say upon the first sip, but Andreas isn't listening, tuning instead to the conversation between Sylvania and my wife. 'So where are you from?' I ask, and then have to ask again a little louder before his head swivels back.

'Basel,' he snorts, 'in Switzerland.'

'Like Roger Federer,' I retort.

'Who?'

'Roger Federer, the famous tennis player?'

'Oh yes, yes. Federer. He is very good, very good.'

But his eyes are not on mine; they are roaming, crawling over my wife like invisible tentacles. Of course, she's not just beautiful, she has money! Is this guy some kind of vampire, is he a leech? More drinks arrive; I'm finding it hard to keep up. After a short burst of conspiratorial, teenage whispering, Jenny and Sylvania both stand up, bags tucked under their arms.

'Off to the loo,' says Jenny with an embarrassed shrug.

'OK,' I reply, not relishing being left alone with Andreas. Clearly he is not keen either and it's only a few seconds before he excuses himself as well.

In their absence, I help myself to some nuts and try once again to read the drinks menu. I find the cocktail and eventually make out the ingredients: sloe gin, apricot brandy, and Jamaican rum. It's not mixing well with the fish in my stomach; I feel queasy, a little drunk and a little sorry for myself. *I* should be talking to Sylvania, I think, not my wife. I should be asking her about the programme, who else they've asked along for an initial meeting, what stupidity and trauma I'm letting myself in for. But the three of them return together and it's hard to get a word in or make decent conversation with Andreas. He just keeps ordering drinks and ogling my wife.

'We should head up,' I say to Jenny, admitting defeat. She's wide-awake; her eyes are sparkling and, due to Sylvania, I suspect, her tongue and her spirit have been chemically freed.

'Half an hour?' she says sheepishly.

I look at her, exasperated.

'You go ahead,' she adds, 'I'll be right up.'

In the morning, I'm woken by the sound of Jenny moving about in the bathroom. I see light breaking through a gap in the curtains and I look at the clock. It's ten-thirty. I'm surprised she's already up considering she came back to the room at half past four, something she doesn't realise I'm aware of. I can hear the beep of her hair tongs; her GHD's. She's doing her hair. Why? I thought we were having breakfast and then heading straight back down to Somerset. I hear the tri-tone marimba of an incoming text message. It's from her phone in the bathroom. Two minutes later, there's another.

'Who's that?' I shout.

'Oh, you're awake,' she replies. 'It's Raffy, he wants to meet up for an early lunch.'

'Lunch? It's only ten-thirty.'

'Late breakfast then…brunch.'

I sigh loud enough for her to hear. It's not that I don't want to see my son, it's just the earlier we leave, the less chance we'll have of getting stuck in traffic. 'I thought we were gonna drive straight back down to the West Country. I booked the car for noon.'

'He needs his mum. You know what he's like.'

'Oh I get it. He wants to have lunch with you, not you and me. What am I supposed to do, go to an art gallery, the British Museum, the London Eye?'

Jenny comes out of the bathroom for a second. It's hard to see her with the curtains closed. 'Look,' she says, 'why don't you take the car home and I'll come down on the train later.'

'You don't mind?' I ask. 'I'll take your suitcase if you like.'

'No, it's OK, I've got my book in it, might want to read it on the train.'

'What time did you get in last night?' I ask, trying to catch her off guard.

27

There's a pause. 'Oh,' she replies, heading back inside the bathroom where I can't see her, 'must have been half an hour after you, maybe a bit longer. You were snoring your head off. I had to put in earplugs.'

So there's the lie. But what do I do? Hot-headed Italian father, cool English mother, lukewarm, half-English Solomon. Yet I hear my father's voice urging me to confront my wife, call her a liar, *una puttana*, spray accusations, reduce her to tears. What happened in those hours, those missing, secret hours with Sylvania and Andreas? What time did the bar close? No later than two, I'm sure. They went back to his room, it's obvious. There were drugs, they had sex. The way Sylvania was looking at my wife, the way Andreas was looking at my wife, it's fucking obvious.

'Sorry dear,' I reply, 'I was pooped.'

'You've got to do something about it,' she continues, raising her voice from the bathroom. 'It got so bad at one point, I went downstairs and tried to get another room.'

'Really? What time?'

'Must have been about four. No joy though.'

Now I'm confused. Is this an elaborate excuse, a carefully worked out back up plan if I did wake up? What was she wearing? I try and think back. But it was dark, too dark and I was pretending to be asleep. Benefit of the doubt on this one…with reservations.

'Where are you taking Raffy?'

'There's a funky new place in Covent Garden called Machiavelli. A friend of Sylvania's designed it. She says hi, by the way.'

'What? How is she saying hi? Through what medium is she speaking? You exchanged numbers, didn't you?'

'What's wrong with that? We got on really well, and, besides, I may well have made sure that you get to do the programme.'

What the fuck? I think. 'Oh, I see, so I get on the programme not because I can sing opera but because of your sudden lesbian leanings. You're fucking unbelievable.'

'That's not what I meant. Look Solomon, there are more than fifty people auditioning, Sylvania told me. Think of any eighties or nineties pop star whose career has waned and they would have been invited. Think of all the X-Factor winners who sank without a trace, they would have been asked too. Think of all those boy or girl bands that are no longer together, it's a huge catchment area. Anyway, why are you so hostile this morning? I was the one being kept awake all night.'

'I bet you were,' I say, under my breath.

'Don't want to argue Solomon. I had a fantastic time last night and I'm not going to feel guilty because you didn't. Enjoy your breakfast. I'll tell Raffy you send him your love.'

And with that, Jenny puts on her coat, grabs her small suitcase and heads out the door.

'You've left your GHD's,' I shout, 'I can hear them beeping.' But she can't hear me and she's not interested. She knows I'll do an idiot check before I leave the room, an idiot doing an idiot check.

CHAPTER 4

'Travelling on your own, Solomon?' I'm in the back of the car heading home to the West Country when Fran's girlish voice suddenly pops into my head. 'Jenny staying up in London?' he adds. I know what he's trying to do, he's trying to get under my skin, to reinforce the doubts in my head. I always felt he was jealous of Jenny and me.

'Yes, Fran,' I reply, as though he's sitting in the car beside me, 'she's having lunch with our son, Raffy. You never met him, did you? It's a shame, you have a lot in common.'

I realise I'm dreaming, albeit lucidly – must have drifted off listening to my latest download, *Seasons Of My Soul*, the debut album from a sultry voiced woman called Rumer. The music has stopped but my headphones are still in my ears and there's a strange buzzing sound coming from the one in the left.

Fran dismisses me with a chuckle. 'She's up to something... you know she is,' he continues, 'always liked a bit of a threesome, our Jenny.'

'Fuck off, Fran!'

'Is everything alright, Mr Capriati?' asks Mo, the driver.

I open my eyes and catch his look of concern in the rear view mirror. 'Oh, yes,' I say, 'sorry, must have been talking in my sleep.'

Last time I looked out the window we were on the A303 hurtling past Stonehenge, now, we're stationary; engine running, momentarily parked in front of a pair of black, wrought iron gates. My mood suddenly lifts, this is my sanctuary, my castle, this is where Jenny and I raised the kids, where we hide from the big, bad world.

It's not a mansion but it's certainly impressive. Sunnymore, a handsome, nine-bedroomed rough-stone building, parts of which date back to 1467. The previous owners added, what was considered at the time to be, a modern wing. God knows how they got planning permission. But because they did, we've been toying with it ever since and we really have the best of both worlds, cottage charm in certain areas and a large, bright, marble-floored, half-dome conservatory with breath-taking views across the valley. There's also an outbuilding, which, until recently, was a recording studio with every conceivable electronic toy, thirty or so guitars, and pretty much the history of the electronic keyboard scattered in workstations around the walls. The big recording console was bought from Paul McCartney; I had a live drum room and a dry booth for vocals and guitar. But that's all gone now; Jenny decided one day it was a waste of space. Now, it's been turned into a swanky, architecturally designed two bedroom, guest accommodation, with state of the art kitchen, a small gym, a 68-inch TV, and a walk-in shower room with blue limestone walls. I still call it 'The Studio' but Jenny has renamed it 'The Pad.' I just think she has an obsession with feminine hygiene products.

There's also a gatehouse cottage where our lovely family from El Salvador live: Rosa, our housekeeper, Ernesto, her aging husband, who tries his best to look after the grounds, and there's the four girls: Antonia, who's six, Elena, who's nine (ten any day now), Olivia, who's fifteen, and Consuelo, the oldest, who is eighteen. It's like having a second family; they're so warm and open, so damn polite. Here they are now – all except Ernesto – waiting as the gates open, despite the mizzling rain, waving at me and smiling like I've just returned a hero after years at war. I wave back and see Rosa and Consuelo follow the car up the drive and to the house.

'No Mrs Jenny?' asks Rosa as I drop my bag in the hall.

'No,' I reply, 'she stayed in London to see Raffy. He's having a bit of a hard time at the moment.'

'Oh, Raffy,' coos Rosa with great affection, her coos echoed by Consuelo, 'is he OK?' They adore him, all the girls do, even

Ernesto, with his shady El Salvadorian past, does. It was so rewarding watching them grow up together, watching the girls chase Raffy around the garden, swim with him in the river, play catch on the tennis court, his sister looking on from a window in disgust. It's a shame that Mili did not feel the same, a shame she's the only one that refers to the Velasquez family as staff.

'Yes, he's OK, nothing to worry about, just stuff at college.'

'Oh, good. And when Mrs Jenny return?'

'Some time this evening. She's coming down on the train.'

'I will prepare chicken and red peppers and avocado for this evening?'

'Sounds wonderful.'

'Are you hungry now?'

'I am a little, yes.'

'I make you a sandwich.'

'Oh, actually, do we have any soup, tomato soup? I'm on a diet.'

'You don't need to diet Mr Solomon,' says Rosa, who, one might argue, does.

'No, it's just…for a TV show. I'd like to look a little more slim.'

'A TV show? Oh, Mr Solomon, this is good news!'

The kitchen in the main house is vast, with rough antique flagstones on the floor surrounding a sturdy central oak-topped island crowned with decorative copper pans. There are hanging bulbs of garlic and onions, and bowls of fruit that never gets eaten and always gets replenished. I'm sitting in one corner, in my favourite wing back chair in a seating area surrounding the only modest TV in the house. I hear the sounds of panting and the pitter-patter of feet as the dogs scamper in and up to me – a barrel-chested Jack Russell called Smooch and a grouchy lurcher called Kipper – tongues lolloping, tails wagging, desperate for attention or food. Consuelo, I notice, puts some dried food in their bowls and they scamper off to see if it's worth eating. She doesn't miss a trick, Consuelo. She's like her mother, so attentive and servile, spoiling me like I'm her lord and master. But she doesn't look like her mother, she has Ernesto's slim frame, his piercing green eyes.

While I wait for the soup, I pick up my laptop and start browsing iTunes. What I'm looking for are the most famous operatic arias sung by a baritone, with the intention of downloading them and burning them onto a CD to listen to in the car. I'm hoping that if I play them over and over again, they will sink into my subconscious and become as familiar as the furniture in this room. I listen to a few excerpts and one aria in particular stands out because I sang it in a competition, which I won, when I was seventeen years old. (Although there were only two people in that competition.) It's called *Non Più Andrai* and it's from Mozart's *The Marriage of Figaro*.

Mozart seems to me to be the most accessible of opera composers. The jump from Gilbert & Sullivan's comic operettas to Mozart's comic operas is not a huge one, aside from the change in language and the lack of spoken dialogue, of course. His melodies are structured and logical, easy to predict. *Non Più Andrai* is no exception and is sung to the rhythm of a march. In the aria, the main character, Figaro, is teasing the young, flirtatious Cherubino, who, as punishment for his womanising, is being packed off to join the army. Figaro sings mockingly about the glories of war to a frightened young man who is usually – or unusually – played by a woman.

The soup arrives courtesy of Consuelo, who places the tray on the coffee table in front of me.

'You're listening to opera, Mr Solomon,' she says, 'I've never heard you do this before.' Consuelo speaks with a strange, soft, West Country accent marked by the odd Spanish inflection, perhaps from constantly switching to it when talking to her parents.

'No,' I reply, 'I'm doing a bit of research. It's all quite exciting. I'll tell you about it later.'

'Yes please,' she says.

'How's it going at Cloud Nine?' I ask.

Consuelo has a part time job at a hairdresser's and beauty salon in Wells. She wants to be a beautician, and for a month or so has been practising her manicures, pedicures, eyebrow plucking, facials and foot massages on Olivia, Rosa and Jenny. She's offered to do the same for me on several occasions (not the eyebrow plucking) but I find it a little too Nabokovian, the thought of some eighteen-year old girl, who I've known since she was ten, rubbing lotion into my feet.

'Very well,' she replies, 'I did my first bikini wax yesterday.' And then she just smiles and walks away. It's amazing how innocent these girls remain; that's Catholicism for you.

Back in these familiar surroundings, I lose all the morning's suspicions and paranoia. I look at the clock on the laptop. It's five twenty-five. I wonder what train Jenny's on and think it would be a nice gesture to pick her up from the train station, maybe give Rosa the night off, and take my wife out to the pub instead. I take the phone out of my pocket and go to call her, but think better of it. She might be napping on the train. So I text her instead, then she can just ignore it and go back to sleep.

Twenty minutes later, I've downloaded and am listening to *Di Provenza il mar, il suol* from Verdi's *La Traviata*. I translate the words in my head pretty much as I hear them. It speaks of destiny taking you away from the place you love. I think of my father as a young man volunteering for the Italian army, of him being torn between loyalty to his country and loyalty to his faith. I remember his stories about fighting the French in the Alps, stories of red blood on white snow, of friends dying or losing limbs, of deafening explosions, and frostbite. Those experiences must have been trauma enough, but when news seeped through that Italian Jews were being stripped of their citizenship, the irony made him physically sick. He made his escape in a Red Cross ambulance through France and then with the help of the French Resistance via the Channel Islands to England. He never returned to Italy and never saw his family again. He also didn't live long enough to see me enjoy success. He died of a heart attack when I was eighteen, a bitter, angry man.

At ten to six I realise Jenny hasn't replied and I'm getting a little anxious because Rosa has begun spicing the chicken thighs. I close the laptop and take my phone with me to the study. I call Jenny, but it goes straight to voicemail. I'm irritated, not quite sure what to say. I hang up and almost immediately she rings back.

'Where are you?' I ask, trying not to sound too pissed off.

'Still in London,' she replies. 'I took Raffy to buy some new clothes; he's so chuffed. Oh, and I bought myself a couple of things as well. Then we went to his flat and I helped him tidy up…what a mess! You would have thought with two female flatmates, it would at least get hoovered and dusted once in a while.'

'Oh, I see, it's just…Rosa is about to cook. Do you want me to delay her? What train are you catching?'

'Actually, darling, I was thinking of staying up another night.'

The suspicions slowly creep back in. 'Why?' I enquire, the word squeaking out of my throat because I'd like nothing more than to command her to return home immediately.

'Um, Sylvania has tickets for *Anna Nicole* at the Royal Opera House.'

Sylvania, I think, of course. 'Since when did you become a fan of opera?'

'Must be catching. It's supposed to be amazing.'

'And I suppose Andreas is going?'

Pause. 'Not that I know of.'

She means yes.

'What's going on between those two?' I probe, trying to eke out any information, any sniff of a *ménage à trois*, 'Are they an item?'

'Sort of. He's going through a messy divorce…lots of money involved.'

'There's a surprise. What does he do?'

'He's kind of a middle man…'

Yeah, right in the middle between you and Sylvania, I think.

'…he sells small companies to big companies and big companies to bigger companies.'

'Great, if he carries on like that, there'll only be one giant company left, then what will he do?'

Jenny doesn't bother to answer.

'So where are you staying?' I continue.

'Oh, I may crash at Sylvania's…she has a spare room.'

'As if you'll need one,' I mumble.

'Look, I'll be back first thing,' she says, 'back before you're even up.'

'You forgot your GHD's,' I say.

'I know…I bought some new ones. See you tomorrow. Love you.'

Wait a minute, at what point did she realise? At what point did she open her case and notice her hair tongs weren't there? Where did she open her case? Where did she leave it? She wouldn't have lugged it around London, that's for sure. She's up to something; Fran was right. I'm beginning to regret staying at the Savoy. It's like history is repeating itself, but with the shoe – the very expensive Christian Louboutin shoe – firmly on the other, size five and female, foot.

CHAPTER 5

There's a big hole in our garden, a swimming pool-sized hole. And it keeps filling up with water. It took six attempts over eight years to get planning permission for a swimming pool. It was only when our architect submitted plans for an eco-pool that we were finally given the green light. By eco-pool, I mean one without chemicals that essentially looks like a natural pond with the odd newt swimming about and tall reeds and lake plants camouflaging it within its natural setting. But then the eco-pool company, Natureflow, went bust. Since then our architect has been going back and forth with the receivers in an attempt to buy up some of the organic seaweed-polyester pool lining that makes the pool not officially a pool. But until he does, the hole remains.

Last December was one of the coldest on record. The bottom of the hole became an ice rink. I tried to stop the Velasquez kids from skating on it but Jenny said she didn't mind as long as Ernesto kept an eye on them. But now it's turned to mud again. I'm worried that someone might fall in – even Smooch: with his big belly and short legs, he'd never get out – so I've had Ernesto put an orange safety fence around it, just in case.

Rosa takes the news of Jenny staying in London stoically. She doesn't ask questions; she just smiles, 'Yes, Mr Solomon,' and gets on with preparing the supper. Consuelo, however, makes eye contact with me in a way I can't quite read. Is it concern? Maybe the arguments between Jenny and me have not been as private as I thought. I try and lighten the mood by suggesting that Ernesto, Antonia, Elena and Olivia come up and eat with the three of us. There seems to be a lot of food, but I know Ernesto is too proud and too shy, and that, as their mother prepares dinner here, Olivia and Elena are cooking *pupusas* or *tamales* in the gatehouse cottage.

There's some short instruction in Spanish from Rosa to Consuelo, and Consuelo asks me if I'd like a glass of wine. I accept graciously and, over the next hour or so, sit at the island and tell them both about my time at ITV and our stay at the Savoy all those years ago.

'I can't believe Mrs Jenny had green hair,' says Consuelo, 'and she was only eighteen…my age now.'

'Yes, and I was only twenty-one.' I expect Consuelo can't imagine me as a young man. 'I have some pictures somewhere,' I add, 'probably in the attic. I'll have a look tomorrow.'

The house phone rings and cuts the conversation short. 'I'll get it,' I say, in case it's Jenny, and rush off to pick it up in the study.

'Hello?'

'Dad?'

'Raffy!'

'No, it's Mili.'

I keep doing that. Their voices are identical, which secretly I think is a problem for them both.

'Oh, hi Mili, how are you? How's Aberdeen?'

'Bloody freezing. How's the swimming pool coming along?'

'Ugh! One big muddy hole still. Probably won't be ready till May.'

'Just in time for the summer. Um, what are you and Mum doing next weekend?'

'I'm not sure, why?'

'I was thinking of popping down with Eric, my new boyfriend.'

I cover the mouthpiece and groan. 'Right. What's he like?'

'Very tall, Scottish…he's a drummer in a band, wants to play you some of their demos. He thinks you'll like it, they're like a modern version of Big Country.'

'I hate Big Country.'

'Dad, why are you being so mean? Anyway, he wants to play you at tennis.'

'Why me? Surely he should be playing you, you're the one who had coaching since the age of eight, you're the daughter of Jennifer Capriati.'

'Old joke, Dad. We have played, but he can't get a game off me.'

'That good is he?'

'Big serve but weak backhand.'

'I'll bear that in mind.'

'Can I have a quick word with Mum?'

'She's not here. She's in London. You might want to try her mobile…in fact, call her on her mobile and ask her who's she's with!' I sound fretful and Mili can hear it.

'Is everything alright, Dad?'

I try and regain my composure. 'Yes, just being silly. Look, I might be doing a TV show…'

'Which one? Where Are They Now?'

'Ha ha. No, it's called Popstar to Operastar. Not sure if you saw the last series?'

'I saw the first show with Alex James,' she replies. 'I hope they're paying you a lot of money to make a fool of yourself like that.'

Money? I didn't even think of that. 'Well…it's not certain, yet. Just toying with the idea.'

Two hours later and I'm back in the study, feet up on a footstool, and with a second bottle of Amarone perched next to me on the side table, by the light. There is an aria playing quietly on my laptop – something demonic in German, which isn't really helping my mood. I'm not really listening to it because of the various strands of thought rattling around my brain, and because I can hear Rosa and Consuelo chatting and whispering in Spanish, doing the last bit of cleaning in the kitchen. Very soon I will be alone in this big old house and I'm preparing myself for the vacuum, for the creaks from upstairs, for the random gurgling from the pipes. I'm not sure why but I feel scared and contemplate asking Rosa and Consuelo to shut the downstairs shutters. But I don't get the chance; I hear the front door close and both of them carrying the leftover food back down the driveway.

To quell the impending silence, I turn the volume of my laptop up and skip on to the next track, a feisty, spirited aria, *Il Cavallo Scalpita* from Mascagni's *Cavalleria Rusticana*. The musical introduction is nervy, nail-biting stuff, slowly building in tension and punctuated randomly by the sound of a whip being cracked. While I listen, I idly surf the Internet. I have a quick read of the Yahoo front page, a glimpse at Google news, and then, once I'm sure of my solitude, navigate to YouPorn. I spend the next minute checking out the thumbnails of the latest additions until I find something I like the look of: a blonde woman, like a younger Jenny, being tossed around a bed by a bronzed, six-packed stud. Suddenly, I don't feel so alone. The sound of a woman being fucked really hard is mixing with the opera, both coming out of my small laptop speakers. There's that crack of a whip again, or is it that guy's hand slapping the woman's arse. I'm surprised no one's thought of this before – a porn opera, a porno with an operatic score, or perhaps they have? Or maybe a series: Pornstar to Operastar, or vice versa. It's perhaps because of these drunken thoughts, because of the laptop's volume, that I fail to notice the footsteps on the gravel drive, the front door open. But I do hear the tap on the study door. Immediately, I slam the laptop shut, killing the ecstatic moans and the masterful warbling of an opera singer long since dead.

'Hello?' I say.

The door opens and Consuelo pops her head through the gap. 'Are you OK, Mr Solomon?'

'Er…yes…yes, I'm fine.' I'm flushed with embarrassment and hiding a rapidly deflating erection under my laptop.

'It's just…it sounded like you were having an asthma attack.'

Such innocence. 'Oh…that. No, just, um, breathing exercises. If I do this show, I'm gonna have to get my lungs working to sustain all those long notes.' And then I cringe at my own ridiculous lie.

'Oh, I see,' says Consuelo who is now feeling safe enough to open the door completely. She looks somehow different from earlier, as though she went back, re-styled her hair, put on a tight tee shirt and applied eye make-up. But I can't be sure; I'm a little drunk and I've been watching porn. She slips further into the room and closes the door behind her, leaning back against it as though she's preventing anyone else from entering. 'Is everything OK with you and Mrs Jenny?' she asks.

'Yes,' I answer automatically, 'why do you ask?'

'You…you seemed upset when you found out she was staying in London.'

My face drops. I can feel it. I'm unmasked by this innocent interrogation. You learn so quickly as a child to hide your feelings. You grow into a young adult and in a safe environment pour those feelings into songs, share them with your partner, exorcise the darker ones in therapy. But then you have kids, and they're the ones with emotions, they're the ones who need looking after; you become the manager, the caretaker, responding to their every whim. Yet here is a girl even younger than my own kids and I feel like a prisoner receiving a visitor for the first time in years. I don't know what to say and I'm desperate not to break down in front of her.

Consuelo ends the silence. 'Would you like a foot massage to relax you before you go to bed?'

I take a deep breath and say to myself, Just go to bed, Solomon, just go to bed, but then I think of Jenny and what she might be up to right now. Fuck it, I think, why the fuck shouldn't I?

'Wakey, wakey, I've brought you a cup of coffee.'

I look up from my pillow. Jenny has been true to her word and has returned home before I'm even up. She places the mug down on the bedside table and sits on the bed beside me. I really have to shake myself awake. I was dreaming about Fran again, we were playing table tennis in some heavenly environment and he was beating me – something he never managed to do when he was alive. He said he'd been having lessons from an American Ping-Pong champion called Dick Miles. One of the perks of the afterlife, I guess.

'What time is it?' I ask Jenny, propping myself up on one elbow.

'It's almost eleven. How was the foot massage?'

'Huh?'

I thought I explicitly asked Consuelo not to mention it to anyone.

'I had a phone call from Mili last night,' Jenny explains, 'she said you sounded uptight, so I rang through to the cottage and asked Consuelo to help you relax a bit while your shameless wife was out on the town having fun.'

Like a madam pimping a young girl, I think to myself, like a puppet master pulling my strings from afar. 'Oh, that. Yeah… it was OK. I just, well, you know me, not a great fan of people touching my feet.'

I'm lying, it was amazing. I didn't even have to unlace my own shoes, I didn't even have to wash my own feet, Consuelo did it all. She even suggested I put on some opera quietly in the background, which I did after erasing my browsing history, and while she was in the bathroom fetching a warm, damp flannel, a towel, and some of Jenny's expensive hand lotion. She was so delicate with my toes, pushing four of her fine fingers through the gaps, bending them backwards and gently rotating my foot at the ankle. She explained how various points on the sole of the feet correlate to the internal organs. She pushed one really hard on my right foot and I yelped. She said that was my liver. She pushed another on the left and it had the reverse effect. I asked her what that was and she just giggled.

'How was *Anna Nicole*?' I ask, keen to deflect the attention, keen to know the intimate details of Jenny's evening.

'Good, but very long. I wanted to nod off in the second half so badly, there's only so much of that kind of music I can take.'

'And how was Andreas?'

I've caught her by surprise, I can see, even in the dim light. There's an uncomfortable pause. From the floor below comes the distant sound of marimbas repeating the same melodic pattern over and over again.

'Oops, that's my phone,' says Jenny jumping up.

How convenient.

I finish the coffee and then get dressed into a dry-fit tee shirt, sweatshirt, tennis shorts, trainers. We have a small gym in the studio with a treadmill, some free weights, a couple of yoga mats and an exercise ball. I haven't done any exercise since October, not even running or tennis, but I reckon I've got 'til mid-May, that's almost three months, to get seriously back in shape.

I don't even bother to brush my teeth, I'll do that a little later. I go down to the kitchen where Jenny is seated at the kitchen table, reading glasses on, her laptop open, phone by her right hand. Smooch is lying under the table, resting his head on her right foot. She loves that dog. Kipper, by contrast, is sulking in his dog bed, clearly desperate for a walk. I grab some more coffee, lean against the island, and try and judge her mood.

'So where did you end up staying?' I ask.

Jenny is busy tapping away at the keyboard. 'At the Savoy again,' she replies without taking her eyes off the computer screen.

'The Savoy?' I repeat, voice cracking slightly.

'Don't worry, it wasn't a suite, and, besides, Andreas paid for it. I didn't ask him to, but I got down to reception this morning and they told me everything had been settled.' She notices what I'm wearing and fails to hide her amusement. 'Playing tennis in the rain?'

'No, I thought I'd get on the tread, try and get rid of some of this,' I grab hold of the spare tyre around my stomach and wobble it crudely.

'That's not like you to worry about how you look naked,' she replies. 'He's invited us skiing, by the way…Andreas, Sylvania too. He owns an eight-bedroom chalet in Verbier. Now *that's* exercise.'

What, I think to myself, hopping from bed to bed?

Jenny knows I hate skiing. I've only been twice. I twisted my ankle the first time and broke a thumb on the second. She, however, does the moguls and the black runs with efficiency and grace. She also knows there's not a chance in hell I'll go.

'When?'

'Next weekend.'

'But that's when Mili's thinking of coming down.'

'I know,' she sighs, 'but you know what she's like, always wants you to herself.'

I'm getting a strange sinking feeling as I stand here in my shorts. Jenny's always been strong-willed, business-like on occasions, but now she seems to be detaching herself from me, and mourning it no more than the loss of a clipped fingernail. Is she falling out of love with me as I approach fifty and the siring and raising of her children is done? Is she getting everything she needs from Andreas and Sylvania, or is my obsession with the TV show simply making matters worse? I decide to find out.

'I've been thinking,' I say, 'about the show…Raffy doesn't think it's a good idea, Mili doesn't either…' I pause and wait for Jenny to offer some kind of encouragement, to protest, or at least indulge me. But she doesn't. 'Maybe I should forget the whole thing,' I continue, 'maybe I should just say no…right now.'

'OK,' says Jenny, picking up her phone, 'I'll text Sylvania.'

She starts plugging letters into her phone.

'No!' I shout but she keeps plugging away. 'No, don't do that…' I put down the coffee mug and rush towards her. Smooch immediately jumps up and starts yapping. There's a small, pathetic struggle that only lasts a couple of seconds as Jenny tries to hold me off, and I try and grab her phone but all I manage to do is make it fly out of her hand and onto the stone floor. It lands with a nasty crack.

'Solomon!' she screams, 'For fuck's sake, I was only joking. What's the matter with you? I know how much you want to do it, but it's only a TV show, a stupid TV show…it's not going to change your life!'

Ah, I think to myself, but what if it did? What if it actually made me a household name again, or was a springboard to a second career? How would Jenny feel about me then?

'Sorry,' I mutter, and slink back to the island.

Jenny gets up off her seat and retrieves her phone. She presses a few buttons and then slams it down on the table. 'Fucking brilliant,' she says and then, phone in hand, dashes past me and out of the kitchen with both dogs following closely behind.

'Where are you going?' I shout after her. I hear her in the hall grab her coat and some car keys.

'To get a bloody new phone…I'm due for an upgrade.'

CHAPTER 6

I'm only on the tread for about fifteen minutes, running a measly five miles an hour, when I hear the latch go on the studio door, the gym door fly open, and a manic, rain-soaked Rosa panting and panicking her way into the room. 'Mr Solomon, Mr Solomon! Come quick…Ernesto has fallen in the hole!'

I waste no time; I don't bother to hit the emergency red button on the tread. I jump off, fly past Rosa and out the door a lot faster, it feels, than I'd just been running. I hear Rosa behind me trying to keep up. It's pouring with rain; the wind is swirling in icy breaths, but it barely registers. I race past the workshop, past the greenhouse, and towards the vale below the copse.

I can't see Ernesto at first, but then I notice a gap in the orange safety fence down the far end, the deep end, where Kipper is barking and pacing anxiously. As I near, I see the poor man up to his chest in the thick, muddy water, and holding on to a hollow, orange, plastic section of the fence, which has slipped in either with him or before him. He clearly has his feet stuck in the muddy quicksand; he's breathing hard but in no imminent danger – as long as he doesn't move. Rosa joins me and starts jabbering at Ernesto in Spanish. But she's panicking and he starts to try and claw his way up and out. The fence buckles and the section starts to unhinge.

'Don't move!' I yell. I peer into the depths of the copse, thinking that there may be a stray branch I can use: something for him to grab hold of. But it's raining hard and visibility is poor. 'Rope,' I yell, 'do we have any rope?' Of course we have rope. This is a huge house. There must be rope somewhere.

'Workshop,' Ernesto gasps.

Rosa begins to follow me as I rush off to fetch it. 'No,' I say, 'stay here and try to keep calm.'

I find the rope in the workshop. It's orange, plastic, coiled neatly in a circle and hanging on a nail on the wall. It's about half an inch thick but obviously strong and thankfully long. I grab it and return to the hole. I tie one end of it into a ball of random knots – knots upon knots – and throw it as accurately as I can to Ernesto. After two failed attempts, he catches it with one hand and then puts that hand back where it was.

'Wrap it round your wrist,' I shout, and then mime the action. 'More, yes, that's it, more, and up the arm.'

All the time I'm shouting, Rosa is translating what I'm saying into Spanish, even though I'm sure Ernesto can understand. There's a huge old sycamore up the slope, about twenty feet away. I run towards it and around it, using its trunk as a lever. I then wrap the end of the rope around my hand, arm, and waist, spinning myself in circles until I have the right tension but remain a good, safe distance from the hole. And I pull. It's like a two man tug of war with a tree in the middle. Kipper keeps barking; the ground is wet. I slip and I have to dig in my heels to gain some traction. But it's working, I think, because Rosa's tone has changed to one of optimism and encouragement. Thank God Ernesto is slight. I pull, turn again, wrap more rope around my waist, and pull and pull until, eventually, I see his hands grasping the orange cord, the top of his head and then his shoulders. Rosa bends down and tries to assist her frail husband further. Covered in mud, drenched in self-pity and embarrassment, Ernesto finally clambers out of the hole.

I can see he's lost his shoes or boots, or whatever he was wearing. I know for a fact that he is proud and stubborn, but his grief seems out of proportion to what has just taken place. He's on all fours, head bowed, in tears. Rosa, too, is in tears. They are talking quietly to each other as though they are partners in some secret tragedy. I get an almighty feeling of terror as I wonder whether Ernesto had been trying to rescue someone or something from the hole.

'Where's Antonia?' I scream, thinking of their youngest, most minuscule of daughters.

They both turn their heads. '*Escuela*...school,' snuffles Rosa. Of course.

'Take Ernesto back to the cottage,' I say, 'make him some tea... tea with sugar. Put him in a hot bath. No more work today.'

The pair tramp slowly off, Rosa with a supportive arm around her husband's waist, Ernesto limping slightly. After all the drama, the cold suddenly hits me and I begin to shiver. I look at my feet, legs and shorts, thick in mud; my hair is flattened by the rain.

'Come on Kipper,' I yell, then jog back to the house. But it's only when I begin to take off my muddy trainers that it dawns on me, where's Smooch? In a frenzy, I return to the hole, Kipper running beside me. I look at the earth beside the broken fence in search of any tiny paw prints, and then at the water's surface, pricked a thousand times by rain. I search the copse, the workshop, the studio, all the time shouting, 'Smooch! Here boy!' I run to the gatehouse cottage. The front door is unlocked and the ground floor deserted. I hear Rosa and Ernesto in a room upstairs. 'Smooch!' I yell again. I want to run upstairs and ask them if they've seen him, if that's what all the fuss was about. But another part of me just wants Ernesto to get his strength back.

It's no use, I can't find the little Jack Russell anywhere. Back in the house, I ring Jenny – there is a small chance she might have taken him with her – but it goes straight to voicemail, she doesn't have the new phone yet, or is between SIM cards. It's like Schrödinger's Cat, or rather Schrödinger's Dog; I open the box one second and see Smooch mummified in mud, I open the box the next and there he is grinning and wagging his tail. But one thing is for certain, if Jenny's precious mutt is dead, then so am I.

Half an hour later, I'm showered and changed and sitting at the island in the kitchen, nervously picking at a cheese and pickle sandwich. I'm working my way through the second half, when I hear the front door open and Jenny drop her keys into the basket, then the sound of Jenny removing her coat. I pray that any minute now, I will hear the scampering of a tiny, fat dog. But I don't. Jenny walks into the kitchen with her handbag in one hand and a paper bag bearing the Vodafone symbol in the other. She dumps them both on the kitchen table.

I feel too sick to eat.

'How was the tread?' she asks, innocently enough.

'Oh…fine.' I don't really know what to say. I don't want to mention the incident with Ernesto, because that would lead to the inevitable question.

'How's the phone,' I enquire, 'manage to transfer your number OK?'

She looks a little sullen as she takes the phone out of her handbag.

'Yes,' she replies, 'the new iPhone. It uses a different SIM, a micro SIM.'

'Yeah, I know, same one as the iPad.'

'So I can't put my old SIM card in there.'

I don't know what's going on here. I'm worried about a dead dog and she's worried about her SIM card.

'No, but if you sync it with your laptop, all the contacts and emails should go straight across.'

She's seems really unhappy, and I'm not sure why. Maybe Kipper is picking up on this because he starts whining. Oh, no, I think, she's gonna notice…she's gonna ask me a question I don't want to answer.

She looks at Kipper. 'Shit!' she says, jumping up. 'I've locked Smooch in the car!'

It should feel like a relief, but it doesn't. All that anxiety and guilt I'd been experiencing is transmuting into cold rage. She has no idea what I've just been through…none! I make a decision, right there and then, and as Jenny comes back through the front door with Smooch charging ahead, she sees me putting on my overcoat.

'Where are you going?' she asks.

'To Bath, to see a man who can coach me in opera.'

'Isn't that a bit premature? Shouldn't you wait until you're formally asked?'

'I thought you said it was in the bag.'

Jenny becomes suddenly coy. 'I've lost Sylvania's number,' she says, sounding strangely like a little girl. That probably means she's lost Andreas' as well.

'You didn't sync your phone with your computer, this morning?'

'No.'

'What about text conversations?'

'Gone.'

'Aw, what I shame,' I say sarcastically, while feeling an immense sense of power.

'Please, Mr Solomon, I know you have it, just give it to me.'

She only uses 'Mr Solomon' when she wants something. Sounding like Rosa or one of the girls usually works. But not this time. 'Blow me!' I yell.

'OK,' she replies, unperturbed.

What? I can't believe it, Jenny's agreed to end our sexual drought just to get Sylvania's number. I'm about to ask if she's being serious, when I hear the tri-tone marimba of an incoming text from Jenny's new phone on the kitchen table. She hears it too. I've never seen her run so fast. I walk back and stand in the kitchen doorway.

She waves her phone at me. 'Never mind,' she says with a cold, vengeful smile, 'I just got it.'

CHAPTER 7

I'm still seething as I drive the Boxster out of the garage. I'm revving the engine high, making the wheels spin and the gravel fly everywhere. I've forgotten the bloody opera CD as well. It would have fitted my mood so perfectly to have the windows open and opera blaring as I made my way down the drive. I've just saved an old man's life, for Christ's sake, and a dog's. OK, so those statements aren't entirely true, but that's how it feels. It's not till I've circuited Wells that I begin to calm down. I'm listening to Radio 4, about the loneliness and the conditions of life on Lundy Island, a tiny atoll in the Bristol Channel; the habits, the hobbies of the inhabitants, how they manage to survive the strange weather patterns and the once-a-day ferry. They should try being married to Jenny. I'd swap places with any one of them.

The Georgian city of Bath is twenty-four miles away and I may well be on a wild goose chase, but something about this feels right. Yesterday, while I was drunkenly downloading more arias, I browsed the Internet for opera coaches. There's a website called Mozartline, which has the contact details of pretty much every singing teacher, voice coach, and accompanist throughout the UK and even beyond. The directory is sectioned region by region. I read through the CVs of a couple of ladies, one in Bristol, and another who coaches both in Bristol and London. I looked at their pictures, both motherly and blonde. And then I thought that maybe one of them might be the actual coach I'd seen at ITV. What was her name? Jo, that's it. I certainly wanted to keep my mission a secret, I mean, some people would call it cheating, getting a head start. And so I settled on a man who lives, not too far away, just east of Bath, a man who surely has nothing to do with ITV, Dr Eugene Sparks.

51

His CV was certainly impressive: a distinguished international operatic baritone, The Royal Opera House, Covent Garden; Metropolitan Opera, New York; Teatro alla Scala, English National Opera, San Francisco Opera, etc. I read through his Wikipedia page and saw that his first major performance was in 1961, the year I was born. Having said all that, the guy is now eighty-three years old and lives on a barge on the Kennet and Avon canal.

I sent him an email introducing myself, explaining my situation; that I had sung pop professionally but now, in my middle years, wanted to learn to sing classically, that in some ways, it was my destiny. I didn't get a reply and so I rang his number. His voicemail greeting was an incredibly well spoken croak asking people to leave a message for him or Tilda Sparks, his wife. I left my name and number, but, once again, received no reply. He could be dead, I realise, but there's only one way to find out.

Forty minutes later, and thanks to the satnav, I find myself on the road adjacent to Hampton Wharf. I park the car behind a grubby ice cream van, obviously stationed there for the winter. I retrieve a small brolly from the boot and, with the rain just a light drizzle, head down the steps towards the canal.

Even in the depths of winter, the foliage by the canal path is thick and overgrown. The canal is filled to the brim. Ducks and moorhens interweave innocently as though one breed is oblivious to the other. It's an idyll, like that frieze in The Savoy, an idyll of a golden age. You can barely hear the traffic from the road above; it's a compact, protected space. I see only three barges on this stretch, the third one being a lot wider. They're all painted different colours, one burgundy and black with patches of white, one, royal blue with a sage green deck, and the third, creamy yellow with a black hull. Perhaps they haven't been painted since the summer but the many, thick coats are holding up well.

I stroll past each of them in turn, noting their names: Morgana, Lost At Sea, Almaviva. Take your pick, Solomon. I skip onto the first barge and knock gently on the door. There's a little commotion from within, but eventually a scruffy looking bloke with matted dreadlocks opens it.

'He's not here,' he says. His breath smells of skunk.

'Who?'

'Glen, he's not here.'

'Oh, no,' I reply, 'I'm looking for Dr Eugene Sparks.'

'The Dutch barge, third boat down, the one with the wheelchair ramp,' he gabbles and then closes the door.

'Thanks,' I say, but he's already back inside.

Almaviva is the boat he's referring too, and I'm rather glad, because it's the largest and the cleanest by far. I walk down the ramp and, under a small awning, shake my brolly free of rain. I then tap at the round pane of glass in the door. About thirty seconds later, the curtain behind the window is drawn back and an old man with thick black glasses, heavy eyebrows, and a large nose peers at me through it. He seems to recognise me, perhaps my email did get through?

The door opens and Dr Sparks is revealed as a very tall, unshaven, shabbily dressed man, his height only lessened by the way he stoops. He has a remarkable head of hair for his age; grey, mostly, but with a stubborn streak of black running right down the middle. A good quality purple scarf is tied around his neck and tucked into a thick, baggy, coffee-coloured cardigan. His trousers are clearly pyjama bottoms and there are large tartan slippers on his feet.

'Did you manage to park your van any nearer this time?' he asks with an unnerving leer.

'Van?'

'Your Tesco delivery van.'

'Oh, no. Sorry, my name is Solomon Capri...I sent you an email, left a message on your answering machine?'

'I see,' he replies, clearly confused. 'My daughter-in-law collects and reads me my emails...anything important, but her computer was stolen from her car. The bastards broke a window. And our telephone...is somewhere on the boat. I hear it ringing, but I still can't find it amidst the clutter.'

'Never mind,' I reply, 'let me explain. I found your name on Mozartline. Dr Eugene Sparks, yes? I'm looking for some voice coaching. It's for a TV show, you see, that takes pop stars – I'm a pop star by the way – and teaches them how to sing opera. You may have seen it?'

Dr Sparks seems disinterested. 'Hobnobs,' he says, 'we ran out five days ago. When I saw you at the door my stomach started rumbling.'

'No, look, I'm not from Tesco,' I chuckle. Here we go again. 'My name is Solomon Capri, I've sung professionally for years and – in my youth – had opera lessons for about six months and now I'd like to get back into it. It's for a TV show, Popstar to Operastar. It's a golden opportunity, I'm really excited about it, it feels like my destiny...'

The old man suddenly bristles with rage. He's clearly upset by something, perhaps because I didn't bring any Hobnobs.

'Destiny?' he bellows.

I'm shocked by this sudden change in demeanour. The meek, forgetful old man is now sounding strangely demonic. And the tone of his voice, the power, the volume, is like nothing I've ever heard in my life.

'What do you know about destiny?' he growls. 'My son got on the wrong bus, was that his destiny? And my wife...' Dr Sparks stands back, opening the door completely to reveal, down the far end of the barge, a woman in a wheelchair, the top half of her body wrapped in an off-white shawl, one side of her face drooping badly. I assume she's suffered a stroke. '...Fifty five years we've been married,' he rages, 'Tilda was one of the finest mezzo-sopranos ever to play Amneris – she made the role her own. Is this a destiny fulfilled? Our son got on the wrong bus…it was the wrong bus. Now get off our barge, you fool, and pursue your destiny elsewhere!'

'Wait!' I yell. I really should leave this man to his forgetfulness and his bitterness, but something stubborn inside me can't bear to be turned away at the door. 'My father sang with you,' I blurt, 'he's Italian.' I'm lying, of course, about my father being a singer, and relying heavily on this octogenarian having a few blind spots in his memory. 'In Milan.' I try to remember whether Dr Sparks had actually sung in Milan, whether that was on his CV. Surely every noteworthy opera singer has sung in Milan. Then I do remember – La Scala, of course. 'He adored you,' I continue, 'said you were one of the most brilliant men he'd ever met. You bought him supper…when he was…hungry.'

Sparks peers at me distrustfully. 'When was this?'

'Sixty-three, sixty-four or five, seventy something, I can't remember exactly.'

'What was his name?'

'Er…Joe.'

'Joe,' he repeats bitterly, almost gagging on the word, as though he knows exactly who this fictional character is. 'He was a tenor, yes?'

'Yes, a tenor.' I may well have struck oil.

'A stout man with curly hair. Big hands.'

'That's it.'

'Joe,' he repeats once more with a dark and murderous tone. He looks at Tilda, who is smiling, or at least half-smiling. 'Do you remember Joe?' he asks her. She really can, that smile is lighting up half her face. 'That dirty philanderer couldn't keep his hands off you could he? Yes, I remember Joe. Where is Joe now?'

Jesus, I may have struck oil, but I've also, in the process, penetrated a fault line in the earth's crust.

'Oh…dead. A long time ago.'

The old man starts to chuckle. It sounds hoarse and evil. 'Dead? Did you hear that Tilda? Your boyfriend is dead.' Her face drops… even more.

Sparks seems ecstatic. 'How did he die?'

'Hanged himself with some orange plastic rope,' I reply, hoping that with this succession of lies I have not damned myself to hell.

'*Il destino*,' says Dr Sparks, '*Il destino di Joe*. Please. Come in, sit down. I am sorry to hear about your father. It is very sad. Were you young?'

'Oh, about five or ten at the time.'

I enter the barge and sit on one of the barge's sofas, a foam mattress covered in, what I would describe as, hippy fabric, and resting upon a fitted plywood base. There seems to be a solid lump beneath the foam just to make sitting that little bit more unbearable. The barge seating area is symmetrical, like a hexagon split down the middle. Dr Sparks sits opposite. I'm surrounded by flowerless plants, pale and leafy, some sprawling onto the floor, while others climb along the window frames in search of moisture. There are manuscripts and magazines in tottering piles covering, what I believe to be, their dining table. There is a small kitchen area, and an upright piano, again with manuscripts stacked on top. A circular wood-burning oven bisects the long room, gun grey with a chimney that shoots through the wooden ceiling. It's also freezing. I don't know why anyone would choose to live like this. Perhaps they have no choice, or perhaps this is an annex to a Bohemian, itinerant lifestyle, and that they have residences, or barges, all over the world?

'Can I offer you some coffee or tea?' says Dr Sparks, now completely calm and extremely well mannered. He sounds a little like Christopher Lee when he's at his most charming. 'We're out of milk, but I have chamomile or mint or Earl Grey, if you prefer.'

'No, er, no thanks. I'm fine.'

'How about some spliff?'

'No,' I chuckle. That surprised me. 'No, I'm good.'

'So,' he continues, 'tell me about this TV show.'

I repeat what I said earlier, but deliberately omit the word 'destiny.' I explain that it's a competition and when I mention that Rolando Villazón is involved, Dr Sparks seems momentarily impressed.

'So, you are a pop star. Are you famous? Do people ask you for autographs?'

'Only in Tesco.'

'And have you made millions from pop music? Do you live in a great big house in the country?'

'I've done OK over the years, and, yes, the house is pretty big.' I do not mention, of course, that Jenny's paid for most of it.

'And now you want to sing opera. Have you ever tried singing opera, seriously?' he asks.

I confess to the little I've done, the review in the Evening Post, my stellar role as a teenage Pirate King. All the time, he's nodding, nodding and squinting and pulling questioning faces. Tilda, I notice, has dozed off.

'Are you a tenor like your father?'

'No, bass-baritone.'

'Let me hear you,' says Dr Sparks pulling himself up slowly and then sitting on the piano stool. He rearranges several pieces of manuscript on the piano's music stand. 'What do you know?' he asks. 'Anything you particularly enjoy? Stand up, stand up, don't be shy.'

'I know *Non Più Andrai* quite well,' I reply, rising and positioning myself next to the piano.

'That's a start,' he replies, and then hammers the introduction really loudly on the keys. The piano almost sounds like a honky-tonk piano; the moisture and cold clearly having played havoc with the tuning.

'Er, do you have the music?' I ask, 'I don't know it off by heart.'

'Hmm,' he grunts as he stops playing. For the next five minutes he searches for the sheet music on top of the piano, and through the piles on the small dining table. Eventually he finds some tatty pieces of paper and hands them to me. There's a coffee stain running through the bottom right corner of all three pages.

Without hesitation, Dr Sparks starts pounding the keys again. I join in and sing no more than a few lines when he stops.

'Take your hand off your hip.'

I didn't even know I had it there.

'Uncross your feet, stand upright, push out your chest, retract your jaw, stand like an emperor delivering a speech to the masses, you're slouching like a teenager.'

Christ, this guy is confusing me, it's like I've mastered the social foxtrot, now I'm suddenly having to learn the cha-cha-cha. He starts again and I join in at the right moment. This time I get a little further. I sound great, I think, but he's playing more and more gently as though he's dissecting my voice. Naturally, I follow his dynamics.

'No, no, keep singing out,' he urges, '*forte, forte*, perform, perform!' And then he sings along and in that instant I realise the gulf between us. This octogenarian has lungs. He has echoic caverns hidden deep within his body. His vibrato, control and sustain are remarkable. I stop singing. He's made his point.

Somewhat crestfallen, I slump onto the sofa, right onto that hard lump which suddenly starts vibrating.

'I think I've found your phone,' I say, reaching under the mattress and pulling it out. The vibration becomes a ring, which stops almost immediately. I must have cut whoever it was off.

Dr Sparks swivels on his seat. 'So that's where it was, thank you.' He seems displeased. 'Do you always give up this easily?'

I rise again automatically.

'No, no, sit back down,' he says and then returns to sit opposite me. 'When is this television programme?'

'It airs live at the beginning of June.'

Dr Sparks shakes his head. 'You don't have anywhere near enough time.'

'What, not even if I have lessons two or three times a week?'

'Hah!' he guffaws, 'Not even if you have lessons every day. There is no connection between your voice and your soul, no connection to the pit of your stomach, your guts, to the pain and the passion in your life. You have pain and passion in your life?'

'Yes,' I reply, thinking of Jenny.

'Your breathing is shallow, your tone is thin,' he continues, now sounding more like Christopher Lee playing Saruman in *The Lord of the Rings*, 'your vibrato, inconsistent. You're not using your chest. Your voice sits in your throat and then jumps into the mouth when you try for the high notes. You say your father was Italian. Was he from Puglia?'

'Somewhere near there.' I'm not enjoying this dressing down one bit and there's a strange smell coming from somewhere.

'You have inherited his bad habits. You sing Italian like a country boy. It has to be sung like a noble from the north.'

'It's only a TV show,' I interject.

'A live TV show,' he replies. 'Were you nervous when you were singing?'

'Not really,' I admit.

'You will be when you perform on television in front of the cameras, your efforts beamed live into people's homes. Your heart will be beating fast, you will be sweating, and your mouth will be dry. Everything you will have learnt will desert you. You will crumble, and your voice will be weak. You will prove to the world that pop stars cannot sing opera. You will fail. But the question you need to ask is whether the journey is more important than the destination. Will these efforts make you a better man? Will you have learned something about yourself? If the answer is yes, then I may be able to help.'

It's been here for a few minutes now, this odd smell, and Dr Sparks notices I've noticed it. 'But now you must go, my wife has soiled herself.' He rises and so do I. 'Think about it,' he adds, 'think about it, long and hard.'

'Shall I ring you?' I ask, as I pick up my brolly, which I'd left just inside the door.

'Be here at eight o'clock tomorrow morning, that way I'll know whether you're serious. Oh…and bring some Hobnobs.'

It's approaching six o'clock and my stomach is rumbling. I'm heading back into Bath along the London Road, thinking that the longer I stay away from home, the better. I should give Jenny some space, a chance to reflect, a chance to miss her husband. I decide to drive into the centre and get something to eat.

Waitrose car park is virtually empty. I park the Boxster on the ground floor and walk out across the road and up Broad Street, cutting through Milsom Place. Da Vinci's is my destination. I like this restaurant, it's simple, fresh, well-cooked food. On display are the sumptuous joints of Parma ham they cut to wafer thin slices, and the huge rolls of Parmesan and pecorino cheese; the kitchen is open – generally a good sign; the menu shows great variety and a knowledge of regional Italian cuisine. It's also somewhere you don't mind eating alone, somewhere you can find a private corner.

I'm just about to head up the steps, eyes to the ground, when someone calls out my name: 'Hey, Solomon!' I recognise that faux mid-Atlantic accent immediately and secretly groan. I turn round and see a gaunt middle-aged man wearing a black leather cowboy hat, his hands in the pockets of a black leather coat, tinted glasses hiding his eyes. It's Perry Lighthouse, lead singer of early-eighties Goth band, *Cast Of Hawks*.

'Oh, hi Perry.'

Now, I know Perry, but not very well. He's more of a friend of a friend than a friend. He's also a fully paid up member of the West Country Semi-Retired Pop Stars' Club. We're all supposed to get along, with our big houses, home studios, dogs and kids, and so much time on our hands, but I'm not sure if we, as individuals, have any more in common than a dentist does with a gynaecologist, or a taxidermist does with a vet. I find Perry a tad holier-than-thou, to be honest, a bit preachy, and I can never forget the fact that FFTB were replaced at the last minute on the Live Aid bill by Perry's band. Someone, somewhere took a bribe. Nowadays, though, he's harmless enough, as is his wife, Miranda – or Cruella, as Jenny likes to call her – who walks up beside him.

'Hi Miranda.'

'Hi. How's Jenny?'

'She's good, yeah, very good. How are you, Perry? You look unusually tanned for this time of year.'

'Yeah,' says Perry, 'I just got back from Africa. Was out there with a few celebs distributing medicine.'

'You've done that quite a bit over the years, haven't you?'

'Ever since Live Aid.'

Bastard...bastard for mentioning Live Aid!

'That's right,' I reply, 'that's why they gave you an MBE.'

'OBE,' he says, correcting me, 'for that, and my charity work for Nordoff Robbins, and Elton John's AIDS Foundation. So, what are you up to these days, Solomon, any new music on the horizon?'

'No, no music. We've turned the recording studio into this incredible high-tech chill out pad. I've sold all my gear, now I spend most of my time meditating and practising tantric yoga.' I'm certainly not going to tell him about the TV show. 'How about you?' I enquire.

'Oh, the lads and I are working on a new Hawks album.'

'Nice. I suppose that X-Factor guy getting to number one with a cover of *Highway to Venus* has rekindled a lot of interest, put you back in the spotlight.'

'Yeah,' says Perry, looking like he was just caught stealing, 'got a bit lucky with that.'

'I suppose you'll be touring with the new album, doing a few summer festivals?'

'I expect so, but I might be doing a bit of TV as well...'

'Really? What, Celebrity Big Brother?'

'No, it's called Popstar to Operastar, not sure if you caught any of the last series?'

Huh? Perry's words reverberate through my head as though they'd been shouted in a cathedral. I feel like a fool – everything Jenny said was true. They've cast a large net into an ocean of yesterday's men and they're hauling them in by the boatload, selecting the bigger fish and casting the sprats aside. I hear Dr Sparks' sinister chuckle in my head. I see my wife's cynical smile.

'Doesn't ring a bell,' I say, 'what's the premise?'

I listen as Perry explains what I already know, recounting almost exactly what I went through at ITV.

'I really liked the producers, got on very well with them,' he says.

'Yeah, they were nice guys...I mean, I'm sure they are...nice. Have you ever sung opera?' I ask.

'No, I don't really know much about it.'

'Then why do the show?'

'Gets my face back on TV, I suppose.'

Gets my face back on TV, I repeat, scathingly to myself.

'When do you find out?' I enquire, trying to hide my self-interest, my irritation and my envy.

'Beginning of March, then it's just a matter of agreeing the expenses. I'm trying to get them to pay for a nice hotel for Miranda and me.'

Not The Savoy! I scream internally.

'Well…good luck with it,' I say, 'I look forward to hearing your Puccini.'

'My what?'

'Doesn't matter.'

CHAPTER 8

The first thing I do when I sit down at the table is order a Dirty Martini. I have to explain what it is to the waitress, but when she comes back with drink in hand, she informs me that the barman knew exactly what it was, and now, thankfully, so does she. There is fish on the menu, there are salads, either of which I should be choosing, but I can't. Not right now. I go for a huge plate of penne in a thick *Amatriciana* sauce. Not what the doctor ordered, not on my list of dietary foods, but I'm determined to stuff myself, to rid myself of this gnawing void.

I've gone into meltdown. What's the fucking point of even entertaining the idea of the show? How many eighties pop stars will I be lining up against? What if they're all eighties pop stars? What if someone dropped a bomb on the studio? The eighties would be gone in a flash, forever, up in operatic smoke. How am I going to stand out amongst all that lot? Am I really going to compete with Perry? I mean he may have screamed some high notes on *Highway To Venus* but what good will that do him during the climax of *Nessun Dorma*? If he nicks this one off me, like he did with Live Aid, I'll kill him.

With the martini glass drained of its slurp, I order a large glass of Montepulciano, and then the food arrives. I know I'll be over the legal limit to drive, but I can't help myself. The more I eat, the more my mood changes. The more Montepulciano I drink, the more Machiavellian I become. I start looking at the positives, at my two secret weapons – Jenny and her relationship with Sylvania, and Dr Eugene Sparks. I realise that I shouldn't be so jealous about Jenny and her new Best-Friend-Forever. I should be positively encouraging it, turning it to my advantage, sealing my place on the show. Then, I realise that no one else will be as prepared as I will be; no one will be singing opera every day with such an enlightened taskmaster as Dr Sparks. I can use this humiliation, I can turn it into the most professional, operatic tone to ever have been heard from the lungs of a novice. I have to stop thinking about the past, about my peers. If I look back, it's just depressing. If I look forward, who knows what I can achieve? I'm no longer a pop singer, I tell myself, I'm an opera singer, and there's no turning back. I decide there and then to grow a goatee.

When I arrive back at Sunnymore, I head straight to the kitchen only to find Rosa toying with various unprepared ingredients in anticipation of cooking a meal. I immediately inform her that I've eaten and ask whether she's seen Jenny and suggest that Jenny might be hungry, even though I'm not.

'Mrs Jenny is in studio,' she says. I glance at the empty dog beds and surmise that Smooch and Kipper are with her. 'She say she may have snack later.'

'Oh, OK, that's fine. How's Ernesto?' I ask.

'He is much better, thank you Mr Solomon, thank you so much for helping. He wants to thank you too. He is very sorry for falling in the hole.'

'Honestly, it was nothing.' I pause and think back to Ernesto's breakdown after he'd hauled himself out. 'Why was he crying earlier?' I enquire, 'I mean, he wasn't in any real danger.'

Rosa seems reluctant to answer as though that answer might summon more tears. She sighs. 'He lost his wedding ring in the water. It must have slipped off when he was trying to hold the rope. It means so much to him, that ring. He has not taken it off since the day we married.'

'Oh my God,' I say.

I feel terrible. It all makes complete sense.

'I see. I'm so sorry.' And then I think of an immediate, if somewhat overly romantic solution perhaps inspired by the lack of romance in my own relationship. 'You know,' I suggest, 'I have an idea. I'd like to buy him a new one. I'd like to buy both of you a matching set of new rings. Perhaps we can have a party, a celebration of your marriage? Renew your vows, right here at Sunnymore?'

Now Rosa really is in tears. She's sobbing and, naturally, I want to comfort her. I approach her and put my arms around her. Her sobs increase. I don't notice Consuelo's presence in the room until she asks her mother what's wrong. Rosa replies, between sobs, in rapid Spanish, and then Consuelo puts her arms round us both and starts weeping too. After a few seconds Rosa peels away to blow her nose on some kitchen towel. But Consuelo does not. She puts her arms around my back, her head on my chest, and squeezes me tight. 'Thank you, Mr Solomon,' she says, sniffing and snuffling, 'you saved my father's life.'

'Really,' I reply, 'he wasn't in any danger.'

Now I know how Superman feels.

I try and break away, but Consuelo is holding on a little too forcefully, a little too passionately. She's comfortable in this embrace and it feels odd. It's like, in this apparently innocent show of gratitude and affection, she's trying to reward me, to reinforce my protective instincts, to instate me as the new provider for her and her family, as if, by the simple act of falling in the hole, her father is no longer fit for the job. It's only when Rosa blows her nose loudly and crudely like the sound of a wet fart that the deadlock is broken, that the clench loosens. Consuelo laughs out loud and so do I. The tension is released, even though there wasn't any – except in my imagination. And I realise, once again, how ludicrous my thoughts are. Why do I always have to invent a conspiracy, a secret motive? Why do I always have to read so much into everything? This is Consuelo, for God's sake, she's an innocent Catholic girl.

A minute later we're still laughing, even Rosa is laughing. 'I'd better check on Jenny,' I say, and promptly leave the room.

I walk down the drive and into the studio courtyard. Thankfully the rain has finally stopped. The lights are on both outside and inside the studio. I lift the latch on the studio door and find it unlocked. This is a good sign. If Jenny were in a foul mood, she would have locked it and all the other doors. There's music playing, drifting quietly out of every speaker in every room, the source being Jenny's phone in the iPod dock. It's the flower duet from *Lakmé* by Delibes – not such a good sign. They play this music on British Airway flights just before take off. Jenny plays it whenever she wants to escape.

She's sitting on a barstool at the studio kitchen's massive island. To her right are the indoor barbecue and the deep fat fryer, both, covered in neat, brushed steel hinged tops. By her hand is a box of tissues. Her laptop is open and even through her thick reading glasses, I can see she's been crying. What is wrong with these women today? It's not even a full moon.

'Hi,' she says, as I grab a wine glass from the cupboard.

'Hi, gorgeous,' I reply, 'everything alright?' Jenny chooses not to answer. I pour some red wine from a half-empty bottle and park myself opposite her; four feet of thick, clean oak and a single gas hob between us.

'How did it go with the coach?' she asks.

'Difficult to tell. He's a real character; eighty-three, lives on a Dutch barge. The place is a complete mess, it's freezing, it smells, his wife sits at the back in a wheelchair. I'm pretty sure she's had a stroke.'

'Sounds grisly. I can understand why you wouldn't want to go back.'

I study Jenny closely and wonder how long she'd been crying for. The more I look, the more time I spend in her presence, the more the tears threaten to resurface.

'Want to tell me what's up?' I ask.

Jenny sighs in resignation. She's clearly struggling to find the right words or maybe doesn't want to tell me what she's really feeling. 'I don't know,' she admits finally, 'I've been thinking about us, about the two of us. We're not getting on very well, at the moment, are we? Haven't been for quite a while.' She reaches for a tissue from the box and I grow immediately worried. There is no flash of anger like the prelude to an argument, instead her voice is tinged with regret. 'I was so young when we got married,' she confesses, 'I followed you around the world like a lost puppy. The band was so successful, then Fran got ill and died; it was awful. Things weren't the same after that. The shine went, it's like the sun disappeared from our lives.'

I'm not sure if I like the sound of that. I know Jenny and Fran were close, all three of us were. There were times when we'd stay up all night doing cocaine, and I would have to leave them to it in the end. They'd chat away sometimes like I wasn't there. One crazy night, we all ended up in bed together. I wasn't jealous, I knew what Fran's preference was. Plus he never fucked Jenny, not properly. I must admit though, I'd never seen her so turned on. I don't think I have since.

'Then we had kids,' Jenny continues, 'brought them up. We've been so lucky with money. Look at all this, it's like a glorious prison. Now the kids have gone, I feel even more trapped.' She blows her nose. 'I just feel I haven't had time for myself. I need a break, Solomon.'

'You're having a break,' I say, increasingly concerned where this outpouring is leading, 'you're going skiing.'

'I mean a break from my life as it is. Come on Solomon, admit it, you're bored too, you're bored with me. When was the last time we fucked?'

And now I have to think. It was probably November last year after our fireworks party. 'About four months ago?' I reply, 'what's that got to do with anything?'

'No, not – sorry love I've gone a bit soft – fucked, but really fucked, with passion, with intensity?'

This is all news to me. Jenny never seemed too worried about it at the time.

'Every man experiences a few difficulties at this point in their life,' I try to explain, 'it's the drop in testosterone that occurs as you hit your late forties. I can get some Viagra, if you like?'

'Maybe you're just tired of me, maybe I don't turn you on any more?'

I don't really know what to say, because I don't really know what's going on with me physically, whether it's age-related or not. Maybe she's right? We've been going through the same sexual ritual, the same positions in the same order for more than twenty years, and lately there's been no satisfying conclusion for either of us. We just kind of give up.

'We can't carry on like this, Solomon, we're just gonna get old and die. We have to spice things up somehow.' Jenny pauses and I really fear what's coming next. 'I think we should be free to try out other partners,' she says, dropping the bomb.

I feel the blood drain from my face. How did we get here? How did we get from 'not getting on very well' to the need for an open relationship, so quickly?

'You're kidding me?' I say.

'No, I'm deadly serious. Wouldn't be the first time.'

'Come on, that was years ago,' I protest, 'we were young. There were no kids. People could get hurt now, it could become a complete mess.'

I can see my protests are merely feeding Jenny's resolve. But she wouldn't mention it now, she wouldn't bring it up unless she had something in mind.

'You lied to me the other day,' I say, 'about what time you came up to bed. You didn't go down and try to book another room at all, did you? You came in at half past four.'

Jenny has steel in her eyes. 'So what,' she says, 'so what if I had fun? They had a bit of coke, that's all, good coke. I haven't done coke in ages.'

'Two weeks ago with your nutty American friend, actually. And I guess you all went back to Andreas' room. I mean, Sylvania wasn't staying there. I can only imagine what happened next.'

'Imagine all you like, I'm not going to give you the gory details.'

'Why not? Isn't that what an open relationship is all about? Ask questions only if you want, only if you dare, but if you do, you get an honest answer. No possessiveness, no jealousy.'

Jenny shrugs. 'It must have been cut with ecstasy,' she admits, 'the coke…it all got a bit silly, a bit loved up.'

'Loved up?'

'Sylvania showed me her piercing…down there.' Jenny nods at her own lap. 'And then we were like teenage girls in a bedroom, just showing and touching and that kind of thing.'

'And where was Andreas while this was going on?'

'Asleep,' says Jenny. I can see by her expression that she knows how implausible that sounds.

'So, you were all doing coke, Andreas was in a hotel room with two gorgeous women making out with each other and he managed to fall asleep.'

'He may have opened his eyes once or twice.'

I feel if I delve any further, I might explode.

'I've got some if you want to try it? The coke. Sylvania gave me a gram as a little present. Horny stuff. Might do you some good.'

I'm tempted, but I just feel numb and detached right now.

'No thanks,' I reply, 'I've got a really early start.'

'How so?'

'I've got to be back at the barge for an opera lesson at eight.'

'Christ, you're keen.'

'I am resolute and determined.'

Jenny mutters something under her breath that I can't quite hear.

'I bumped into Perry today, by the way,' I say.

'Where?'

'In Bath, I was starving. He said he'd been for a meeting at ITV for Popstar to Operastar. What a coincidence.'

'Oh yeah,' interjects Jenny, 'I remember Sylvania mentioning it.'

'Thanks for telling me.'

'It's none of my business,' she replies. There's an uncomfortable pause. 'Well, if you're going to bed early, I'm gonna sleep here tonight.'

'Whatever, I suppose you need your toothbrush?'

'It's OK, I already brought it over.'

'Other partners,' I mutter to myself as I stomp up the drive, 'other fucking partners.' This is Jenny's revenge for Anki and Panki and all the others after and in between. She wants the rock star lifestyle now; feminine hygiene is the new rock and roll. It's alright for her, she's got her fuck buddies already lined up and in place, what am I going to do? Internet dating? Go to a nightclub and pick up some young girl? Then what? Where am I going to take her, to a hotel, back to the studio? What if I go soft again, what if I'm just useless in bed? Do I use a condom? That's only going to make it worse. No, this is not going to work for me.

I'm furious and I still don't understand what she meant by, 'the sun disappeared from our lives.' It's like she's saying she was happier when Fran was around, as though being in some kind of *ménage à trois* is her natural state. I mean, whenever there was tension between me and Jenny, when the bickering and arguments would start, one girlish chuckle from Fran would dissipate the whole thing. And then he said something on his deathbed. He said he wanted to come back, to be born again as our child, to have Jenny and me as his parents. It was freaky when Raffy came into the world. I always expected him to pick up a guitar and start instinctively strumming away, but he never did, because he's not Fran. Fran is dead.

I grab another drink in the kitchen. The house is completely empty. Rosa is probably sitting with Ernesto and sharing the good news. They're probably laughing and crying, the whole family joining in the celebration, singing my praises. 'Thank our Lord Jesus Christ for Mr Solomon. Let us say a prayer for him.' Yes, I can save a man from a hole, but I can't sustain an erection. 'Thank our Lord Jesus Christ for Mr Solomon. Let us say a prayer for his erection.'

Jenny's no doubt texting or talking to Sylvania or Andreas, sharing the revelation of her new semi-single state. She's probably getting high, doing coke, thinking back to the night (or nights) at the Savoy. She'll have her vibrator with her, that's for sure, and it won't be me who's pounding away at her in her head. Fuck it!

It's only nine o'clock, but if I start drinking now, I won't stop. I'll spend an hour or two on my own, then, in a moment of weakness, head back to the studio and ask Jenny if I can try that coke. Then I'll drink even more. I'll feel like shit in the morning, my voice will be rough, and Dr Sparks will sound like Saruman again. But I have a choice. I can choose the path of righteousness. Well done, Solomon, just pour the drink down the sink and go to bed. That's exactly what I do.

An hour later and, even though the room is pitch black, there's no way I'm going to sleep. I never go to bed this early and I keep replaying my conversation with Jenny over and over in my head, thinking if there was something I could have said that would have made her see the damage she's causing. Nope, can't sleep. Blackout curtains or no blackout curtains. Pillow's too flat, two pillows, too high. I do have a solution though. Jenny keeps some sleeping pills in her bathroom drawer: Ambien. She only really uses them on long haul flights. I'm not allowed to use them because it makes my snoring even worse and Jenny finds it embarrassing, especially on a plane. But I'm alone, no one to disturb, and they are absolutely guaranteed to send me off to sleep.

Back in bed, I feel the pill's influence almost immediately. I enter, what feels like, a semi-dream-like state where my thoughts become images, scenes that morph effortlessly into each other, while fragments of conversation interweave like the ducks and the moorhens on the canal. I have two distinct scenarios co-existing at the moment. One is Tilda Sparks in her wheelchair and she's doing some kind of wheelchair race with a bunch of other stroke victims. Strange, I know. They're in a park and screaming with excitement as they race. The other scenario is Jenny, Sylvania and Andreas in his room at the Savoy. I try and let the second one take over, try and put Tilda out of my mind. What's nice is that I don't feel jealous right now, just sleepy and dreamy and slightly horny. The second scenario is becoming more and more vivid as though I'm hovering outside their window and watching every titillating act. Christ, I've got a hard-on, a proper rock star hard-on. If only Jenny were here to witness it.

But I'm falling asleep. I turn over onto my belly and feel the solid flesh between my groin and the sheets and I don't care about doing anything about it. Perhaps the Velasquez family did say a prayer for my erection after all.

I'm not sure how long I've been asleep, or whether I've just been half-asleep and dreaming, but I hear and feel Jenny slip into bed beside me. Maybe she'd had enough of being on her own in the studio, maybe she regrets what she said. I'm lying on my side now with my back to her, and I still have this hard-on. Amazing. She snuggles up and, with her firm body, spoons me. I realise she's naked. She puts an arm around me. It feels so good to have my wife back. Perhaps there is something to be said for following the path of righteousness. 'I love you,' I whisper drowsily.

'I love you too, Mr Solomon.'

I chuckle lightly in my sleep. She only says that when she wants something. I feel her hand reach down for my cock and there's a quiet coo of surprise as she wraps her fingers around it.

CHAPTER 9

Last night I had the most vivid dream that a succubus entered my bedroom, fellated me until my cock was the size of a giant horn, and then mounted me, riding me maniacally until I shot my seed deep inside her. Her aim achieved, the she-devil peeled herself off me, flipped backwards onto the floor and walked naked out of the room on her hands, my sperm already racing to fertilise her demon egg.

It's six-thirty a.m. and the alarm on my watch is sounding. I'm not entirely sure what happened last night, if anything happened at all. I sweep my left hand across the bed in search of Jenny and, to my disappointment, find it empty. Even if she had been there at one point, she would have left because of my snoring, so that doesn't really answer my question. I turn on the bedside light and examine her pillow. There's no sign of any blonde hairs, just a few long dark ones of mine.

After a quick shower, I go into the walk-in closet to pick out some thick winter clothes for that freezing barge. But while I'm pulling out drawers I notice a lot of Jenny's clothes are missing. If we did have sex last night, it must have been some kind of pity fuck, because it's clear that she's making the studio, my studio – a place I used to record music – as a base for her new, open marriage.

Depressed and confused, I head downstairs, make myself some toast and a large cafetière of coffee, then open my laptop and check the news on Yahoo's front page. I notice I have an email. It came in yesterday evening around nine, from Martin our architect, addressed to both Jenny and me.

Dear Jenny and Solomon,

I have some good news re: the pool. As you know, I've been going back and forth with Natureflow's receivers and, lately, their asset strippers, and they are finally in a position to sell us a substantial amount of the organic seaweed-polyester pool lining at a discount price. I've also sourced some Columbian beech for the sunken deck area plus (most importantly) the Icelandic lava pebbles for the filtration system. Doing this ourselves should bring the project in under our proposed budget. With your permission, I'd like to get the bulldozer back in, along with the drainage unit, to clear the unsettled mud etc. I believe we're about to enter a drier spell next week, so that would be a perfect time to pour the cement and seal in the liner, which has to be done on the same day. Sorry this has taken so long.

All the best,
Martin

Hallelujah! This may sound optimistic and quasi-spiritual, but I have begun to view that hole as a metaphor for my marriage. It's like the problems surfaced the moment the digger started digging, as though the hole itself is malevolent, as though we'd disturbed consecrated ground. Was it a coincidence that it took the wedding ring from Ernesto's finger? I don't think so. I honestly believe that this email could be the turning point, where things slowly come back together. A few weeks, I'm guessing, and that hole will be teeming with new life. I'm tempted to reply to Martin immediately, but I know Jenny likes to deal with him because he, like so many men round here, is part of the Jenny fan club. Still, that's put me in a better mood as I grab my phone, my coat and the car keys…oh, and don't forget the CD of famous arias. There it is.

Today I decide to take the Range Rover. We have four cars, a black Range Rover, a purple Boxster, a brown Mini Clubman, and a white Audi R8 – last year's birthday present from Jenny, which, due to its awesome power and its colour, doesn't get driven much, certainly not in the winter. But the Range Rover has a great sound system and I intend to exploit it to the max.

It's still dark as I wait for the gates to open. The studio and its courtyard are obscure in the twilight, but the gatehouse cottage has the lights on downstairs. I think I see Rosa looking through the window to see who's up and leaving so early, probably castigating herself for not at least offering to make me breakfast. I haven't told them about the coach or my lessons, but I wave at her to tell her that everything's alright.

I arrive at Hampton Wharf about ten minutes early. I've managed to get through fifteen of the twenty-one arias I have on the CD and while I wait, I listen quietly to number sixteen: *Al Sen Ti Stringo* from Handel's *Ariodante*. This is about as sedate as it gets. I know the singing is in Italian but the music is so reserved, so polite, so English. I listen to the harpsichord – no blood and guts there. I forget about my English side, or, at least, I take it for granted, but it's the side that tries to remain in control, that is tolerating my wife's craziness right now, sweeping it under the carpet. I just wonder what would happen if I allowed my Italian side to react, to dictate my actions? Would I end up committing *un delitto passionale*, a crime of passion? Would Jenny's body end up under the cement, under the organic seaweed-polyester lining of the swimming pool?

Hmm, I'm not quite sure where that idea came from. Maybe that dream of the succubus has affected me more than I'd care to admit?

Promptly at eight o'clock, I knock on the barge's porthole window. It takes about five minutes and several almost window-breaking attempts before Dr Sparks finally answers. He's wearing his purple scarf and a brown stripy dressing gown.

'Oh, it's you.'

'You said eight o'clock.'

'I remember. You really are serious. Did you bring the Hobnobs?'

'Shit!'

'Oh dear, oh dear. There is a garage just down the road; you may have passed it on your way. Be a good man and go pick some up…some milk too, oh, and some logs for the fire. It's freezing in here.'

Ten minutes later, I'm back with all the requested items. The door is slightly ajar and Dr Sparks is attending to the kettle in the small kitchen area. He fills a French press with instant coffee. Why? There are two mugs on the counter and no sign of a wheelchair or Tilda. I assume she's still in bed, in the small room at the far end of the barge. He seems very pleased about the logs; they're obviously a good size. He spends the next five minutes stoking the wood burner. It's not until it starts to emit any heat that I dare take my coat off. We sit, just as we did yesterday, opposite each other. Sparks is holding a cup of what he described as, coffee, a plate of Hobnobs on the seat next to him; me, with a badly-stained cup containing, what I would call, insipid instant muck.

'So, you were clearly not deterred by my assessment.'

'I was very impressed by your voice. I'm very keen to go on this journey.'

Dr Sparks nods in deference. 'I too am impressed, by your punctuality. Well, before we start, perhaps I should get to know a little more about you, the famous pop star. Are you married?'

'Twenty six years.'

'Happily married?'

There's a pause. 'Yes.'

'Children?'

'Twins, a boy who's studying fashion in London and a very sporty girl who's up at Aberdeen University.'

'I see, so you and your wife are rattling around a big, empty house wondering where all the silence is coming from, wondering why your life is so empty.'

Is this intuitive, or has he been speaking to Jenny?

'I suppose so,' I reply, 'though we do have a family from El Salvador living in a cottage in the grounds. They've been with us for years. The woman cooks and cleans and the husband does the gardening, plus they have four charming daughters. They're like a second family. They really keep the place alive. How about you... you mentioned a son, I think, yesterday?'

This is the first time I've sensed any regret from this tough old man. He takes an age to answer. 'We had a son,' he replies, 'who was tragically taken from us. It is the worst trick God can play on you, to survive your own children.'

'I'm sorry, that must have been terrible.'

'For everyone,' he replies sullenly, lost in memory for a second. Then, suddenly, it seems, he remembers our conversation from yesterday. 'You said your father was Italian...Joe, a tenor, yes. How good is your Italian? You were singing it yesterday, but do you speak it well?'

'I'm pretty fluent. I can converse quite well when I'm on holiday.'

'And your mother?'

'English.'

'Ah, so your mother kept a lid on things, kept everything together while your father was a cauldron of passion, sitting around the kitchen in his vest, crying into his pasta, expressing his rage, his disappointment when Italy loses in the World Cup semi-final. Which language do you prefer? They're very different, their values.'

'I've never really thought about it,' I reply, 'I suppose Italian is the language of hyperbole; everything seems bigger and better, more colourful, more full of life.'

'You know,' says Dr Sparks, 'when Tilda and I were studying in Milan with the great Romani, we were not allowed to speak one word of English in his presence. It was, what that fat ogre called, *la lingua di scuse.* "Sorry, sorry, sorry," he would say in his ridiculous voice, prancing around the room, one hand on his hip, handkerchief flicking away the flies, "Pardon me, excuse me, I do beg your pardon." The German students, he didn't mind, but all the British students were made to speak, at all times, *la lingua di passione.* Do you understand what I'm saying, do you understand the difference?'

'Of course,' I reply, 'the language of apology, the language of passion.'

'But do you really understand?' He pauses. '*Non si capisce davvero?*' He's raising his voice, staring at me through his thick black spectacles, and spitting Italian in a perfect accent.

This is getting tiresome; bad coffee and a freezing barge. I just want some singing lessons, I want to be fast-tracked to operatic greatness, not sit here and listen to an old man's recollections. I'm tired, still trying to work out what happened last night, and dying for a pee. I reply with a shrug.

'Are you a robot? Mr…'

'Capri, Solomon Capri.'

'Talk to me in Italian.'

'No, *non sono un robot.*' What a stupid question.

'Does your English side douse that Latin fire?' He keeps pressing. 'Wait,' he notices my irritation, 'why are you clenching your jaw, what's upsetting you right now?'

'Nothing.'

'I don't believe you.'

'I'm not upset, really, I'm fine.'

'Talk in Italian, come on you spic, tell me what's bothering you.'

'*Questo caffè gusti come merda*!' I spit back, losing my composure for a split second.

'Ah…at last, some honesty, some Latin fire, and our first phrase. Shall we?'

Dr Sparks crosses to the piano and perches on the stool. He strikes a low note and sings that same note, in his rich, dark tone, repeating what I said in Italian about the coffee tasting like shit.

'OK, ready?'

Frankly, I'm finding this ridiculous, but I play along just in case he actually is a genius. I stand next to the piano; he strikes the same note and waits for me to sing. Weakly, I submit.

'*Questo caffè gusti come merda.*'

'And again, louder.'

'*Questo caffè gusti come merda.*'

One note, a heavily vibratoed, soulless monotone. This carries on for about five minutes. The notes get gradually higher and I feel like an idiot every time I criticise his coffee in an operatic voice. He, on the other hand, seems to be enjoying himself, not stopping once to offer advice. Finally, we're at the top of my range and my voice begins to crack.

'Don't force it,' he says, 'don't believe for one minute you have reached the ceiling…there is no ceiling. Come on, come on, this coffee tastes like shit!'

Every time I try it, my voice cracks, but then Sparks just hammers the same note over and over again until I'm forced to find a new place in my throat and manage to sing it somewhere between head voice and falsetto.

'*Bravissimo*,' he shouts, 'That is a top A!'

'What?' I say. I was looking at the wall not the piano keyboard.

'You, my boy are a tenor.'

'No, no,' I protest.

'What's wrong with being a tenor?' he asks, 'Was it because your father, Joe, the philanderer, the good-for-nothing, was a tenor?'

'Look, I made that up. He was never a singer, he didn't know you, and his name was not Joe. But he was Italian.'

Dr Sparks chuckles malevolently just as he did yesterday. 'I know,' he confesses. 'Do you think you are the only bullshitter in the world, Solomon Capri? Do you think you have a monopoly on bullshit? You have met your match, my boy. Now take some of your pop star money and go and buy me some decent coffee!'

'Are you serious?' I ask. I'm really beginning to think that this guy's a maniac. I'm going to give it a few more hours and then, if he continues like this, I'm going to call one of the opera ladies from Bristol.

'Yes,' he replies, 'and, anyway, I have to feed Tilda right now.'

So that's what all the baby food jars are for.

'Oh, I see. You know, I might dash into Bath, I know a good coffee shop there. Anything else you need?'

'Well,' he says with an opportunistic shrug, 'some cheese, some red wine, perhaps a few cold meats?'

'Leave it with me. Oh, can I use your loo before I go?'

Sparks hesitates, he seems embarrassed. 'Um...Tilda's in there.'

'What, all this time?'

'It saves on the diapers.'

Colonna and Smalls Espresso room is about a ten-minute walk away from Waitrose car park. The smell inside is overwhelming with enough floating molecules of caffeine to wake even Sleeping Beauty. I stand there for a second just breathing it in. There are a couple of attractive middle-aged Bath women sitting at a table. They seem happy, it's becoming a rare sight. I'm tempted to sit down myself, but I don't. I buy two packets of freshly ground Italian coffee before heading up the hill to Chandos Deli. Here, I buy some aged pecorino, a good quantity of freshly sliced, thinly sliced Parma ham, and a variety of salamis. They also have a good Chianti; black cockerel on the neck, raffia around the base. It's cheap, but it's sweet, light and evocative. I take two bottles. Finally, I buy some ciabatta, a bottle of good extra virgin olive oil and a large bulb of garlic.

Bags in hand, I chug down the road, and in The Kitchen Shop, pick up a small wooden chopping board and a serrated knife large enough to cut the ciabatta but fine enough to slice through the cheese. On the way out, I almost walk into a woman pushing a double pushchair. She has pink wrapping paper in a roll poking out of the back like an antenna. The colour alone is enough to remind me that today is Elena's birthday – Velasquez daughter number three. There's a shop in New Bond Street that sells all kinds of bright, present-type objects, from literature-themed coffee mugs, to Paul Smith wallets, to big plastic Lego storage boxes for kids. I have a quick browse and settle on a Flik Flak Dancing Mouse Watch. It's pink, she'll love it.

It's while I'm paying for the watch, that I first catch the sound of someone singing in the street outside. It's a pure, classical, soprano voice and the song is *Pie Jesu*. I look through the window; it's lunchtime, the streets are filling up. I can see, just across the road, the figure of a woman standing alone, a ghetto blaster, playing the backing music, by her feet. I leave the shop, walk in her direction, and the closer I get to her, the more I find myself mesmerised by this creature. She's like an angel in a thick winter coat and woollen hat. She has fine features; high cheekbones, pretty, clear blue eyes. I've never seen a busker like this before, someone who, to my ears, sounds like she should be on TV, not on a street. But maybe I have, maybe I've just never noticed. I know psychologists probably have many theories as to why, when we find a new obsession, events occur that seem connected. We pick up on them and believe they're more significant than they probably are. That's how I feel right now. I feel this is significant. There's a collection box, and as I near, I see that it's for a charity, the Stroke Association. I immediately think of Tilda. Could it be a coincidence? The woman is still singing as I put down my shopping bags, take out a fifty-pound note from my wallet, and put it in the box. She doesn't seem to notice, her eyes are focussed on some distant object, on her singing. She doesn't look at me, not even for a split second.

I walk back along New Bond Street towards the car park, and even one hundred yards away, I can still hear her. She's not singing loudly at all, but her tone cuts above the bustle of the shoppers, the noise of traffic. Five minutes later, I'm in the car wondering whether I've just given fifty quid to a ghost.

CHAPTER 10

Back at the canal, as I walk past the first barge, Morgana, I catch sight of the dreadlocked guy coming out of his door. He notices the bags and shouts out, 'Got you doing his shopping, has he?'

I look to the heavens and give a kind of nonchalant, macho shrug. I haven't seen any signs of life in barge number two, Lost At Sea, yesterday or today; maybe they are? But as I approach Almaviva, I hear Sparks' raised voice from within. He sounds like a man possessed. I stop for a while and listen but only make out fragments, something about taking a taxi to somewhere, not taking a bus. I'm wondering who he's talking to. Is he on the phone, or is he screaming at Tilda? The bellowing continues and the only way I know it will stop is if I bang loudly on the window.

'You're back,' says Dr Sparks as he opens the door. He seems surprised and breaks into the most polite smile.

'Why, did you think I'd done a runner?'

'The thought did cross my mind. Come in, come in, let me have a look.'

Tilda has been returned to the position she was in yesterday. There are no tears, and she gives no impression that she has suffered in any way. Sparks takes the bags off me and seems bemused and slightly offended that I bought a chopping board and a knife. But he surrenders the offence when he smells the coffee.

'Mmm…' he says, and then promptly puts the kettle on.

After we drink the coffee – and he accepts that it is a huge improvement – he picks up a bottle of wine.

'Is it too early, do you think?'

'Well, I've been up since six-thirty, so it's not too early for me.'

'That's what I want to hear.'

He then rattles around what must be a cutlery drawer for a worrying amount of time. I'm just praying he has a corkscrew because that is the one item I forgot.

'There you are,' he finally announces and goes to work on the foil.

We spend the next hour doing simple vocal exercises, scales in a variety of vowel sounds similar to what I did with the coach at ITV, with the odd bit of staccato madness thrown in for good measure and a concerted effort to get me to move from chest to head voice without pulling a strange face. Every now and again, we stop and sip some Chianti and the wine seems to lighten the intensity between us. It's charming too when Sparks gets up and pours a little into one side of Tilda's mouth. She seems to appreciate it even though a few drips end up staining her shawl.

The atmosphere has been lifted; there is a rapport, I believe, between all three of us. While Dr Sparks recounts another story about Romani, I get to work preparing a simple snack of toasted ciabatta rubbed with garlic, topped with the Parma ham and anointed with olive oil. I slice some of the pecorino, and put it on the same plate as the salami.

Dr Sparks opens the second bottle of wine; this is the most relaxed I've seen him. We talk for a while about what we would have done if we hadn't gone into music. I confess that I'd had ambitions to be an actor and Sparks explains how close he came to studying architecture. It feels so vital, these exchanges, and he even includes Tilda in the conversation, although her contribution is understandably confined to a half-smile. When he's had enough of the food, he sits back down at the piano and starts playing freely. I vaguely recognise the music, it's Mozart, I'm pretty sure. It's gentle, measured and quite staid. He plays for a couple of minutes, and then takes a sip of wine. He places the wine glass back down on top of the piano, and starts singing in that remarkable baritone of his.

'*Il core vi dono, bell'idolo mio…*'

I let the round, fulsome timbre of his voice wash over me, hoping that perhaps by osmosis it will improve mine; the wine, the music, the barge; it's all beginning to make sense; even the fire is pumping out the heat. There's a musical pause as he comes to the end of the phrase: '*…via, datelo a me.*' I expect him to continue, but what happens next is akin to seeing someone pronounced dead suddenly open their eyes. Tilda, previously mute, starts singing, replying to her husband's words in the most heartrending, celestial tone. I watch, half in shock, as this invalid somehow manages to produce this sound, her lips, her chin, quivering with the vibrato, the rest of her as lifeless as dough. And I listen in awe as this old, married couple slip back into their shared, glorious past. They're in sync, in harmony; there is understanding and unspoken acknowledgement regardless of Tilda's stroke, and it makes me realise, just in that moment, how at odds, how discordant Jenny and I have become. By the time the song ends I am close to tears – the poise, the beauty, the effortless performance. I notice Dr Sparks is not saying anything, not turning around; I suspect he is feeling the pain too.

'How does she do that?' I ask.

'They don't know,' he replies, finally turning to face me. 'And the strange thing is, she will not remember any of her solo arias, just the duets.'

There is a knock on the porthole window. Dr Sparks gets up and answers the door. 'Oh, hello Glen. Let me get your money.' He returns inside and disappears into the back room. A second later and he is handing over some cash to Glen, whose face I can't quite see, but whose military-style jacket, I can. He then closes the door and comes back in holding a bag of pungent dried leaves.

'Same time tomorrow?' he says.

'I'll be here,' I reply. I pick up my coat and the bag containing the small pink watch, and leave.

Back at home, after a long nap, I go down to the kitchen and grab myself a large glass of iced water. As far as I can tell, there's no one in the house, although, like she's trying to cement my feeling of loneliness and isolation, Jenny is in the studio and has company. When I drove in, I noticed a blue BMW parked in the studio courtyard. It looked vaguely familiar, and I tried to work out which of Jenny's friends it might be. Was it Lexi, perhaps, her lusty, busty, American cougar pal, or April, her stick-thin vegan Pilates instructor? I open the fridge door to see if there's anything to eat, then I hear footsteps in the hall. It's Rosa. She's holding two large bags of shopping and seems troubled.

'Hello Rosa, how are you?'

'I am fine, Mr Solomon, how are you? You leave early this morning.'

'Yes, I'm having opera lessons from an eighty-three year old man who lives on a barge just outside Bath. It's very sad, his wife's in a wheelchair, I think she's had a stroke. But she can still sing beautifully. Fifty-five years they've been married; sung together in virtually every opera house in the world. What a life, eh?'

'They must love each other very much.'

'Incredible,' I reply, 'I wonder if Jenny would look after me like that if I ended up in a wheelchair?'

Rosa's expression sours. She doesn't want to look at me. This is the first time since the day she walked in here that I sense private opinion and disapproval with no attempt to hide it. I try and lift her mood.

'Good news about the swimming pool,' I say, 'they're going to drain it next week then pour the cement.'

I don't think she quite understood what I meant. '*Piscina, el cemento,* hole *no mas,*' I say in bad Spanish using my hands to elaborate.

'Oh, *si,* very good. Ernesto, very happy,' she replies and then begins to unpack the food from the bags.

'No Consuelo tonight?' I ask. The girl always helps her mother.

'She is lying down.'

'Oh, not ill is she?'

Rosa's face lights up. 'No, Mr Solomon, she is very well, she is in love.'

This throws me slightly. 'Wow, that's…good news. Nice lad, is he?'

Rosa gives me a remarkably coy look and puts one finger to her mouth to indicate it's not something we should be discussing. Fair enough, I think, the relationship is obviously in its infancy.

'So, what's on the menu for tonight?' I ask.

'I have all ingredients for chilli con carne,' she announces proudly.

'Nice and spicy for Mr Solomon?'

'Very spicy!'

'Wait,' I suddenly remember, 'I almost forgot…it's Elena's birthday today.'

'Yes, Mr Solomon.'

'I bought her a little present when I was shopping in Bath. It's nothing much really, and I haven't had a chance to wrap it. Look, I know I've asked you a hundred times, but why don't you go and get your whole family and we'll have a little celebration for her?'

Again, Rosa looks troubled.

'Rosa, come on, talk to me…I've never seen you like this. What is it?'

It takes a while but reluctantly she confesses. 'Mrs Jenny,' she says with regret, and then her tone changes to one of outrage, 'she is with a man!'

Fuck. I'm not so much jealous as deeply concerned. The rift between Jenny and me is affecting everyone and I realise by the Velasquez family staying in their cottage, and getting on with their usual chores, they remain neutral. But by coming up to the house and socialising with me, they stand the risk of alienating Jenny; alienate Jenny and their whole position is in jeopardy.

There's been less and less for Rosa to do since the kids grew up, and now they're away at uni, there's half the washing and half the cooking and cleaning. Jenny has been complaining about Ernesto for more than a year now. She says the grounds are too big for a frail, old man. She complains about the vegetables he plants, about the gaudy choice of flowers. So she hired a landscape gardener in the summer, and confined Ernesto to trimming branches and cutting the grass.

'You know what,' I say, on reflection, 'maybe I should just give you the present and you can give it to Elena, wish her a happy birthday from me.'

I can't believe how sad I feel as I say this. It's like I'm not allowed to have any fun. It's like it would be OK if I went out and picked up some woman then brought her back to the house, but I'm not allowed to just sit down and relax with Rosa, Ernesto and the girls. Parity is my only option. I cannot appear to be benevolent because, by definition, it makes Jenny seem like the bad guy. And she's not doing herself any favours either by bringing blokes back to the studio and flaunting it in my face. There's something wrong here and I can see by Rosa's eyes, she feels it too.

'Give me five minutes,' she says and then heads back to the gatehouse cottage.

Elena loves the watch. I knew it. The kitchen is full of life and laughter as Olivia, Antonia and Elena pass it around, chuckling away at the dancing mouse. Even Ernesto is smiling, sitting at one end of the kitchen table and drinking a glass of red wine. He raises his glass to me. 'Thank you, Mr Solomon.'

Everyone is relaxed. The only girl missing is Consuelo, but I've been told she'll be along any minute.

Rosa is busy in the kitchen and, although the girls ate earlier and gorged on birthday cake, she is making a little, not so spicy, chilli for them, perhaps to put by for tomorrow. I decide to put on some music, a compilation of Quincy Jones' early jazz, and film scores. It's bright and quirky and old enough for Ernesto to remember. It's during *Soul Bossa Nova*, that I start to dance rather stupidly and the girls start copying my moves, and when Consuelo walks in.

I stop dancing immediately. I can see the superficial enhancements – a little more eye make-up, lipstick, and highlights in her hair. But there's something altogether more predatory about her. She's producing pheromones, her eyes are sparkling, and her skin is so smooth. She *is* in love. She's also holding a clutch bag, as though she's about to go out to dinner or a nightclub. I feel a little jealous, I have to admit. I don't want her to go, don't want this glamorous being to leave and go out into the night.

Thankfully, she sits down at the kitchen table, to the right of the vacant end, puts her clutch bag on the seat next to her, and is soon overwhelmed by the attention of her sisters. They're chattering away in Spanish and showing her the silly little watch. And it looks like she's staying to eat as well, because, after a short conversation, Rosa brings her a glass of wine. I've never seen this before. The girls have always been raised to look after themselves, to do things for themselves, to do things for their parents, but now it seems that Consuelo's newly found sexual charisma is allowing a certain privilege. It's as though she's ripe all of a sudden, fecund, ready for the picking, the carrier of the Velasquez seed.

The food is ready and everyone sits; me at one end, Ernesto at the other, Rosa to his right, Consuelo to my right. Rosa stands and distributes the food from several pans, large portions of meat and rice for Ernesto and me, then less and less, and less spicy, as the ages decrease. Ernesto attempts to say grace, but the youngest two girls can't stop giggling and it's so infectious. They seem to be teasing Consuelo in Spanish. At one point, Rosa snaps at them to speak English. They can, perfectly, but I think they speak Spanish so that their father can more easily understand.

I realise I haven't actually spoken to Consuelo or looked her in the eye, so I do, or at least try to. 'Hot date?' I ask, trying to sound informal and younger than my years.

'He is very hot,' she replies, looking directly back at me. She shows no aspect of the servile young girl she was yesterday. Her eyes are large and all encompassing.

The girls start teasing her again. I hear words like, 'YouTube' and '*guapo*.' I assume they're talking about Justin Bieber or Enrique Iglesias. And then Consuelo snaps, jabbers in Spanish. The girls shut up immediately, freeze. Consuelo is fierce. I remember Mili, who used to challenge anyone, especially Raffy, always backing off when Consuelo was pushed to the limit. Her green eyes, just like her father's, are piercing, her temper, sharp and to the point.

Rosa brought some cake up from the cottage. It's really just a token, I think, for my sake more than anyone else's. She tidies it up and puts a small amount on seven plates. As she delivers it to the table, I start to sing 'Happy Birthday.' Soon everyone joins in, changing it halfway through to '*Feliz Cumpleaños*' in a delicious cacophony. I'm not the first to notice the presence of an outsider; I see the look on everyone's face as though the fun police have just walked in. The song comes to an embarrassed halt.

'Oh, hi guys,' says Jenny, 'I was wondering where everyone was. I tried ringing the cottage.'

I jump up. 'Hi babe,' and go across to kiss her as though nothing at all is fractious or strained. But her eyes are glazed over, she's a little drunk, a little wobbly, and trying to appear jolly and sober.

'It's Elena's birthday,' I announce.

'Of course, happy birthday Elena,' she says, addressing Olivia.

'Thank you for the watch, Mrs Jenny,' says Elena.

'Oh, you're welcome.' She then addresses me. 'Run out of wine. I'm just gonna grab a couple of bottles, OK?'

At this point, I hurriedly remove two whites from the wine cooler. I'm desperate to not have a scene, to not have her put me down in front of the Velasquez family. By my body shape and bluster, I usher her out, out of her own home, her old home. Then we get to the hall and the argument starts.

'We've got a meeting with Martin at eleven o'clock, tomorrow,' says Jenny, snatching the wine off me.

'Can't do it,' I reply, 'I have an opera lesson.'

'You are obsessed!'

I ignore her slight and cut to the chase. 'Who the fuck is he?' I yell as quietly and as viciously as possible, right in her face.

'Who? Marcus?'

'You're kidding…not the bodybuilding barman from the Hat & Fiddle? He's only a kid.'

'Twenty-nine, actually.'

'And can keep going for hours, no doubt.'

'According to Lexi, yes.'

'You're making me look like a fool!' I plead.

'Go back to your children's party, Solomon,' she replies, then turns her back on me.

I follow Jenny out of the hall, out of the door, and watch as she walks, occasionally staggers, down the drive. It's freezing, I can see my breath. I watch her all the way until she is hidden from the driveway lights by the shadow of a tree. I don't know how long Ernesto has been standing beside me, or whether he just appeared.

'Things so different in El Salvador,' he says, 'men and women. When a woman does this to a man, she sometime just disappear. Thank you, Mr Solomon, for tonight. My family, very happy. You help me…I help you…*la piscina, el cemento*. God has answered your prayers.'

And then he just walks away with a slight limp back to the gatehouse cottage.

By the time I get back to the kitchen, even though the music is still playing, the party is clearly over. All the girls except Consuelo, who must have left for her date, are helping Rosa wipe down surfaces, load up the dishwasher, replace all the chairs tidily. There are large bowls of uneaten food covered in cling film, ready to go back to the cottage with them.

Soon, the kitchen is spotless. They bid me goodnight, and I sit back down at the table, head in my hands, eyes scrunched tight in frustration. I just want to scream or sob. 'God has answered your prayers.' I wonder what Ernesto meant by that. I am overwhelmed by solitude once again, and would like nothing more than to drink myself into oblivion. But then I hear light footsteps from behind me, feel someone's hands upon my shoulders, hands that begin a gentle massage. God has answered my prayers. I smell her perfume, feel her breath against my neck. The pressure on my shoulders lessens and then the hands move up into my hair, pulling it, nails scratching at the scalp. This is bliss. I feel a pair of arms go round me and mountainous breasts rub against the back of my head. I hear a crude American chuckle.

'Lexi?' I say, as I turn round.

She backs away still chuckling crudely. 'Who the fuck did you think it was?'

Lexi is Jenny's outrageous American friend; her hair, and she has lots of it, is dyed magenta, long and thick, and styled into Medusa-like curls. In her early forties, Lexi possesses an almost cartoon-like hourglass figure: huge breasts, tiny waist, big, round arse, and long, fine legs. She can be crude and very funny, except when she's on Prozac, which she clearly isn't now. She's wearing a figure-hugging black dress with a zip running straight up the middle.

'What are you doing here?' I ask.

'I was in the studio with Jenny, she texted me earlier, just wanted to come and say hi to my favourite rock star.'

'I thought she was with Marcus.'

'Oh, he left an hour ago. Left us a nice little package. Wanna come down and party?'

'Ugh, can't...Jenny hates me at the moment.'

'Come on Solomon, you guys were made for each other.'

'She's talking about an open marriage.'

'So what? Roy and I have an open marriage...well, at least I do. Hey, isn't she going skiing soon? I can pop over and we can fuck.'

'Thanks Lexi but...'

'Come on, Solomon, I know you always wanted to have a go on these mamas. My nipples are like corks.'

'I'm sure they are Lexi, but really...'

She grabs my hand and places it on her left breast. 'One hundred per cent State of Maine.'

'Really, Lexi...'

'He doesn't want to fuck you!'

We both turn. Consuelo is standing in the doorway with a fearsome look on her face. What's she doing here? I thought she'd gone out for the night.

'Who the fuck do you think you are,' yells Lexi, 'one of the fucking Spy Kids?'

'Lexi, please,' I say, standing up to try and placate her.

'No, fuck off, no one talks to me like that!'

Consuelo opens her clutch bag and pulls out a pointed metal nail file. Lexi notices.

'Oh, what are you gonna do with that, give me a manicure, you little bitch?'

'Lexi!' I scream. Now I'm angry. 'Go back to the studio, go on, get out! Consuelo, I want to talk to you...in the study, now!'

CHAPTER 11

'What is wrong with you?' I ask. I'm pacing around the room totally flummoxed.

Consuelo is sitting on the sofa, her head bowed, clutch bag by her side. She's breathing slowly, but heavily, probably with rage. I've never seen her like this, I've never heard her swear. No wonder Mili used to back off.

'Do you realise what's going to happen?' I continue, 'Lexi is going to go back and tell Jenny that you threatened her with a nail file. What's Jenny gonna think: that some girl we know and love has come of age and is now a danger to anyone who walks in here? You've put your whole family at risk, jeopardised your position here.'

Consuelo remains quiet, her stilted breath, the only indication that she is considering what I'm saying.

'Anyway, weren't you supposed to be going out tonight? Hot date? Rosa told me you're in love.'

She looks up at me with fury, confusion and tears in her eyes. 'Why are you pretending?' she asks with unnerving venom.

'What, what am I pretending?'

The house phone rings and I answer it. An inebriated Jenny is on the line from the studio.

'What just happened?' she asks, sounding more drunk than angry.

'Oh, it was nothing. You know Lexi…she was all over me, tits in my face, the usual. Consuelo was being protective of you, that's all. She's in tears now…'

I look at Consuelo and pull a face that says, 'This is the story if anyone asks.'

'She didn't want to upset anyone, just looking out for you, really.'

'Lexi says she threatened her with a nail file,' says Jenny.

I can hear Lexi in the background cursing and yelling.

'Come on Jenny, you know Consuelo wouldn't hurt a fly.'

'That's what I said,' she replies. There's a pause. 'Alright, drama over.'

I put down the phone but it's all too much for Consuelo. She grabs her clutch bag and storms out of the room in tears.

The next morning, I rise again at six-thirty and repeat the same hygiene regime. There was no need for a sleeping pill last night and in spite of the bad taste in my mouth from having to tell Consuelo off, I slept incredibly well. When I get down to the kitchen, Rosa has beaten me to the punch. She has hot coffee in the cafetière, and bacon and eggs ready to go.

'Good morning, Rosa,' I say, 'you don't have to do this, I'm fine with some toast.'

'No bacon?'

'Alright, a little bacon.' Even my father couldn't resist bacon.

Rosa lights one of the gas hobs and fetches a frying pan.

'Is Consuelo OK?' I ask, 'Only, there was a scene last night, one of Jenny's friends was a bit drunk and Consuelo took offence.'

Rosa sighs deeply, no smile to mask her concern. 'She was very unhappy, Mr Solomon,' she admits, 'crying, crying, crying. I ask her what is matter, but she won't say. Just crying, crying, crying.'

'Oh dear,' I reply, 'I hope I wasn't too hard on her. I had a little word in the study, may have said the wrong thing. Maybe I should speak to her when I come back from the opera lesson? When does she finish work?'

'Today, five-thirty,' replies Rosa.

'OK. Actually, maybe I should pick her up from the salon? From Cloud Nine? Take her for a coffee, have a bit of a heart-to-heart?'

'You are very kind, Mr Solomon.'

'Not at all.'

At the barge, Dr Sparks seems happy to see me, even happier when I tell him that our housekeeper, Rosa, has made us some *tamales* for our lunch. They're wrapped in silver foil and only need reheating.

We start off with a long period of warm-ups, the same ones as yesterday, but, from time to time, Dr Sparks stands up and pushes my shoulders back, tucks my chin in, changes my posture slightly, straightens my back and angles my arm in front of me like a waiter holding a cloth. I don't really know what this is supposed to do, but he tells me at one point that a cloud has left the horizon, that the transition between chest and head voice is less of a step. He also seems to be less grouchy and more optimistic.

We take a break around the same time as we did yesterday, where Dr Sparks retrieves Tilda from wherever he's hidden her, and feeds her some baby food. To give him some privacy, I take a walk along the canal. It's a mightily cold day, but at least it's dry. I have a scarf and I'm careful to protect my voice.

While I'm walking, I take out my phone to check for texts from Jenny – I should be so lucky – and emails. Aside from the usual junk, there is one of alarming importance:

Hi Solomon,

I finish here today at ITV on to pastures new. So please touch base with Marissa Young who will be taking over and is cc'd on the email. Hope it all works out and once again it was a pleasure meeting you.

Sylvania.

Not even a kiss. Fuck! I realise that this is a generic, probably ITV-monitored email – no mention of Jenny or anything personal. In a panic, I ring Simon, my agent.

'Simon, have you heard anything from ITV?'

'No, why?' There's a pause. 'Hold on,' he says. I can hear him clicking away at the keyboard of his PC. I visualise him wearing that silly Bluetooth earpiece. 'Oh yeah,' he says, 'there's an email from the celebrity producer saying she's moving on.'

'That's what I got just now. Have you been in contact with anyone about the show?'

'No, I wasn't sure whether you wanted to do it.'

'Simon,' I shout, 'I'm fucking having opera lessons on a fucking barge on the fucking Kennet and Avon canal!'

'Keep yer 'air on,' says Simon, 'I'm not fucking psychic!'

'Sorry,' I reply, 'I should have told you. Look…do me a favour, will you, and email Marissa Young – she's cc'ed on the latest one – tell her how nice it was to meet her – from me, obviously – tell her how keen I am etc, etc. Can you do that? I *have* to do this show.'

When I resume with Dr Sparks, I am no longer the same person. We attempt an aria from Gounod's Faust, luckily, or so I think, track number four on my CD. But nothing I do is right, whatever progress I may have made has been immediately wiped out by Sylvania's email. I can see him getting frustrated. We start to bicker a little; I'm talking back, making excuses, complaining about how high one of the notes is, the fact that the aria is in French. He tries his best to be civil, but one cracked note too many and he slams down the piano lid. Even Tilda flinches.

'No more, no more!' he rages. 'What is wrong with you? You cannot sing with your head full of shit. Whatever is eating you up inside, get it out, get it out!'

'I'm just worried,' I yell back. 'I'm just worried they won't pick me for the show!'

There, I said it and I know how pathetic it sounds. Here is a man who has been through the mill, has lost a son, has a wife in a wheelchair, and lives in a leaky, freezing barge, and I'm the one complaining.

'Oh,' he says in that evil, Saruman-like tone he adopts when he's at his most spiteful, 'so there is a chance that you may not be picked, that I am training some buffoon, some glory-hunter, who, if things don't go according to plan, will abandon this new little hobby of his, will drop it like the proverbial bad habit. Oh dear, oh dearie, dearie me. I was acting in the belief that this was your destiny. Now heat up the *tamales* and stop your stupid whingeing!'

After lunch, Dr Sparks seems reluctant to do any more voice coaching. He lectures me for hours, almost, it seems, in an attempt to lower my expectations. He tells me endless stories of long stints in theatres doing the same show every night, having to wait for ages backstage, not listening or following what is taking place on the actual stage, of reading, reading, always reading so many books, then getting a knock on the dressing room door, performing robotically (his word), and then returning to the book as though there had been no significant interruption. He makes my touring experiences sound utterly glamorous.

After the third time I look at my watch, he notices my fatigue and confesses, 'I hope they pick you for the show, Solomon. But if they don't, remember, there are so many more important things in life: your health, your happiness. And don't forget…keep your loved ones close; make sure they don't get on the wrong bus. See you tomorrow?'

I can't wait to get home. I drive like a mad man, park the Range Rover in the garage, then march over to see Jenny. I know exactly where she is. I unlatch the studio door and spot her instantly at the island, reading glasses on, laptop open. She doesn't even look up.

'You didn't tell me Sylvania was leaving ITV,' I fume.

'Oops,' she replies, clearly not giving a damn.

'You're just hell bent on my destruction aren't you?'

'Oh,' she gasps theatrically, 'Mama mia!'

'Fuck you!'

'Actually, I think she was fired,' she says, removing her glasses and placing them on the island.

'Really, why?'

'Too familiar with the celebrities, if you know what I mean.'

'Oh…OK,' I begin to calm down. 'How did it go with Martin today?'

'Good. He wants to bring the heavy machinery back a little sooner, in a few days' time. I told him it was OK.'

'It's fine by me.'

'So…I thought I'd get away a little earlier than planned to coincide with the building work; you know I can't stand the disruption.'

'Where?'

'Skiing, I told you.'

'With Sylvania?'

'She needs a lot of emotional support right now.'

I shake my head in disbelief. 'Look, can we talk?'

'We are talking.'

'Can we talk about us, about this rift? Aren't you tired of hiding in the studio? Don't you miss your home, the home we spent so much money on making so fucking plush, the home we raised two children in?'

'Oh,' says Jenny, 'no, I don't miss it…moment you're gone, I'm over there like a shot. Spend most of the day there. I had Rosa change the sheets on our bed…a few bloodstains. Have you got piles again?'

The very mention of the word causes a needle-like pain in my rectum. 'Actually,' I reply, 'I think I have. But wait…piles are not the problem. There's something else isn't there? And it's not to do with Sylvania or Andreas or experimenting with other partners. I've known you since you were seventeen; there's something else going on. Come on, just tell me the fucking truth.'

Jenny's expression becomes very business-like. 'I've had a buy-out offer for the patent from a pharmaceutical company in Germany.'

'When did that come in?'

'Yesterday.'

'So what? You had one six years ago, what was it, seven million? You turned it down, quite rightly.'

'This is fourteen million.'

That does sound like a lot of money, but there are so many stories of lottery winners, through their avarice and stupidity, ending up with nothing.

'Jenny,' I plead, 'you'll be left with one huge sum on which we'll have to live for the rest of our lives. Have you thought about the tax you'd have to pay? No one's paying interest any more; house prices are stagnant, the share indexes have flat-lined, what are you going to do, invest in gold? You're selling the family jewels!'

'Andreas thinks it's a good idea.'

'God!' I rage, 'I suppose he's the middleman? He's just after his commission, can't you see that? You're a cash cow to him. Jenny, I may be a musician, I may sometimes act like a fool, but I do know a bit about money.'

'Oh, I know you do. Remember our pre-nup?' she says, like she's had it in mind for some time.

'Oh, come on Jenny, we've been through this a thousand times...I was twenty-three years old, making loads of money. My business manager made me do that.'

'Yes, but you never had it annulled did you?'

'Well, since 1993 you've insisted on keeping it like that,' I reply.

'Yes, it works in my favour now. Anyway, there are lots of ways to get round the tax. Whittaker Holdings has always been an offshore company and I can become ex-pat before the deal is done. Andreas has opened a Swiss bank account for me already, just in case.'

I feel numb. This is serious. It's not about the sex, it's not about me going soft, it's about the money. She wants it all – a nice Swiss bank account, and a Nazi to go with it.

'What did I do wrong?' I ask like a hurt child. 'I've always been loving, giving, understanding; I've always been there for you... always good with the kids...'

Jenny looks at me like I'm some drunk sitting on a pavement begging for coins. 'Yes, you were always good with the kids because you're a kid yourself, Solomon. You're not gonna change,' she continues, 'and this TV show you're so obsessed with proves it; it's more of the same, the same childish need for attention.'

'What? Hang on,' I argue, 'when I met you, you were a fan, another girl in the audience, a groupie even. You didn't have a problem then.'

'That was a long time ago,' says Jenny, 'some of us have grown up.'

Fuck, I think, when did my wife become the establishment? When did she join the Third Reich or the Puritan Army?

'You have no idea what music means to me, do you?' I say, starting to feel like I'm arguing against a brick wall, 'no idea about what it's like to be possessed by a lyric or a melody.'

'Hah!' Jenny scoffs, 'You don't even make music any more.'

'I don't have a recording studio!' I yell.

'You were barely using it!' she yells back. 'How many hits have you had since Fran died? Two or three minor ones? This refurb has put about four to five hundred thousand pounds on the value of the house.' And then her expression tells me she's done with arguing. 'Solomon,' she says, 'I'm still young, I've still got my looks. There's a whole world out there waiting to be explored. I'm sorry, I want out.' And then she slams the lid down on her laptop as though that's going to hasten her exit.

I can't believe what I've just heard. She's never dismissed me like that before, not even in our worst moments. 'Two days ago you wanted an open relationship,' I plead, 'now you want a divorce? What happened in between?'

Jenny won't look at me. She just gets up and pours herself a glass of wine as though I'm not even in the room. There's nothing I can say. I can't look at her either; I just walk out the studio and back to the house like I've just been handed a life sentence.

I try and do some sums. I try and work out what it would mean if Jenny walked away with all the money, whether my royalties and touring income would be enough to run this place and pay for the Velasquez family. But the house is in Jenny's name. I suppose she would cut me a deal of some kind unless she, and her advisors, got really aggressive. I'd have to work a lot more, that's for sure; sell a couple of cars, maybe some artwork, I don't know.

I'm not really in the best of moods and I've just remembered I'd promised to pick up Consuelo from the salon. What was I thinking? All I want to do right now is jump in the hole, inhale the muddy water, and sink into its depths.

Like a zombie, I meander to the garage, open the door and stare at the Audi R8. It looks glorious, so clean, and so white. This may be the last time I get to drive it, I think. So I do, down the gravel drive and into Wells. I park it right outside the salon so everyone inside can see. Consuelo certainly sees it and gets visibly excited. The other beauty therapists and hairdressers are fussing over her, all of them gawking at the car. This will cheer her up no end. I see her put on her coat and head out of the salon door, all her co-workers waving as she leaves.

She jogs round in tiny steps to the passenger door and, after waving back to everyone, gets in. People are pressed up against the window trying to look into the car. Consuelo grabs my face and plants a big kiss on my lips. She then hugs me, though I know she's waving behind my back to her friends in the salon.

'Mr Solomon,' she says, 'I can't believe it. This car is amazing. My friends can't believe it.'

It's strange how easy it is to make one person ecstatic and how impossible it is to make another person feel even the slightest joy. There must be some kind of universal law or balance there. Consuelo's mood is rubbing off on me; it's infectious.

'Do you fancy a coffee?' I ask, 'or a glass of champagne?'

'Champagne?' she asks. 'I can't believe it!'

CHAPTER 12

I park the R8 in a public car park two streets further down, across two spaces so that no one else can park too close. There's a wine bar that Jenny and I sometimes go to; it's called La Chapelle – strangely enough, an old converted chapel – and it's only one hundred yards away back towards the salon.

It's bloody chilly tonight though; Consuelo is walking with me arm-in-arm, but it's a struggle as we're both trying to grab as much warmth from our own coats as we possibly can. I hear the occasional, 'I can't believe it,' yet I sense her trying to appear grown-up, an equal, not the daughter of a family my wife and I employ, not the tearful young girl I castigated last night.

Inside the wine bar, I choose a table in a corner near the fake pulpit and away from the cold window. There are low-hanging tungsten bulbs with red lightshades that issue a warm, almost seedy glow. The walls are dark purple painted wood, the tables, covered with red-checked tablecloths, the chairs, simple pine. It's not quite the Savoy Grill, in fact, it's nowhere near, but if you're eighteen and have just been picked up in a white Audi R8, it probably seems like you've been whisked away to paradise.

There's not a lot of choice on the menu, champagne or sparkling wine-wise; one Freixenet, which is a Cava from Spain, one Asti Spumante, and one non-vintage Moët et Chandon – which is what I order. The Moët arrives in an ice bucket; the waiter pops the cork and recognises me from having been in there before.

'Would you like to taste it?' he asks, in an Antipodean accent.

'Actually, let Consuelo taste it,' I reply, 'this is Consuelo, by the way.'

'Hi, I'm Reece,' he says. 'Don't you work in Cloud Nine?' he asks.

'Yes,' says Consuelo.

'I think you know Angie, my girlfriend.'

'Angie? I can't believe it. She did my hair today.'

Wells: it's a small world.

We clink our glasses and Consuelo just can't stop smiling. She's completely different to the smouldering psycho she was last night. She seems relaxed as though all the crying has taken away the intensity, as though she's thought long and hard about what I said. Having said that, she has spent a lot of time on her make-up – or perhaps one of the other beauty therapists has – and, I'm pretty sure she, or Angie, has added a few more blonde highlights to her hair.

'I'm really sorry about last night,' I say, 'I didn't mean to raise my voice like that.'

'No,' says Consuelo, 'you don't have to apologise, Mr Solomon, I do. I'm sorry I got so upset. I couldn't stand seeing that woman molesting you, pushing her titties in your face.'

'Thank you, Consuelo, but, you know, I can look after myself.'

Consuelo looks at me with a skewed mouth as though she finds that hard to believe. I guess my oafishness and openness with her and her sisters has led to the impression that Jenny is the grown-up and I'm some helpless, cuckolded clown. That's what Jenny just said, and there may be an element of truth in it, but Consuelo was still out of order last night. 'Lexi is a bit of a tart though,' I whisper, to put her at ease.

Consuelo giggles just like her sisters did at the table. 'And she has enormous titties,' she says, 'not like mine *or* Mrs Jenny's.'

I really don't want to get into a discussion about breast size right now, not with an eighteen-year old girl.

'I'm sure your breasts are lovely,' I say, before immediately wishing I hadn't.

She's giggling again, this time without opening her mouth; the noise is coming out of her nose. It's so charming. 'You're so good at pretending, Mr Solomon. I can't believe it.'

She said that last night – about me pretending. Maybe I am? Pretending that there's nothing wrong between Jenny and me, putting on a clown's face. It's just, I don't want to think about it, don't want my face to drop, don't want to become a snivelling wreck. We've been through these phases before. But it must be odd for the Velasquez family, after all this time, seeing my wife and me sleep in separate buildings. I wonder if they know how bad things really are.

'So,' I say, trying not to think further about it, 'have you heard about my opera lessons on a barge with this really strange guy?'

Over the next five minutes or so, I entertain Consuelo with my tales about Dr Sparks and Tilda. She's a willing audience but seems to be drinking quite fast and trying to top me up. But I'm driving – a beast of a car that I don't trust myself with – and am constantly having to put my hand over the glass.

'Mr Solomon,' says Consuelo, when I finish telling her about Tilda's unexpected and amazing singing, 'can I ask you a question?'

'Sure, go on.'

'How old were you when you made the *Dust in the Attic* video?'

'Oh…about twenty-four. Why, have you seen it?'

'Lots of times, on YouTube,' she replies. 'I can't believe it's you, lying on a bed with just a sheet draped over your privates; you have a great body.'

'Had,' I immediately interject.

'I bet lots of girls want to fuck you.'

'Wanted,' I correct her. That's the second time in two days she's used the F -word and it's the second time I've seen her with a drink in her hand.

Consuelo then starts singing, 'Dust in the attic, there is dust in the attic…' loud enough for the two other couples in the wine bar to turn their heads.

'Alright, not now, not here,' I whisper emphatically. 'Please, look, maybe we should get back to the house? I can show you how the car performs, take it down a few country lanes?'

It's a relief when I get back to Sunnymore. I managed to drive fast enough to scare Consuelo into small screams, but not fast enough to drown out the sound of the radio she insisted on putting on; Tynchy or Tinie somebody blaring out the speakers. She kept playing with the seat, trying to get it flat. But this is an R8, the seats don't go back that far.

I drop her at the gatehouse cottage and she insists she'll see me later to help her mother in the kitchen. Not that she offered much help last night, but at least she behaves herself in front of Rosa, we'll have a bit of normality. I drive as slowly as possible past the studio courtyard and am confused and dismayed to see the building in complete darkness. What does it mean? Has Jenny left already, or has she popped out to see one of her mates? I waste no time in finding out. I park the Audi in the garage and, when I realise that all our other cars are there, I immediately head for the kitchen to question Rosa.

'Have you seen Mrs Jenny?' I ask.

'Mrs Jenny gone,' she says rather callously, unless I'm misreading her.

'When?'

'I don't know exact time, Mr Solomon…perhaps after you left to meet Consuelo?'

Obviously, I think to myself.

'Did you see a taxi, a car…like the one that comes to pick us up sometimes, a big black one?'

'No, Mr Solomon, I was cleaning in the house.'

'What about Ernesto, did he see a car?'

'I have not spoken to Ernesto.'

I can see I'm getting nowhere. I rush out into the hall and look for the studio keys, hoping to check whether her things are still there. But the keys are nowhere to be seen. I rush back in.

'Have you seen the studio keys anywhere?' I ask Rosa.

'No, Mr Solomon.'

I can't believe that Jenny would take them with her and lock me out of my old recording studio, bar me from its use, like it's her newly adopted shag palace in the country. What's she intending to do, buy a place in Monaco and occasionally grace us with her presence? Fly in on a helicopter?

I head to the study, pull out my phone from my coat, which I have yet to remove, and ring Jenny. It's really no surprise when it goes straight to voicemail. I leave a garbled message, cursing her for taking the studio keys, and letting her know I'm getting a locksmith in, in the morning. She's bound to ring me back about that.

In my haste and franticness, I decide to go down to the studio to see if there's a window or a door accidentally left open, to break in if I have to, and discover the truth.

Down the gravel drive I jog, setting off the automatic lights of the studio courtyard. The building seems pretty secure at the front. I try the latch on the stable door and then the glass, retractable doors but there's no give in either, so I dart through the bushes to try the door at the back. It's dark and I have to get out my phone to use as a torch. I'm fumbling with the passcode, when I'm startled. I hear someone moving in the bushes. I catch a glimpse of a silhouette. Whoever it is, is standing about ten feet away and wearing a hat.

'Ernesto?' I ask, flashing the light in his face.

'Oh, hello, Mr Solomon,' he says, putting up a hand to block the light from his eyes.

I direct the phone's light lower down and notice he has the orange rope, or a length of it, in his hand. 'What are you doing?' I ask.

'Tying up a broken branch,' he replies.

'Can't it wait till the morning?'

'I have done it now, it's OK,' he says.

'Did you see a car arrive,' I ask, 'to take Mrs Jenny away?'

There's a pause as he calmly gathers the rope. 'I think I hear car, yes.'

This is hardly answering my question.

'It's not a bad thing that Mrs Jenny is gone,' Ernesto suggests with the eerie calm of a gravedigger, 'You are a kind man, Mr Solomon, a good man. You look after my family; you help me, I help you.'

CHAPTER 13

Last night, I managed to slip off to bed without saying goodnight to Rosa or Consuelo. The food was excellent, but the scene that followed gave me indigestion. Consuelo insisting on playing all the old Fortune Favours' songs, dancing, singing along to them; she knows every word. How? Why? Does she think I'm flattered? And no one noticed my mood, my silences, my desperation, no one mentioned the fact that Jenny had left without saying goodbye – that's if she left at all, that's if she's not wrapped in a sheet and bound with plastic, orange rope awaiting her burial under the cement of the swimming pool.

Ridiculous, I know, but I couldn't make any sense of what Ernesto said while he was dodging the torchlight from my phone. It sounded ominous, final, fatal, but then so many things round here are lost in translation.

I spoke to Raffy, briefly. I asked him if he'd heard from his mum and all he kept saying was 'Mum's the word,' as though the pair of them had some secret pact. I wanted to push him, I wanted to scream at him, but I know what he's like, he probably would have ended up in tears.

I couldn't sleep, of course, so I took two of Jenny's pills. I'm surprised she didn't take them with her as well. And I had that strange dream again; the one about the succubus. But there was a major difference, no matter what the demon tried, she could not get my penis erect. I lay there in a state of semi-paralysis and never was I more proud to be impotent. By my impotence, I had rendered the succubus powerless. It was a victory for erectile dysfunction. I wonder if I'll see her again.

The alarm goes off at six-thirty, but I can't move. That was one pill too many and I feel as though the blankets are made of lead. My ambitions, my obsessions are no longer relevant. I am a log of flesh with a mind of mush. An hour later and I still haven't moved. From the mush, I hatch a plan. I'll call Dr Sparks, explain the situation and try and reschedule for later in the day – maybe tempt him with some more food and wine. I just hope he hasn't lost his phone again.

Sluggishly, and in my dressing gown, I head downstairs. Rosa is waiting patiently; a cafetière of coffee has been made, but has no doubt gone cold.

'No opera this morning, Mr Solomon?' she asks.

'Oh…maybe a bit later. I'm a little concerned about the studio keys. I'm gonna wait a while and call a locksmith.'

'No need, Mr Solomon,' she announces proudly, 'Ernesto has found them.'

'Where?'

'Under rock in studio courtyard.'

That's weird, I think, it hasn't been light for very long.

'Would you like some breakfast now?'

'God…yes, the full monty if you have it?'

'Of course.'

While Rosa is frying bacon, I head to the study to call Dr Sparks. Thankfully after five or six rings I hear his voice.

'Dr Sparks, it's Solomon.'

'Ah, my budding protégé, I'm so glad you rang.'

'I'm sorry, I overslept. I'm going to be a little late if that's alright?'

I hear a sharp exhale of disappointment.

'I'm afraid there's no point you coming,' he explains.

'Why? Was I that bad?'

'No,' he sniggers, 'it's our barge…we have a leak. It has to go into dry dock for repair; the bilges need cleaning, you see. Glen has kindly offered to arrange it for us.'

'Right. So where are you staying?'

'The barge next door, Lost At Sea. We know the owners, we have a key, but…alas, there is no piano. I'm sorry to let you down like this.'

'Surely we just need a room with a piano?' I reply, but it's too late, he's already hung up. I call him back and, frustratingly, there's no reply. I'm beginning to feel utterly abandoned. My wife won't answer my calls, and now my mentor, my lifeline to vocal greatness, is suddenly unavailable.

After breakfast, once I've showered and put on a pair of jeans and a thick blue sweater, I go down to check on the studio, looking for clues, I guess, that might explain my wife's sudden disappearance. Ernesto, as I anticipated, has left the keys in the door. I let myself in and head straight for the larger of the two bedrooms. In the built-in wardrobes are some of Jenny's clothes; the Chanel suit she wore at the Savoy, the Christian Louboutin shoes, but it's all looking a bit thin as though a lot of her winter clothes have been removed. In a perverse way, I feel relieved. My ridiculous notion that Ernesto had done away with her was pure fantasy. Easier to accept, in some ways, than the truth; that she might not actually need me anymore.

From the wardrobe, I move to the bed. I want to know if she's cleared out the bedside cabinet drawer of any personal items or left them there to mark her territory. I open it. Depressingly, it's the latter. There it is, like a reminder of my own failings, there for all the world to see, her vibrator, an eight-inch plastic phallus with life-like veins, permanently erect, immune to dysfunction. Next to it are a pair of withered wax earplugs. I despair. Jenny may not care who sees it, but I certainly do. Christ knows what Rosa must think. I pick it up, put it in my trouser pocket and throw the earplugs in the bin.

I'm about to head back to the house when there's a knock on the door. Before I have a chance to open it, it opens anyway and in walks Lexi, full make-up, black winter coat, high-heeled boots and black leather handbag.

'Solomon,' she squeals with surprise, 'aren't you supposed to be off doing your opera thing? Is Jenny around? I thought she might like to go shopping with me in Wells, maybe catch some lunch.'

I'm suspicious about Lexi turning up like this. I wonder if this isn't Jenny once again pulling my strings from afar. Before I have a chance to say anything, Lexi puts her handbag on the kitchen island, her arms around me and kisses me gently on the lips. I'm surprised how delicate and sensual she can be. I immediately sense movement in my trousers, it's Jenny's vibrator in my pocket and I hope Lexi hasn't noticed. I self-consciously adjust my sweater to cover it.

'She left last night,' I say, looking at Lexi searchingly, 'Didn't she tell you?'

'No. Kept that quiet, secretive cow.' Lexi sounds convincing, I'll give her that.

'She's not answering my calls,' I admit, 'I've been worried sick.'

'Do you want me to try her now?'

'Yeah, actually, I would.'

Lexi takes her phone from her handbag and rings Jenny. 'It's gone to voicemail,' she says, holding her phone up as though I can somehow see inside. She then leaves Jenny a teasing, expletive-ridden message. 'And now you're on your lonesome,' she says, putting her phone back in her bag. 'You know, I'm sorry it got a bit ugly the other night, but I was a little…' she taps her nose, '…out of it. Anyway, if you want some company at any point,' she adds, 'don't hesitate to call.'

'Thanks Lexi, I'll bear that in mind.'

There's a pause while Lexi looks sultrily at my groin and then at the ground. 'Solomon,' she asks, now looking sultrily into my eyes, 'can I ask you a personal question?'

'Depends what it is.'

'Have you taken Viagra?'

Here we go, I think, what's Jenny been saying now? 'No, never.'

'It's just, I couldn't help but notice…you've had a fucking hard-on since I walked in the room.'

I suppose I could have owned up, but in light of recent accusations and rumour, I decide it can only enhance my reputation. Once I've dispatched Lexi, who's now more curious about me than ever, I head back to the house, shoot upstairs, wrap Jenny's vibrator in a hand towel and hide it on top of a wardrobe. I then return to my study and try Dr Sparks once more. After the fifth attempt, I begin to fear that I've lost him for good. I go to my laptop and search Mozartline again for the names and numbers of those other two local opera coaches. I'm only online for a second when an email comes in. It's forwarded to me by my agent Simon and he's retitled it, *'When it rains, it pours…'*

Dear Simon,

I am currently working on a new programme for the BBC with choirmaster Malachi Jones called 'Malachi Jones Goes To The Royal Opera House.' The idea of the show is to take singers from the world of pop, past and present, and have them perform a newly written opera. Shot in an informal documentary style, Malachi will meet and coach the participants and then choose who gets to sing solo before the Royal Opera House panel; the successful participants would then perform the opera at the ROH in July. Although there is an element of competition involved for the leading roles, as with all Malachi Jones' programmes, the human side will be very much to the fore. I would be keen to meet with Solomon Capri to discuss this opportunity.

Regards,
Petra Cornellisen,
Open Road Productions.

Quite honestly, I don't know what to think. Maybe this opera thing is not destiny but more like a tunnel from which I can't escape until I find its conclusion, a tunnel I'm being squeezed through, like a birth canal. Right now I can't even see a flicker of light from the opening. Having said that, I was born by caesarean section, so maybe I never will. Yet, I know for a fact that Malachi Jones makes great TV programmes, superb human stories about the uniting power of music, the healing power of music, and, after all, he is the centrepiece; the pressure and spotlight are firmly on him. I don't suppose it would hurt to meet with the producer. I am, if nothing else, slightly more prepared than when I met Steven…I mean Steve and Paul at ITV. Besides, it's never a bad idea to have a plan B. I ring Simon to see what he thinks.

'What do you reckon?' I ask, 'I mean, I can't do both shows, or can I?'

'Well, I like Malachi Jones,' replies Simon, 'he makes great TV, plus it's never a bad idea to have a plan B.'

'That's what I thought.'

'Do you want to reply to her, er, whatever her name is, personally?'

'Yeah, actually, I think I will.'

So I send Petra an email saying how much I admire Malachi Jones and how great the idea for the show sounds. She gets back to me immediately and asks whether I live in or near London, or if not, when I'll next be in town for a possible meeting. This is all very informal. I was told the day and given a choice of strict half hour slots for Popstar To Operastar. Maybe that's the way Open Road Productions works? I like it. I tell a little white lie and say I have to be in London tomorrow to see my accountant. She then writes back, *Great. Fancy meeting for lunch? 1:30, Soho House, my treat?*

Love to, I reply – even more informal, familiar even. *How will I recognise you?* I add, expecting her to come back with some quip about wearing a red rose or carrying a brown umbrella.

There's a five minute delay before she replies, *See you tomorrow. Petra xxx.*

I hate being late, and I realise I'm going to be. The train I'm on pulls into London Paddington at five past one having run on one engine alone for the last eighty miles or so. Tedium. At least now I'm in the back of a cab, peering through the window at an ominously dark sky, and the rain, which is unfortunately slowing London's traffic to a crawl. I take out my phone and send Petra a short email to say I'm on my way.

In Soho, the taxi drives down a street with unexpected road works. There's a diversion. The cabby shouts from behind the wheel that he's going to have to go back round and down Shaftesbury Avenue, but he won't charge me extra for it.

'But Greek Street's only over there,' I shout back, 'it'll be quicker to walk.'

'Up to you mate,' he replies.

Disgruntled, I pay the man and leg it. The rain is beating hard and those proud locks of mine, so carefully coiffed this morning, are slowly being pummelled into a ridiculous Georgian wig. I dodge the puddles and pellets of water until I arrive at Soho House, not in the best of shapes or moods. I sign in at reception, hand them my coat, and tell the receptionist I'm meeting a lady for lunch: last name, Cornellisen. A second girl leads me upstairs into one of the dining rooms and straight to the table.

'God, I'm so sorry I'm late,' I say, 'Look at me, I look a sight, my hair's a mess. You must excuse me, I got caught in the rain. Sorry. Petra…pleased to meet you, Solomon.'

Petra is chuckling at me. 'At least you still have your hair,' she says. She seems naturally carefree and full of the joys of spring, even in winter. A large lady in her late forties, Petra has blue eyes, plump rosy cheeks, shiny skin and thin, possibly overly-plucked eyebrows. Her head is covered by a brightly coloured headscarf. She's wearing a substantial amount of ethnic jewellery around her neck and on her fingers. Her face is vaguely familiar. I must have seen her in here before. Soho House is a private members club. I'm a member, I assume she is too. I offer my hand, which she takes briefly.

'Don't worry, Solomon, relax, sit down, please sit down.'

There's a slight sing-song quality to her voice – Danish, Swedish perhaps? She's smiling at me strangely, as though she finds my sense of panic amusing. 'Would you like a drink?' she says.

'Yes, I could murder one,' I reply.

Petra waves at a sprightly young waitress who promptly arrives at the table and takes our drink order – red wine for me, a white wine spritzer for Petra. While we wait, we study the menus.

'So, are you taking every candidate out to lunch?' I ask cheekily. 'You must have a big budget. That's a lot of food.' That was a stupid thing to say, Solomon, she obviously does eat a lot of food. Petra doesn't answer, she just glances down at the menu. I'm slightly unnerved by her constant knowing look, her secret smiles, and this indefinable familiarity. She seems in no hurry to interview me. 'Do you mind if I ask who else you've approached for this programme?' I say, trying to coax her into at least talking about the show.

She looks up, surprised by the question. 'I don't mind,' she says, and then starts reeling off a series of household names. The list is endless, containing all the usual suspects. I'm beginning to prefer the way I was dealt with at ITV. No one put it there on a plate for me like a regurgitated curry, no one punctured my balloon.

'Aren't you afraid it might look like the ageing cast of Band Aid?' I suggest, rather cynically.

Petra chuckles again. 'Malachi was talking about that only the other day. Don't worry, there will be lots of younger artists, all shapes and sizes, all colours...like a Benetton ad.'

'Right...' Like a Benetton ad? Is she serious?

'Solomon,' she continues, more forcefully, 'we're asking a lot of people, I admit, because we know that a lot of people will drop out. In some ways, it's no different to filming kids from a rough council estate. Because of the style in which we shoot, there is little order. Things are decided as we go along, that's what makes it interesting. We rely on trust, goodwill, and spontaneity. There are no contracts, at least not to begin with; the people who end up going along with it will be the people who most enjoy it, who believe in the project. It's that simple. But you must meet Malachi, because he really is inspirational.' She takes a sip of her spritzer. 'Anyway, it should be easy for you, you used to sing opera when you were a kid, right? I remember you singing opera in the dressing room.'

Dressing room? What's she talking about?

'You really don't remember me, do you?' she adds.

I'm confused, and it shows.

'Have I really changed that much?'

I'm still confused...and worried.

'I know,' she admits, 'I got fat, my hair is just starting to grow back. My maiden name is Wolters. Petra Wolters? Petra and Anke, remember?'

CHAPTER 14

Oh my God, it's Panki from Anki and Panki, the Dutch girls who were always down the front. She used to be gorgeous, absolutely fucking gorgeous. The two of them were absolutely fucking gorgeous. And what a fucking tag team, slim, blonde, firm breasts, wonderful lashings of dark-blonde pubic hair. They would do each other. They would do me. I would do them. Life was good. Life is strange. What happened to Panki? What happened to us all?

'Petra,' I say, gushing. I stand up, reach across and hug her, then kiss her on the lips. 'I can't believe it…I just…now I understand why we're not meeting in some office somewhere. God, it's been so long. Fuck, twenty-eight years? You haven't changed,' I lie, 'I mean…we're all a little older. What happened to Anke, is she still in London?'

'You didn't know?'

My expression answers that question.

'She died in ninety-six. Car crash just outside Rotterdam. Not her fault…stupid lorry driver. She left a young daughter as well. It's so sad.'

'I'm so sorry.'

'Life can be cruel,' she replies. 'You must have felt sick when Fran died?'

'Sick as a dog,' I admit, 'I'm not sure if I ever recovered. I'm not sure if my wife ever recovered. It kinda changed everything.'

For the next hour or so we roll back the years, completely relaxed in each other's company. The wine is flowing. I tell her about my kids and she tells me about her three daughters, her short-sighted sixty-seven year old husband, her battle with cancer and how awful the chemotherapy was. I feel for her and completely forget what I'm here for.

'You know,' she confesses, 'you don't have to worry about me or what happened in the past. If I'd wanted to, I would have contacted you years ago. But you got married and I respect that. This is purely professional. I don't want anything from you, I'm not after your body any more.'

'Probably wise,' I suggest.

'But, if you do agree to the show, I will look after you. I'll make sure you get treated with respect. I owe it to Anke.'

'Anke. God, I still can't believe it. Look, while we're being honest, I have to tell you I've been contacted about Popstar To Operastar. I went along for a meeting.'

She seems unperturbed. 'What do you think of the show?' she asks.

'Well…I don't know…it's a bit cheesy.'

'Malachi loathes it. He believes the show is set up in such a way that only the opera singers come away with any kudos. He also believes they will run out of steam. There are only so many times you can have someone sing *Nessun Dorma*. They rely on familiarity. The programme we are making won't be like that.'

This all sounds fair enough. 'What about this new opera?' I ask. 'Has it been written yet? Do you know what it's about?'

'Have you seen the play, *Jerusalem*?'

'No.'

'You should. It's playing at The Apollo Theatre on Shaftesbury Avenue at the moment. We've been talking to the author about turning it into an opera; it would be perfect.' She pauses, looks around the room to see if anyone's listening, then lowers her voice regardless of the fact that no one is. 'I'm not sure how busy you are at the moment, Solomon,' she says, 'but it would be really helpful if you see it before you meet Malachi…'

I suppose with no wife to go home to, and no opera coach to force me to get up early in the morning, I may as well stay in London a little longer – maybe stay the night or take the late train home. After I leave Soho House, I walk in the drizzle for about ten minutes until I reach the Covent Garden Hotel. I ask at reception if they have a room, which they do. I check in, and then ask the concierge if he can arrange a ticket for the evening's performance of *Jerusalem*.

Up in the room, I've just got out the shower, trying once again to fix my poodle hair, when the phone rings. It's the concierge saying he can get a ticket but it's pretty much at the back of the theatre and will that be OK? I tell him it's not a problem. To be fair, I just want to say I've seen it; I may even leave early if it gets a bit dull.

I have a lot of time to kill, I realise. I watch a couple of the in-house adult movies, hit the mini-bar for two gin and tonics and a beer, and leave about five messages on Jenny's voicemail in tones ranging from rage to remorse. I do not tell her, however, that I'm in London or that I had lunch with Panki of Anki and Panki fame. That would only make matters worse. Around six, an envelope containing the ticket is slipped under my door. That's good service. They've had a runner go to the box office and deliver it to my room. An hour later, I'm making my way to the theatre to get there a little early, have a drink in the bar, and order one for the interval. I then find out that there are two intervals and that the play is around three hours long. This better be good. I down two glasses of cheap white wine, and head for my seat right at the back of the stalls.

The house lights go down; the stage lights creep up. We see a curtain bearing a faded Cross of St George. A teenage girl wearing fairy wings appears and sings William Blake's *Jerusalem* in a meek, deliberately self-conscious way. OK, now I see where the play got its name from, not the city in Israel or, indeed, the artichoke. The girl is interrupted by the sound of a thumping bass sequence. She runs off stage and then the scene explodes into life. Loud rave music is bursting through the speakers. I know this song, I've heard Mili play it at home – it's *Invaders Must Die* by *The Prodigy*. Lights are flashing, people on stage are going mad, jumping up and down, spliffs on the go, cans of beer; it's fantastic, visceral, then suddenly, it falls quiet. We hear the sound of birdsong.

The setting is a woodland. At the back of the stage is a huge silver Airstream caravan, at the front, a scrap heap of cheap, worn furniture, logs of wood, an old fridge, a smashed flat screen TV, and empty beer cans. Very quickly, we learn that the central character is a wayward, lawless, drunk, drug-dealing gypsy, and that the council – funnily enough, the Kennet and Avon council – is trying to evict him. It would be a lot simpler if he lived on a barge. There follows some fantastic dialogue, some wonderful gags, and a fuck of a lot of swearing. I look around at the mainly middle-class, middle-aged audience, and I see that some of them, possibly the tourists, weren't prepared for this kind of language. I'm also trying to work out how it would translate into opera. Would they write in all the swear words? And then I remember my first proper lesson with Dr Sparks when he had me singing, 'this coffee tastes like shit,' albeit it in Italian. And then there are the accents; the play is based in Wiltshire and pretty much everyone is adopting a strong West Country lilt.

The first third goes by in a flash. I'm not sure if it's an hour or forty-five minutes long, but you can't take your eyes off the main character, played superbly by Mark Rylance. The lights go up. A lot of people around me immediately get up and head for the bar and so do I. I stand, and glance down at the people at the front, some of whom are also making their way out. And then I see two people that look so much like Jenny and Andreas that I feel my skin begin to prickle and my heart pound in my chest. I follow them with my eyes all the way to the exit. Is it them? I can't be sure. Now I've lost them. Surely, I'll find them in the bar.

I realise I'm nearer and will get there first, approaching from the opposite side of the theatre. I can stand to one side of the entrance and watch as they walk past me. I'll be hidden, or at least unseen. And that's what I do, though admittedly, I have no idea what to say or do if it is them. The seconds evaporate as I study, like a paranoid hawk, everyone who passes. My heart is still going crazy, and my jaw is clenched tight as wave upon wave of shivers grip my body. And then they stroll nonchalantly by, blissfully unaware of my presence. It's them alright, and my wife is holding hands with my nemesis. I feel such a cold rage. I sneak up behind Jenny – she has absolutely no idea – and very calmly, very sinisterly say, 'You never call…you never write…' She lets go of Andreas' hand and turns round. The shock on her face gives me immense satisfaction and then I let loose. 'I thought you were dead! Dead for fuck's sake!' I scream.

'Solomon, what are you doing here?'

'Watching a play, what else?' I reply, not taking my mad eyes off her.

'Are you stalking me? How did you know I was going to be here tonight?'

I'm stuck for words at this point. I'm breathing hard and my anger is clear for everyone to see. In fact, everyone in the bar is watching. Then Andreas steps in. 'Maybe it would be better if you left,' he says.

The gall, the cheek; I am outraged. He's now positioning himself between me and my wife, as though I might do her harm. 'Why should I leave?' I reply to the big man, 'I have a ticket. Why don't you leave? Why don't you go back to Switzerland, go back and put your jack boots on, you fucking Nazi!' And then stupidly I take a swing at him. I'm not a violent man, nor am I known for my boxing skills. One swerve of his big head, a reflex jab to my stomach and I'm doubled up on the floor. Minutes later, I am escorted by security out of the building.

CHAPTER 15

I feel humiliated. I don't even bother to check out of the hotel. I hail a cab and head straight for Paddington. Why did I do that? I keep asking myself on the train journey back. I lost control, lost my dignity. I didn't even get to find out what happens in the play. It's like a sudden curse has been placed on me by someone, somewhere. I think back to that night at the Savoy, how Jenny and I split up not long after the first time we stayed there. Now, it all seems to be happening again, while at the same time, Panki, or Petra, is suddenly back in my life.

But what do I do? Do I lie down and die, or do I fight back? My stomach is hurting and I'm not sure if it's from the punch Andreas threw or the fact that, aside from a few mini bar snacks, I haven't eaten anything since lunch. I decide to take one option out of the equation and slink along to the train buffet where I buy a microwaved lasagne and a small bottle of rosé wine. I then return to my seat.

I can't help it; I keep replaying the scene over and over in my head. If I was worried before, I'm even more worried now. I'm worried about Jenny's resolve, worried about losing the house. For that ridiculous moment, I identify with the lead character in *Jerusalem*, and the threat of him being turfed out of his own home. Squatter's rights, that's what I need. Except, I'm not a squatter. Maybe I can hire a few? After burning my tongue badly on the nuked lasagne, I realise I have no alternative but to fight back. I make a vow, there and then, to order the script and find out what the fuck happens in that play.

The next morning, after an anxious sleep, I wake around seven, beat Rosa to the punch, grab a piece of toast and a cup of coffee, then hop in the Range Rover and head for Hampton Wharf. I park behind the grubby ice cream van, get out the car, and walk down the steps to the canal.

At least Dr Sparks wasn't lying. Almaviva has gone, and I see movement through the windows of Lost At Sea. I jump onto its hull and start hammering at the front door. After a few seconds, the old man opens it. He seems rightfully surprised to see me.

'Solomon,' he says, raising his substantial eyebrows, 'what brings you down to the canal this morning? Clearly, it's not for an opera lesson; I told you there's no piano here.'

'It is for an opera lesson. Look,' I explain, 'I've had an idea. Why don't you and Tilda come and stay with me while your barge is being fixed? I have an empty guest house, it's on one level, no steps, perfect for a wheelchair; there are two bedrooms, en suite bathrooms, a kitchen, plus an upright grand piano. You can live in luxury and I can get back on track.'

I can see the cogs of pride whirring in the old man's brain. I can also picture Jenny's look of horror should she find out.

'I'm afraid that won't be possible,' he replies, as noble as ever.

'Think of Tilda,' I argue, 'It's freezing here, my place is so plush, so comfortable.'

'You're very kind, but I can't possibly accept.'

'I have some excellent Italian wine, super-Tuscans, cases of the stuff,' I say, tempting him further, 'I have a cook who is quite frankly underworked. Look, I'll even buy you a year's supply of Hobnobs...'

'Hmm...' 'Come on. What's stopping you?'

'Will I be able to smoke spliff in there?'

'Ha!' I guffaw, 'I'll even light it for you.'

I suppose the only time I begin to regret my decision is when I'm hauling Tilda, who is heavily bundled in blankets, in her wheelchair up the steps from the canal to the road. Luckily, the dreadlocked guy, who I now know as Gavin, is giving me a hand and taking the bulk of the weight by being the lower man down.

He may smell, but he's wiry and strong. Even so, due to the angle, this is killing my back. Finally, we get Tilda on the pavement beside the Range Rover and manage to lift her onto the back seat. By this time, Dr Sparks, wearing a heavy coat and brown trilby, has arrived with a suitcase and a number of manuscripts. He places them in the boot along with Tilda's collapsed wheelchair. He then joins Tilda on the backseat and does up her seatbelt for her. He removes his hat and places it on his lap.

There isn't much conversation during the journey, just Dr Sparks telling me how kind I am and that they won't stay long, they won't be a burden. I put on, in the background, *Avant de quitter ces lieux* from Gounod's *Faust* – the aria I struggled with the other day, just to remind Sparks where we'd got to in our last lesson. Literally, the title translates as, 'Before we leave these places.' Valentin, the character singing, has been called off to war, a thing he's not afraid of due to a sacred medallion he's carrying. In the aria he asks God to look after his sister, and also prays that should he die, he will be allowed to watch over her from Heaven. It is a proud and sentimental aria and the mood is emulated by Dr Sparks as he affectionately takes Tilda's hand.

I turn the volume up slightly as we head south from Bath, leaving the city behind to cut through rolling hills veiled by a light mist of rain, the sky above, pregnant with puffy clouds. The countryside opens up before us, as voluptuous as a Ruben's nude. There are curves and mounds and dips and crevices all in a shade of green that seems immune to the winter.

When the aria finishes, we drive in silence for another twenty minutes. I get the feeling that neither Dr Sparks nor Tilda have been out of the barge lately for any length of time, except, perhaps, to the hospital. And I get a strong sense that the old man is growing fonder of this idea by the second. The car is quiet, warm and my driving is steady. I have become the silent chauffeur, the nanny gently rocking the pram. I look in the mirror and notice they've both fallen asleep.

Finally, we reach the black gates. Rosa has obviously heard the car and darts out in front of us from the gatehouse cottage. My last instruction to her before I went to bed last night was to prepare the studio for some old and infirm guests. It was obvious who I meant, and she couldn't have been happier.

'Here we are,' I say, trying to rouse my passengers, 'welcome to Sunnymore.'

I drive in and park in the studio courtyard as close to the main door as possible. We don't really need Rosa's help but she's offering it anyway and even rearranging Tilda's blankets once we set her in her wheelchair. Within minutes we have Tilda safely inside, parked in the big red kitchen.

'This is Rosa, our fabulous cook and housekeeper...Dr Eugene Sparks and his wife Tilda.'

Rosa seems ecstatic and, in her excitement, is forgetting to speak in English. She takes Dr Sparks' hand and vigorously shakes it, then does the same to Tilda who doesn't seem in any way overawed or particularly aware of her new surroundings.

'This is a lot larger than it appears from outside,' says Sparks, clearly impressed by the Tardis-like space, the swanky fixtures and fittings, and the amount of light, even in winter, from the skylights and the glass doors.

'It used to be a recording studio,' I say, as I lead him into the main room. 'I had a state-of-the-art sound board across here and giant speakers where the mezzanine level now is. The whole place was soundproofed up to the hilt, the ceiling about six feet lower with an air conditioning unit running through the middle. There were tape machines, computers, keyboards and guitars lying all round the place. Hard to believe, looking at this now. I had a real life-laundry session when I cleared this place out.'

Dr Sparks examines every niche and seems to consider what I've just said. 'So, now it's just you and your piano,' he says, 'maybe this is your destiny. May I?'

'Please.'

Dr Sparks moves toward the upright piano, which is flush against the wall beneath the spiral of the mezzanine steps. He opens the lid and plays a few scales. 'And you keep it in tune,' he enthuses. 'It sounds good in this room, a good echo from the stone floor and the high ceiling, perfect, perfect.'

'I know,' I say, 'I have tested out my tonsils in here a few times.'

'And this is just the guest accommodation?'

'Yes, the gatehouse cottage is where Rosa and her family live; the main house is up the drive. I'll show you round after lunch.'

Sparks looks at me wistfully. 'You live like a king, Solomon. Do you understand how lucky you are?'

I'm not quite sure what to tell Sparks because right now I don't feel particularly lucky. 'Actually, my career was one thing,' I admit, 'but a lot of this is down to my wife.'

'I see. Well, I'm very much looking forward to meeting her,' he replies.

Maybe I should have kept my mouth shut.

'Actually, Jenny is skiing with friends at the moment…or about to be,' I say, 'in Switzerland.'

'And does she know she has guests?' he asks, as though he can sense the marital rift.

'Oh yes, she couldn't be happier,' I lie.

Thankfully, there is a welcome distraction. Like hounds to the rescue, Smooch and Kipper scamper up to the glass doors, Kipper scratching at the glass, marking it with a muddy paw.

'Rosa,' I shout, 'can you let the dogs in?' and watch them dart across the courtyard as the latch on the main door sounds.

Smooch, the feisty little fellow, races in and does his usual round of sniffing, probably in search of Jenny, but Kipper remains in the kitchen, strangely infatuated with Tilda. I crane my neck and watch as he goes down on his haunches and makes sorrowful howls as though he hasn't been walked for a week or so. He then approaches Tilda and timidly starts sniffing her blanket and licking her hand. Tilda breaks into a half-smile and I wonder whether she's soiled herself again and that's what's drawing Kipper to her. But then he sinks his teeth into one of her blankets and starts tugging at it as if to pull it off.

'Kipper!' I shout. Rosa moves to intervene.

'It's OK,' says Sparks sidling up to his wife, 'she is too warm. Look, she is sweating. Your dog must have sensed this.'

Sparks loosens both Tilda's blankets, takes out a handkerchief and mops her brow.

'It is very warm in here,' he continues, removing his coat.

'Under-floor heating,' I reply.

While Eugene and Tilda settle into their new accommodation, I walk up to the house to make a few private phone calls. The first person I ring is Jenny. As usual, it goes straight to voicemail. I leave yet another message.

'Hi babe – I can still call you babe, can I? – just wanted to let you know that I'm fine by the way, in case you were worried. That punch didn't really hurt, just caught me off guard. Oh...and we have guests staying in the studio. My opera coach and his wife – their bilges are being cleaned. Don't suppose you know what bilges are. Never mind. Enjoy London.'

And then I hang up. Thirty seconds later I get a phone call and it's Jenny.

'You can't do this,' she says.

'Really? What can't I do?'

'You can't put those people in the pad while their bulges are being cleaned, I'm living there.'

'No you're not,' I reply, 'you're in London with the middle man.'

'We flew to Switzerland early this morning, actually. Anyway, my things are in there.'

'I've had them moved.'

'Personal things,' she adds.

'Oh, don't worry, I found your vibrator but where's your stash?'

'Back of the right hand drawer in the desk on the mezzanine. Touch any of it and I'll kill you. And another thing…I told Mili she can stay there with her boyfriend when they come down.'

'Well I'll just tell her she can't.'

'She'll hate you.'

'She'll hate me even more when I beat her at tennis.'

'Good luck.'

'You don't need luck when you're Solomon Capri!'

And then I hang up. My God, that felt amazing! I'm fighting back!

The next person I ring is Simon, my agent.

'Hi Simon, just wanted to let you know, I met with the woman who's producing the Malachi Jones programme. Turns out she's an old flame.'

'That could come in handy.'

'Yeah, that's what I thought. Looks like we have a plan B, if not a new plan A. Talking of which, did you contact Marissa Young at ITV?'

'Yeah, I sent her an email…'

'I didn't see it. Did you cc me?'

'No, do you want me to forward it to you?'

'No, just tell me what it said.'

'Oh, it was pretty short, just along the lines of what you told me to say. Then she replied very politely but without giving too much away, so I sent her a bunch of flowers…from you.'

'Brilliant.'

'And then I took her out for a drink in The American Bar at the Savoy.'

'Really?'

'Yeah, she's a corker, isn't she? Hit it off really well.'

'And?'

'Well, she couldn't say too much, but reading between the lines, she hinted at the fact that the opera coach at ITV thought you were a potential winner. It's just down to the producers now.'

'Wow, that's great news. Thanks Simon. Beyond the call of duty. The flowers? Excellent idea.'

'Yeah, well, you know...a way to a woman's heart and all that...I'll probably find out a little more when I take her to dinner.'

'Blimey. What about your wife?'

'It's business, isn't it?'

'Sly dog.'

Less than a minute after getting off the phone with Simon, I get a panicky call from my daughter.

'Dad?'

'Hi Mili.' There's no confusion here, I know exactly what this is about.

'Mum said I could stay in the pad when I come down and now she says there's an old couple living there.'

'Yes, my opera coach and his disabled wife, who live on a freezing, leaky barge, are staying there while their bilges are being cleaned.'

'What are bilges?'

'Actually, I'm not sure.'

'But I told my boyfriend, I showed him the pictures of the walk-in shower and the big TV.'

'Mili, as you know, there are plenty of bedrooms in the house. Besides, I'm sure Dr Sparks won't mind you watching the big TV in the studio, he'll even share a spliff with you.'

'Oh,' says Mili, 'that sounds alright. Got some good stuff has he?'

'Huh?' I was being flippant. 'Since when did you smoke pot or weed or whatever it's called these days.'

'Come on Dad, I'm at university, it's part of the curriculum.'

The lesson could not have gone any better. It was so much easier than singing on the barge, where, at times, I could see my own breath and where the low wooden ceiling would creak and sigh in disappointment at my every cracked note. And the echo in the studio, just as Dr Sparks pointed out, is so supportive of my efforts. Strange too to be singing on terra firma. I realise, in hindsight, that the barge rocked gently in the water, but I didn't appreciate how unsettling it was, especially when trying to get my tongue round Faust.

Of course, the good lunch really helped: the rotisserie chicken, the potatoes and onions basted in the chicken fat. Rosa had prepared a roast tomato soup thickened with bread for Tilda and insisted on spoon-feeding her herself. Dr Sparks relished the freedom; the more the bottle of Tignanello got drained, the more humorous his stories became. We sat across from each other at the glass table beneath the mezzanine floor and I saw a glint in the old man's eyes as though a weight had been removed, as though this was his first real break in a while. I told him about Malachi Jones and my trip up to London – not about the fracas in the theatre, though. He seemed really impressed that the opera was to be performed at the Royal Opera House and wished me the best of luck.

After the lesson, and with Tilda positioned – in some way I don't wish to imagine – in their en suite bathroom, I walk with Dr Sparks up the drive and give him a brief tour of the ground floor of the main house. He's quietly appreciative of the space and the décor, and is surprised how different in feel the main house is to the studio. But when we get to the conservatory, his eyes open wide. I admit, the view is magnificent, all the way across the lawns, over great trees and down through the valley. And the conservatory's half-dome shape is unusual too – an idea taken from the Eden

Project, although that half-dome was stuffed full of exotic plants. Sadly, there are none here; in fact, it's probably the most neglected part of the house. Any piece of furniture that we fall out of love with tends to get put in the conservatory along with the brown three-piece suite that sits here now. And it gets cold too, in winter. Then on hot summer days, it gets unbearably humid even with the doors open. Today is not so bad though and Sparks walks to the far end to grab a good look at the view.

'You have a hole in your garden,' he says, as I join him.

'Oh that,' I reply. 'Yes, it's become a bit of an issue. It's a swimming pool – kind of, an eco-pool. It'll look like a pond or a small lake once it's finished, but it's filtered so you can swim in it. And it'll be lined as well with organic seaweed something-or-other. That reminds me, the machinery is coming back in tomorrow. They're finally gonna finish it off. Hopefully the noise won't be too disruptive.'

Sparks turns and examines the room.

'What do you use this conservatory for?' he asks.

'Not a lot, to be honest. We have the occasional party in here, like last year on my birthday – that was the last one. We normally go away, but we decided as it was the kids' first summer back from university, we'd stay in England. It was a fun evening – string quartet, we made everyone dress up; men in dinner jackets, women in ball gowns, that kind of thing. Very grown up, very formal, very nouveau.'

There seems to be something on Dr Sparks' mind, but he's not sharing it. Then, out of the blue, he starts singing very loudly in that remarkable tone of his. He follows the outburst with a series of claps, testing the echo, I assume.

'Have you ever had a piano in here?' he asks.

'No, I've pretty much confined the music-making to the studio.'

'I don't suppose it would impinge too much on the Solomon Capri budget if you were to rent or even buy a grand piano for this space? A good one, a Bösendorfer or a Steinway perhaps?'

'I'm sure I could find the money from somewhere. Why, are you not keen on doing lessons in the studio?'

'I'm not talking about lessons, Solomon, I'm talking about a recital.'

I'm confused. 'What kind of recital?'

'An operatic one, of course.'

'By me?'

'By you…and me, and perhaps even Tilda. Plus I know a very good soprano who could do with a little cheering up. I'm sure she would be delighted to join in.'

'But I've only been having lessons for a few days,' I protest.

'Lessons are one thing, performance is another. You're too comfortable in this nether world of pop-star-opera-star-doesn't-have-to-be-that-good-star. You need a goal, you need an audience. You need to start seeing yourself as an opera singer.'

Sparks pauses and takes a very close look at my chin. 'Is that a goatee you're growing?'

'Um, trying to.'

'Good. Facial hair always helps.'

'But…who will be in the audience?'

'Friends and family. Plus I'm sure there'll be many people in Wells interested in hearing Solomon Capri sing again. You can put flyers in some of the shop windows.'

'Maybe I should speak to my agent,' I say, 'I mean, I'm trying to keep it a secret, my lessons and everything, just in case it doesn't work out.'

'Poppycock. Use a pseudonym. I'll even make one up for you. How about Alberto Balsam?'

'Isn't that a shampoo?'

'Never mind that. Get your head round it, Solomon. I'll see you later.' He then turns and walks away.

CHAPTER 16

'Christ,' I think, 'a recital in my conservatory.' Actually, maybe I should refer to it from now on as The Conservatoire. I wonder what Fran would think? Maybe he's looking down at me from heaven saying, 'Whatever happened to you, Solomon Capri? Whatever happened to the coke-snorting rock 'n' roller, the pop star? Performing operatic recitals to friends and family and a few farmers from Wells?'

I feel momentarily ashamed. I remember Fran on his deathbed, talking about how he'd let the band down, persuading me that this was not the end, encouraging me to carry on and take Fortune Favours The Brave to another level. He had some crazy drug-induced idea that we'd one day be inducted into the Rock and Roll Hall of Fame, and he'd become a myth, a legend like Syd Barrett or Brian Jones; he would become immortal. But I let him down. I didn't manage it. Life became too easy, what with Jenny's money. And then I got old. That's what happens, Fran, people get old when they don't die young.

I don't know why holding a recital seems so demeaning. Is it demeaning? Why, because it's not on TV, or at the Royal Opera House, because it's honest and simple, or bloody middle class? Maybe that's what it is? I forget that opera is a world of posh accents and privilege – elitist. We used to get away with murder, Fortune Favours, singing out of tune, playing out of time. It didn't matter. Listen to Dylan or Lennon. It's not the vibrato; the control, the pitch – it's the message, the personality, the blood and guts.

Now I'm depressed. I admit, when I listen to my opera CD, I can barely tell the difference between one singer and the next. Yes, I know that the tones vary, and the age of the recording makes a difference, but it all seems so…uniform, robotic. Maybe that's what Sparks was talking about, maybe you do need to be a robot to sing this stuff.

Needless to say, my next action is to browse the Internet for a grand piano. And there are plenty of them: I find a highly ornate, custom restored, oak satin Bösendorfer on Ebay worth more than a quarter of a million dollars. I'm tempted to bid for it just to put Jenny's nose out of joint. I can hear her screaming at me already, 'You did what?!' But, sensibly, I call Sulis Pianos in Bath and hire a Steinway. That way if Sparks doesn't like the sound of it – something I'd already written into the equation – I can change it. It arrives tomorrow, some time after the heavy machinery.

After this, I find myself at a loss, alone in a big house. If feels as is if there's a magnet drawing me toward the studio. I'm dying to pop down and share another glass of wine with Dr Sparks, arrange their next meal etc, but I know he's not one for nannying and it's probably best to give him and Tilda some space. Besides, there was plenty of tomato soup left and he's a dab hand with a corkscrew.

I decide to leave it for a couple of hours and then check on them, but my mind keeps drifting back. I wonder what time they go to bed? Early, I'm sure, these old people. I wonder if they watch TV? I mean, there wasn't one on the barge. Or films? I have plenty of Blu-rays. Maybe they'd like to watch a film before going to bed, something in black and white like *Gone With The Wind*? It's probably because of these neurotic concerns that I am suddenly reminded of my pledge to Rosa and Ernesto about buying them new wedding rings. When was it? A few days ago and I haven't given it another thought. I decide that now is as good a time as any to pop into Wells and have a look in the jeweller's.

Five minutes later, I'm in my coat, walking down the driveway to the gatehouse cottage in search of Rosa and, hopefully, Ernesto. I realise I need to have some idea about ring size. What did Jenny used to say? It's always better to buy them too large than too small, that way they can be resized.

I politely knock on the cottage door and then open it. At first glance, there's no sign of Rosa in the kitchen-lounge area although there's a strong aroma of freshly brewed coffee, and a cup on the kitchen table giving off steam. I assume she's upstairs. I enter the cottage, stand at the foot of the small staircase and yell, 'Rosa?' When there's no reply, I get curious. I realise I haven't been upstairs in the gatehouse cottage for years. We've had electricians in, the odd plumber or two, but I've always kept a healthy distance, stayed away, given the Velasquez family a respectful amount of space. That's why I feel slightly nervous as I take to the steps. I feel like an intruder. 'Rosa?' I ask again, trying to justify my presence. No, not a soul.

Up in the small corridor, I pause at the doorway of the first bedroom. This is where Antonia, Elena and Olivia sleep, all together in one tiny room. There are two bunk beds pushed tight against one wall and a single divan only a couple of feet away. There are dolls and cuddly toys on the bunk beds, some teen magazines and posters of a boy band I've never heard of on the wall. The beds are cheap, the room badly needs repainting, there's a crack in the window, and I have a gnawing sense of guilt seeing everything, and everyone, crammed into such a small space. I mean, we spent hundreds of thousands refurbishing the studio; it doesn't seem right. I make a promise there and then to have the gatehouse cottage redecorated ASAP.

Further along the corridor, I notice the door to the second bedroom is slightly ajar. I hesitate. This is Consuelo's room and I really shouldn't be looking inside. It feels like I'm poised, hand hovering over the cover of a teenage girl's intimate personal diary. And yet, perhaps inside lie clues to her recent behaviour. I give the door a nudge with my elbow, like I'm suddenly worried about leaving fingerprints; it opens, and then my jaw drops at what I see.

The walls of Consuelo's bedroom are plastered with images of myself as a young pop star. Her room is a shrine to Fortune

Favours The Brave. Posters are everywhere, framed covers from Smash Hits, Melody Maker, NME, some of them even signed. Where did she get all this paraphernalia? Our attic, on eBay? How come I didn't know about this? On top of a pine chest of drawers is a framed photo of Consuelo and me, just the two of us, taken last year on my birthday. Why didn't Rosa or Ernesto tell me their daughter was so infatuated? Did they encourage it? When did this obsession begin? I feel suddenly trapped, I don't know why, sullied even. I think back to the way she was holding me the other day, the foot massage, the champagne. What have I done?

I hear the cottage door open downstairs. I quickly rush back down to the kitchen. Rosa seems surprised to see me, so I put on as happy and natural a face as I can muster.

'Rosa, there you are, I was looking for you. I thought you might be upstairs. Hey, I'm popping into Wells for a couple of things, so I thought I'd have a look in the jeweller's for those wedding rings I promised you.'

'Oh, Mr Solomon, you are too kind. You don't have to.' She seems unconcerned that I may have been snooping in the bedrooms, and genuinely moved that I hadn't forgotten about the rings.

'No, really, I insist, it's our muddy hole Ernesto slipped into. Can I see your wedding ring to check its size?'

'Si, yes, of course.'

It takes about five minutes and a fair amount of butter for Rosa to remove her simple gold band. Clearly her fingers have fattened since she first put it on and there's a deep, pale indentation around the base of her ring finger. I'm about to suggest that maybe I should get her a slightly larger ring but think better of it. I will, I just won't tell her.

'Do you mind?' I say, as I slip it over a succession of my own fingers to gauge its diameter. Once I feel confident of its size, I hand it back and watch as she struggles to get it back on.

'Where's Ernesto?' I ask, hoping to have him try my wedding ring on to see how well it fits.

'He is showing Mrs Tilda the garden. She is very happy.'

'Really? That's good of him, but won't the wheelchair have trouble with the terrain?'

'He use the wheelbarrow. She is very happy.'

'What?'

'She is laughing and smiling.'

I don't have the energy to protest or the will to imagine. 'Do you happen to know what size wedding ring he had? I mean, compared to yours?'

'Yes, one size smaller: Ernesto has long, thin fingers like Consuelo.'

The mention of the girl's name makes me shudder.

I park the Range Rover in the same place I parked the R8 in yesterday. In order to get to Studleys Jewellers, I have to walk past Cloud Nine, Consuelo's beauty salon, and I'm anxious. I don't want her to see me or think that I'm here to take her for a drink again. So I cross the road, hunch my shoulders, and walk with my head facing the shop windows on the other side. As I approach Studleys, I notice a fair-haired woman in a fawn coat peering into its window; she looks like a young Jenny and I find myself immediately fascinated. But a few feet closer and I realise exactly who it is – the very girl I'm trying to avoid, Consuelo, whose hair has now so many highlights her own natural colour barely shows through. I also have a strong feeling that this is not a coincidence, that as soon as the Range Rover pulled out of Sunnymore, her mother tipped her off.

'Consuelo,' I say, trying to hide my irritation, 'what a surprise.'

'Hello, Mr Solomon,' she replies. She seems sheepish and uncomfortable, as though there's something on her mind. 'My mother called to tell me you might need a hand picking the right size rings. I was only across the road.' A deep sigh follows, but she remains sheepish. I suppose that is a credible enough story and my irritation eases slightly. 'Did you know it's their anniversary on Sunday?' she adds.

'No, I didn't.' Try as I might, I can't get the image of Consuelo's bedroom out of my mind. 'But that could work out perfectly,' I add.

She sighs again like a spurned lover, desperate to get something off her chest. 'I feel like you've been avoiding me,' she says, sorrowful and dejected. 'I've done something to upset you, I can tell. That first night was so amazing, you said you loved me, but now you act like you regret the whole thing.'

'Huh?' My irritation returns. 'Consuelo, I don't understand what you're alluding to. We had a drink together, right? That's all. Can we get back to this later and just get the rings?'

She's getting that fierce look in her eyes again, but it doesn't stop her from locking her arm around mine as we push through the door.

The shop is empty of customers. There are only two shop assistants in view, a man in his thirties with neat hamster-coloured hair, and a handsome, if somewhat stocky, middle-aged woman wearing a light-blue shirt and proudly displaying a large, bejewelled brooch. The woman greets us with a smile; the man glances at us briefly and then looks away. We approach the woman and I self-consciously unlock my arm.

'Hi,' I say, 'I'd like to look at a pair of simple gold wedding bands, please.'

'Certainly, sir, we have plenty. Any idea how much you'd like to spend?'

'Oh,' I reply, 'I'm not really worried about the cost. The best you have, whatever that is, 22-carat or something.'

The man looks up for a second.

'Well,' continues the lady, 'if you're not worried about the cost, how about something a little more elaborate for your fiancée, something with diamonds perhaps?'

My expression freezes. 'No, no, no, sorry. This is not my fiancée, this is the daughter of my employees; my housekeeper and gardener. The rings are for them, they're renewing their vows.'

The woman is staring at Consuelo with concern and I don't understand why until I turn and see the tears welling up in the girl's eyes. Consuelo won't look at me or say anything. She just turns around and rushes out of the shop.

'I am sorry,' I say to the woman, thinking of an excuse for her sudden meltdown, 'she's having a bit of boyfriend trouble at the moment.'

'I see,' the woman replies, 'it's just she was in here earlier trying on some diamond rings, I merely assumed...'

A picture starts to emerge as I leave the shop with two gold rings in two felt cases. There is no boyfriend. There was no hot date. Consuelo is in love, infatuated, obsessed...with me. Fuck. Some gnawing voice inside – Fran? – is telling me I encouraged her, that I'm to blame. And something else is starting to break through from the dark recesses of my mind as well. But it's too sordid to entertain, so I don't.

Back at Sunnymore, I put the rings in a safe place, the same bathroom drawer that Jenny keeps her sleeping pills in. I count how many packs there are left. Christ, there's enough here to send you to sleep forever. That's a scary thought. I grab a tee shirt and use it to hide the contents of the drawer; I then head to the studio to see how Dr Sparks is settling in.

It's a windless, foggy evening. The house I turn my back on is lifeless enough without the kids and their bickering, but even worse without Jenny. I'm really missing her now, Nazi-boyfriend or no Nazi-boyfriend, missing having her around, desperate for some partnership, desperate to have, by my side, someone who may not like me much at the moment, but someone who knows me better than anyone else does; someone who has lived with me through my darkest moments. But as I draw closer to the studio,

I hear music; piano and two voices. Sparks and Tilda are singing together again and it touches me deeply, disperses the loneliness, wipes away the memory of Consuelo's tears. When the aria ends I hear a small clatter of applause and a few high-pitched cheers. They have an audience. I enter the studio, walk through the kitchen, and see the Velasquez family, all except Consuelo, sitting around the table, smiles on their faces. Even the youngest girls appear to be enjoying the opera. Rosa has been busy baking, it seems. There is a chocolate cake on the kitchen island and homemade biscuits on the table. There are two empty bottles of red wine by the sink.

'Don't stop,' I say to Sparks, who greets me with a flash of wine-stained teeth and a flourish on the piano. I grab the chair next to Elena and listen along with everyone else as Eugene and Tilda sing *Dunque Io Son* from *The Barber of Seville*. Tilda's voice soars in the high-ceilinged room. It seems to flit about the heights like a tiny bird before diving down and whizzing past our ears. It must be hard for the girls to appreciate just how infirm she is; that it's a minor miracle she can do this at all. The aria ends to another crackle of applause and then Dr Sparks addresses the Velasquez family.

'Who would like to hear Solomon sing opera?' he asks. It catches me off guard and I make vague, pointless protestations. Of course, the answer is overwhelmingly affirmative. I can see there's no way I'm going to get out of it, so I rise and stand next to the piano, face the small audience and clear my throat.

'Not Faust, please,' I whisper.

Sparks chuckles. 'No, let's start with something well-known, *Toréador*.'

Phew! The *Toréador* song from Bizet's Carmen, or to give it its full title, *Votre toast, je peux vous le rendre...Toréador en garde!* is track number nine on my CD, and although I've listened to it about twenty times, I've only been through it twice with Dr Sparks. I remember the song from my childhood as, 'Stand up and fight until you hear the bell,' from the 1954 film, *Carmen Jones*, starring Harry Belafonte and Dorothy Dandridge. It's passionate, full-blooded stuff but there's a dichotomy for me between the French lyric, which I don't understand, and the Spanish music, which conjures up so brilliantly the scene of a bullfight.

I begin a little tentatively – following Dr Sparks and Tilda is not the easiest of tasks – but, by the end, when everyone is clapping along, I realise there's nothing to feel uncomfortable about. There really isn't anyone here who will judge me more harshly than Sparks himself, more harshly than I would judge myself. If truth be told, I'm encouraged and ready to sing some more. And I do. Next up is *Non Più Andrai* from *Marriage of Figaro* and I lose myself in it, puffing out my chest, gesticulating madly. I'm convincing myself, convincing to the audience. But then I see movement in the kitchen, a shadow, a Stygian presence; it's Consuelo, who has returned from work and quietly and sullenly slunk into the kitchen.

I didn't hear the latch go on the door; her arrival completely throws me off balance. I feel strangely inhibited, the power goes from my voice, the vibrato becomes wayward. Sparks notices what has just taken place and quietly encourages me, but it's no good. I realise I'm beginning to have a problem with the girl on a level I can't fathom. She reminds me of the succubus. My performance peters out, but it matters little to the Velasquez family. They applaud as though it was the best thing they'd heard all evening. Yet Consuelo just stands there, sultry or sulking. Is she close to tears again? I can't tell.

Dr Sparks senses there's something deeply wrong. He stands and announces to us all that he needs to feed Tilda and then get her to bed. We all thank him for the small concert and one by one make our way out of the studio. I hang back a little to avoid Consuelo, then Sparks rescues me further.

'Solomon, could we have a brief chat about your performance?'

CHAPTER 17

'So what's going on with you and the girl?' asks Dr Sparks, 'You went to pieces when she walked in.' Sparks is reheating the tomato soup, having opened another bottle of wine and poured me a confessional glass. I'm seated at the kitchen island staring morosely at the cake.

'Consuelo.'

'So that's her name. Well?'

'I found out today, by accident, that her bedroom wall is covered with posters of me as a young pop star. It's just...I had no idea she's secretly obsessed. It's...crazy, unsettling. I think she's in love with me.'

'Is she the cause of the tension between Mr and Mrs Capri? The reason why your wife is not here?'

'Consuelo? God, no,' I scoff, 'I've never thought of her in that way...until recently, I guess. Unfortunately, it's a bit more complicated. It's about money and freedom – Jenny's money and Jenny's freedom. She inherited a small fortune...her grandfather, you see, invented a patent for a feminine hygiene product. And, well, she's been offered a lot of money to buy her company out. On top of that, she met this couple – funnily enough, the celebrity producer of this Popstar to Operastar programme. Yes, her and this Swiss financier. It's turned Jenny's head.'

'And no intimacy has passed between you and...Consuelo?'

That's a question I haven't dared ask myself. 'It sounds stupid,' I reply, 'but I'm not sure. I mean, all this stuff began to surface when Jenny started sleeping over here. It's like Consuelo has been offered as some kind of consolation, some kind of replacement. And then the other day, one of Jenny's friends was getting overly friendly with me, and Consuelo threatened her with a nail file. I mean, this is nuts, I've watched the girl grow up.'

'And you've given her no encouragement?'

'I don't know…I took her for a drink, champagne. I did hug her, after I hugged her mother. We were all hugging. Ernesto had fallen into the hole; I saved him. I was the big hero.'

'I see. So one of King Solomon's courtiers worships and adores him. There is nothing new or surprising in this story.'

'When you put it like that, no. But…I've been taking sleeping pills lately and having some strange, recurring dreams. One involves a succubus. They're so vivid, I'm beginning to wonder if they're dreams at all.'

'How so?'

'It's hard to explain, but when I see Consuelo, her and the succubus merge into one.'

'Well, I'm no Freud,' Sparks admits, 'but it sounds like her desire is disturbing you greatly. But, perhaps you are fearful of desiring her as well? After all, there is something slightly taboo about it all, having watched her grow up.'

Dr Sparks leaves me to contemplate what he just said. He spoons some soup into a bowl and walks into the main room to feed Tilda.

'Do you mind if I stay here a bit longer?' I ask, 'It kind of feels…safe.'

'Be my guest,' Sparks replies. 'Let me put Tilda to bed and then I'll join you for a glass.'

While Dr Sparks is attending to Tilda in the larger of the guest bedrooms, I sit at the piano and quietly tinkle away. The lights on the mezzanine steps are intensely bright and I have to be careful not to look at them directly. I remind myself to show Sparks how to work the Lutron system; there are switches and dimmers everywhere and they're all programmed to do different things. Mood lighting, that's all it is, settings for the daytime, settings for watching a film, settings for getting cosy with one's loved one, complete black out.

Ten minutes later, the old man reappears, walks past me, taps me on the shoulder and invites me to join him at the island again. He pours himself some wine and refreshes my glass. 'So have you given any thought to what I said earlier, about the recital?' he asks.

'I'm still trying to get my head round it, but I have rented a Steinway. It's coming tomorrow.'

'Excellent.'

'I thought Tilda sounded incredible today,' I suggest, 'you too, of course.'

'Thank you.' He pauses, takes a sip of wine and looks at me slightly guiltily. 'I don't suppose you fancy some spliff?' he asks.

This throws me off a little. 'God, I haven't smoked that stuff in years.'

'It might help you unwind…'

I give it a moment's thought. 'Go on then.'

'I'll be right back.'

Sparks returns from his bedroom with a tin of tobacco, a lighter, some Rizlas, and a bag of dried, green leaves – probably the one sold to him by Glen a few days ago. In less than a minute, he expertly rolls a joint, lights it, and takes a deep puff. Even when he exhales, it's enough for me. My eyes water as his glaze over. He takes another puff and then hands it to me. After a bout of coughing, I remember how to smoke this ghastly stuff. I feel lightheaded immediately and the cake starts to look really good. Using a saucer for an ashtray, we talk for an hour at least, trading stories about our different experiences in music, helping ourselves to large portions of the cake. I tell Sparks about Fran and his illness.

'It was Rock Hudson, I remember. It was when he died that Fran started to freak out. I mean, in those days, people were saying that this was God punishing gays and for a while it looked like that. Christ, if we'd known back then where AIDS would go on to cause the most damage…I dunno…Anyway, Fran was a mess, sitting in the kitchen in our house in Belsize Park, wondering whether he should go for an HIV test or not, convinced he had it. Well, he did go for a test and it proved to be negative. So everything went back to normal, but with Fran being a lot less promiscuous and a lot more careful.'

What I don't tell Sparks, even in my stoned and emotional state, is that Jenny and I also went for the test, and not just to give Fran support.

'We were in the States on the East Coast,' I continue, 'touring on the back of a top ten hit, a slushy ballad called, *Heaven In Your Eyes*, when Fran fell in love, or so he said, with Alan, a publicist in a record company, not our record company, by the way. The band was due to head back home, but Fran stayed. Then, when he did return, he used to fly back and forth to New York constantly. It was a year later that Alan got tested positively for HIV; he blamed Fran. Fran tested positive soon after and blamed Alan. That was just the start though. About six months after that, Fran developed a sore throat, but it got bad. Gigs got cancelled and three months later he was hospitalised. I mean…he was always skinny, but the last time I set eyes on him, he was a blotchy skeleton; he looked like an old man.'

Following that, it seems almost frivolous when I recount some of my best groupie stories. I tell him about Anke and Petra, how I recently met Petra again after twenty-eight years, about Anke's tragic death. At this point, Dr Sparks excuses himself and pops off to the loo.

I'm pretty stoned by this time, and a little bit maudlin talking about Fran. I can hear his cheeky, girlish laugh, his voice urging me on. 'Go on Solomon, chop one out.' He knows me too well. He knows that right now I'd like nothing more than a little cocaine to add some edge to the haze, a little sparkle to the blurriness. I know there's some in the drawer of Jenny's desk up on the mezzanine floor. She told me if I touched it, she'd kill me. Sorry Jenny.

As quick as I can, I shoot up the stairs and pull out the desk drawers until I spy a slim antique pen box shoved to the back and badly hidden under a few blank sheets of paper. That's got to be it. I open it and, voilà, find what I'm looking for; several small balls of white powder, each wrapped and tied in clear plastic. I take what looks like the smallest one, slip it into my pocket, close the pen box and shut the drawers, returning to my stool at the island before Sparks has even flushed the loo.

Now I'm in a quandary. I'm dying to try this stuff, but have no credit card or note. I'm also pretty sure I don't want to smoke any more spliff. But when Sparks returns with a great yawn, he solves my quandary for me.

'It's been a long day, I should go to bed,' he says.

'Me too,' I reply. 'What time do you want to start in the morning?'

'Eleven-thirty?'

'That sounds human.'

'Yes, I have another client at ten.'

'Really?' He catches me off guard again. I sound peeved. I am peeved.

'You're not my only student, you know. I was meaning to run it by you. You don't mind do you?'

'Not at all,' I reply. Actually, I'm feeling a little jealous. 'Er, who is he?' Not Perry Lighthouse, I silently scream, don't say Perry Lighthouse!

'It's a she.'

Phew.

'Her name is Samantha. She's the soprano I mentioned earlier. I've been coaching her for almost six years now. She's an amateur, but if you heard her, you'd never guess. Pop in and say hello if you're about; apparently she knows who you are and is rather impressed.'

'OK,' I reply, sliding off my stool, 'sleep well,' I add and then head for the door.

'Er, Solomon,' says Sparks, hauling me back, 'would you have a moment to show me how this giant TV works?'

'Sure.' I spend the next two minutes explaining how the controller functions, showing him the different categories on Sky TV. 'Sky Arts channel is pretty good,' I explain, 'they show the odd opera. I watched Aida not so long ago.'

'And what do they show under the Adult category?'

'Um...porn, obviously,' I reply.

'Porn,' he repeats, strangely interested, 'hard-core?'

'I guess, but you have to subscribe.'

'And you haven't?'

'Um...no.'

'You have a beautiful teenage girl lusting after you, you have access to hard-core porn which you haven't subscribed to; a man in control of his urges...Ernesto was telling me earlier how kind you are to his family. Are you some kind of saint, Solomon Capri?'

'I'm Jewish, I don't think we have saints.'

Sparks stares at me in disbelief. 'Are you gay?' he asks.

'1-9-6-1,' I reply, 'that's the pin number if you want to watch the porn. See you in the morning.'

CHAPTER 18

I don't think I've had to creep back to my house since I was a teenager, but I'm having to now. I head across the grass to avoid the gravel, petrified that at any moment Consuelo is going to jump out from a bush and confront me. Thankfully, I make it to the door unscathed. I open it slowly and listen. Silence speaks back. Thank God.

The kitchen is empty, save for Smooch and Kipper who don't even look up from their beds, and I see that Rosa has left me a note saying that, if I'm hungry, there's a small steak and ale pie in the fridge that only needs twenty five minutes in the top of Aga. Sensitive woman; she's obviously realised I need to be alone. Another quandary; steak and ale pie sounds good, but, right now, I'm more interested in the chemicals in my pocket.

From the wine cooler, I pull out a screw-top bottle of chardonnay and pour myself a large glass. I take the glass into the study and place it on a side table. After a paranoid peek through the windows, I close the curtains and head back to the front door to grab my wallet and phone from my coat, and make sure the front door is locked. Once certain of my privacy, I return to the study and chop out a line.

I'm not sure if this is the stuff Jenny got from Sylvania or Marcus, but it's pretty damn good. Two minutes and the teeth beneath my right nostril are beginning to go numb. I look at my phone and see that I've missed calls from Raffy and Mili, though neither has bothered to leave a message. Nothing, of course, from Jenny. I also notice some emails pertaining to the Fortune Favours' autumn tour, a couple of synch license requests, plus an email from Petra. I fetch my laptop to read them more easily. Petra's is interesting; she's asking whether I can be in London in two days' time. Apparently, there's a gathering at Abbey Road Studios for all interested parties, the first improvised filming of the show. God, they got that together quickly. Or maybe I was a late addition, an afterthought?

Another line of coke and I realise what Jenny meant when she said this stuff makes you bloody horny, and it's not long before I find myself not reading emails but checking out YouPorn instead. My mind darts back to Dr Sparks' suggestion that I fear desiring Consuelo as much as I fear her desire for me. Actually, I'm not sure I can remember what he said exactly, but I allow myself to at least entertain the idea, to test out the taboo. And with YouPorn it's easy. I refine my search to include Latinos, Teen and (now) Blonde. In minutes, I find someone who looks a little like her and watch as she…as she…mmm. This isn't good, I realise, she's eighteen years old; it doesn't feel right, so I adjust my search to more familiar territory – blonde milfs.

God, I wish Jenny were here now because I'm up and ready. I'm raring to go. I could go all night, the way I feel right now. I must be sending out psychic waves because right at that moment, the front screen of my phone lights up. I have a text.

'Just passing. Want some company?' it reads.

It's not Jenny, it's Lexi. Fuck. I'm horny as hell and she couldn't have texted me at a more vulnerable moment. Of course, I can ignore it and, if I wait five minutes, she surely will have passed. But I don't.

'Love some,' I reply.

Immediately she texts back, 'Is psycho-kid around?'

'No,' I write, 'but park outside and come through the side gate just in case. WALK ON THE GRASS!'

I can't believe I'm having to smuggle her in. I also realise that my short conversation with Lexi is secretive and conspiratorial. We all know where that leads. Five minutes later, I hear a mobile phone go off just outside the house. I panic. It's the bloody *Guns*

'*N' Roses* guitar intro to *Sweet Child of Mine*. I hear a muffled curse, 'Shit!' as the phone is muted. She's here already.

I head to the front hall. There's a quiet rap on the door, as if she needed any more of a fanfare. I unlock it and open it. Lexi is standing there with a calm, determined look on her face. She's carrying a bag big enough to be an overnight bag, wearing a dark blue, high quality overcoat, elegant, coffee-coloured stilettos; her hair is pulled back off her face and her make-up is far more subtle than I've seen her wear in a long time.

'It's fucking freezing,' she whispers, 'aren't you gonna invite me in?'

'Of course, come on in.'

She drops her bag in the hall and then puts her arms around me, her lips firmly against mine. Again, I'm surprised. It's not a brassy, tarty, slutty kiss, it's a sensual, sensitive, teasing one and it connects directly to my groin. Christ, she has no qualms about this kind of thing whatsoever.

'Skunk and chocolate,' she says, removing her coat to reveal a figure-hugging midnight blue dress and her Wells-famous cleavage. 'I didn't know you smoked skunk.'

'I don't normally, it's the guy who's staying in the studio, he smokes it.'

'What, the fucking octogenarian? God, Jenny was so pissed when she found out they were staying there. Have you seen her pictures on Facebook?'

'Jenny's on Facebook?'

We walk into the kitchen where I pour Lexi a large glass of white wine.

'Everyone's on Facebook,' she replies.

'I'm not.'

'Well...you *are*. There are five of you at least. OK, people pretending to be you. God, some of those pictures are nasty. You look so much better now you're older.'

'Thanks. And what are Jenny's pictures of?'

'Y'know, the usual; the Alps, the après-ski. Oh, and a few studs. Lucky bitch.'

'So, she is skiing then,' I mumble. I hand Lexi the glass and then she kisses me again, a little more aggressively.

'Love the facial hair, Solomon. It kinda tickles.' She pulls away and scrutinises my nose. 'Hmm…do I see a fleck of white powder up there?'

'Oh,' I self-consciously wipe it away.

'You've been a naughty boy, haven't you? Skunk and coke, no wonder you wanted company. Care to share with your good pal?'

'It's in the study,' I reply.

I lead Lexi into the study and close the door. We sit on the sofa and I chop out a couple of lines. Lexi goes first, hoovering like a pro. This is my third one, I think, as I follow suit, I'd better be careful or I won't sleep tonight.

'So, if I were to join Facebook, could I see Jenny's pictures?' I ask.

'This is Jenny's stuff, isn't it?' says Lexi, not answering the question.

'Maybe,' I reply.

She tut-tuts and shakes her head. 'She'd have to friend you, or you won't be able to see them. But you can see them on my account. Shall we?'

Lexi picks up my laptop but I remember I haven't deleted my browsing history.

'Oh, it's OK,' I say, grabbing it off her. 'Let's forget about Jenny for one night.'

Lexi looks at me steamily, her heavy breasts heaving along with a heavy sigh. 'That's what I want to hear,' she says. She puts down her glass of wine, stands up briefly, hitches up her dress, and in a smooth, confident move, straddles me. She wraps her arms around my head and kisses me again like she did at the front door.

But it's deeper; she's using her tongue and it feels fucking good. Her kissing personality is nothing like her real personality; it's not brash, it's smooth and lethal.

I'm going nowhere. I put my hands around her waist as she starts riding up and down gently on my groin. Sorry Jenny, enjoy the skiing. She then undoes the zip at the back of her dress, loosening the top, the straps falling down her arms. Her breasts do the rest. Freed, they have a mind of their own and in seconds my face is smothered by her flesh.

I move my hands down to cup the cheeks of her arse and realise she's wearing just the silkiest of thongs. Just passing was she? She lifts herself up off me and her hand slips down to feel the hard lump in my crotch. Somehow she manages to undo my fly with one hand and then, in a brief and slightly painful act of dexterity, frees my erect cock. 'Mmm,' she says, 'there it is, good to go, just like the other day.'

And now there is only one fine piece of silk between us and the point of no return. In a teenage head-rush I thrust up at her but she immediately pulls away. 'Not so fast, Solomon,' she says, 'I'm gonna give you the blowjob of your fucking life.'

And then there's a knock on the door.

'What the hell?' I gasp.

In a flash, Lexi jumps off me and adjusts her dress while I desperately shove my cock back into my trousers. Not Consuelo, please God, not Consuelo.

'Sorry to disturb you,' comes the old man's voice from behind the door, 'but we seem to have run out of toilet paper.'

I can't believe it, it's Sparks. I didn't lock the door when I let Lexi in, he must have just wandered in.

'Er, just take some from the loo in the hall, yeah?' I shout. 'See you tomorrow. Have a good night.'

'Oh, fuck!' I yelp, once I'm sure he's gone. 'Shit, I'm sorry. Look, do you want to chop out another line while I make sure the front door is locked.'

Lexi looks at me and laughs in disbelief. 'Ever thought about kicking everyone out? You're running a fucking hostel here, home for the fucking needy.'

I study her briefly to work out if the interruption has blown the mood. But she looks as though a herd of trampling elephants wouldn't put her off. 'I'll be right back,' I say.

After another line and a few gulps of wine, I suggest we go upstairs, not that Lexi needs much persuading. And we do, rushing up to my bedroom, where I put on a bedside light and lie down on the bed waiting for Lexi to fulfil her promise.

'Shoes, mister,' she says prizing them off my feet and throwing them across the room. She then climbs on the bed at the base, crawls like a cat up my legs until her hands rest on my fly.

She wasn't lying; she wasn't joking or exaggerating her skills. She is a master with her mouth, a true talent with her tongue. I should feel guilty; Lexi should feel guilty. I mean, I like Roy; he's a decent, hardworking multi-millionaire, but right now, I couldn't give a fuck. I'm buzzing, floating on a cocaine high. I'm a rock star and I'm back in 1983, sinless, unshackled, guiltless and free. Until I hear a noise out in the hall.

'What was that?' I ask, lifting my head from the pillow, eyes wide with panic.

'What was what?' says Lexi freeing her mouth for a second.

'That noise in the hall,' I reply.

'I didn't hear anything.'

She gets back to the job in hand and I try and regain my sense of blissful abandon. But then I hear it again.

'There's someone out there!'

'Jesus Christ,' says Lexi, 'you're fucking paranoid!'

Frustrated, she gets up, crosses the bedroom and dramatically flings the door open. I place a pillow over my groin just in case and watch her anxiously as she pokes her head out, looks left and then right and then left again. The door is wide open. She turns round and faces me. 'See, no one fucking there. Now, rock star, let's get naked.'

And then my worst fears are realised. From out of nowhere, the succubus appears, jumping on Lexi's back and holding on to her by the hair. Lexi screams; the succubus screams, an animalistic, ear-splitting howl. I can't believe my eyes. Is this real or is this the skunk-coke combination? Is this my guilt suddenly emerging having been chemically suppressed for the last hour or so? Did I summon this she-devil from the depths of my taboo-fearing psyche? I poke my rapidly withering cock back in my trousers.

'Solomon!' Lexi shouts, 'Do something. Get this bitch off me!'

The next few minutes pass in a blur and by the time I am capable of separating the women, of separating fantasy from reality, I have a distraught Consuelo sitting cross-legged on the hall floor rocking backwards and forwards, and a furious, dishevelled Lexi rushing down the stairs.

'Where are you going?' I yell after her.

'To the fucking police. I'm lodging a complaint. She fucking attacked me!'

'You can't do that,' I shout, rushing down the stairs after her, 'Roy will find out.'

'Fuck Roy, fuck you, and fuck that psycho-bitch!' are Lexi's final words as she slams the front door behind her.

CHAPTER 19

I realise I'm not having much luck with women at the moment, what with my restless, want-away wife, her slutty American friend who's threatening to go to the police, and an eighteen-year old psycho that's become some kind of stalker/misguided bodyguard. Let's not even mention Petra, who's battling cancer, or Tilda, who's had a stroke and is in a wheelchair. Not that either is my problem, but where are the normal women? What have I done to deserve this? All I need now is for Rosa to start putting cut glass in my meals and my terrible curse will be complete.

And what about the men? I don't have many close male friends; maybe that's why I've locked on to Dr Sparks so much. I had a very close male friend once who died. Yes, Fran. Perhaps I have been more scarred by this than I care to admit?

I didn't have much to say to Consuelo, at least, at first. She was shaking with rage, so I wrapped her in a blanket, virtually carried her down to the kitchen and gave her some sweet tea. But when she started smiling at me, as if nothing terrible had occurred, I lost it. I told her that I didn't want her in the house or the studio until she sorted her head out. I said, 'And if your parents ask you why, you can tell them that you threatened and later attacked a friend of the family.'

She looked at me with disgust, and spat, 'And can I tell them you took my virginity?'

Cheeky fucking cow. I screamed, 'If you want us all to go to hell, then tell them I raped you.' I shouldn't have said this, but the coke, the wine, the shock brought out the bastard in me. Any crush she has on Solomon Capri should surely now be crushed.

Once I'd kicked Consuelo out, I started on my mission to appease Lexi. Texts leave such a terrible trail, an admission of guilt, so I began cryptically with, 'On my knees.' I waited for half an hour and when she didn't reply, I left a voice message. I just hope, that in regard to Roy, she's discreet.

It's past midnight. Where did the time go? I'm still wired and have been drinking, no, gulping down Chardonnay to try and ease my nerves. I can't believe what has just happened and I kind of retrace my steps in an attempt to understand it. I end up back in the study and see the credit card and rolled up note on the table, the plastic wrap. There's still some coke left. At least two lines. My first thought is to wash it down the sink and chuck the wrap away, to erase one of the illegalities. But I don't; I decide I may as well finish it and be done. After all, there's enough pills in the drawer upstairs to take me out of this life altogether. Problem solved.

Now that I'm alone, and the shock is slowly fading, I sense a strange electricity in the room – a sudden chill. It's when my head is bowed over the table, a rolled up note in my nostril, that I hear someone's voice.

'Hello Solomon,' it says. It's kind of a fake Cockney accent. Slowly, I look up and there sitting in the chair opposite is Fran, restored to the figure of health he was before his skin was ravaged by that awful disease, replete in stage gear and eye make-up, red winkle pickers, tight jeans, thin leather jacket and a white lady's scarf tied loosely around his neck. Clearly, I am imagining things.

'Fran?' I ask meekly.

Fran chuckles like a girl. 'The one and only.'

'Why are you speaking like that?' I say, 'You went to Harrow, you were posh. What happened?'

'Oh,' he replies, 'it's this guy I've been hanging out with in the afterlife…from the Rolling Stones. Keith Richards. Must have rubbed off.'

'Fran, Keith Richards isn't dead.'

'Must be the other one then.'

'Ronnie Wood? He's not either.' I can't believe a ghost can get it so wrong. 'You look amazing,' I say, 'not like the last time I saw you.'

'No, well, don't want to go around shocking people now do I?'

'Good point…but, why are you here all of a sudden? You haven't come to collect me, have you, like a spirit guide?'

There's that chuckle again. 'Relax mate, your time isn't up yet.' He smiles warmly; a ripple runs through his body as though he's no more real than a reflection on a lake. 'Back to your wicked old ways, I see – the sex, the drugs. Two women in five days? Impressive, at your age.'

'What do you mean? That was one woman and it was just a blowjob.'

'I'm talking about the girl. You took her cherry. She could be up the duff, mate. Three kids…you end up with three kids, that's what it says in the script.'

'What script?'

'The divine script of your life, mate.'

'What the fuck? You've read the divine script of my life? When do I die? How long have I got? How do I die?'

'Mate, I didn't read it all, it's longer than *War and Peace*. Besides I had to break off for a table tennis lesson with Dick Miles.'

'This is insane,' I protest. 'So you're saying I slept with Consuelo…when?'

'The night you took your first sleeping pill.'

'How long have you been haunting me?' I yell, half in outrage, half in confusion.

'Mate, I'm not the haunting kind. I can see it. I can go backwards and forwards in time. It's not like being on earth – where I am, time is more…flexible.'

'Fuck!' I gasp. 'Um, how far forward can you go in time?'

'Christ, I dunno.'

'Can you go forward a few months? Can you see if I make it onto Popstar to Operastar? It's in June. Or end up singing at the Royal Opera House? That's in July.'

'Solomon, the girl might be up the duff and that's all you're worried about?'

'Please?'

'Is it a wish?'

'Yes, it's a wish. What are you, some kind of genie? How many do I have?'

Fran closes his eyes. Immediately, he seems to be in some anguish. 'Oh dear,' he says.

'What is it?'

'That guy from Ultravox – he's lost his hair.'

'Not Midge Ure, no! Who else? Can you see me?'

More anguish. 'I don't recognise anyone; I died in the eighties, right? Hang on, is that the girl from Bucks Fizz?'

'You're kidding me. Are you sure you can't see me?'

'Mate, I could be wrong…'

'Which show is it? Is it at the Royal Opera House?'

'Wait a minute, I'm moving forward. I see a theatre. I see an Airstream caravan on stage…'

'Oh my God. That's it…that's *Jerusalem*. Can you see me?'

'I'm not sure, mate. I see a guy with a moustache, he's wearing a Prussian helmet…he's got huge biceps, doesn't look like you…'

Fran shudders, ripples, then opens his eyes. 'Sorry, can't take any more of that. Never did like opera…which brings me to my next point. What are you doing with your life, mate? Jenny's tamed you, castrated you. Look at yourself, you need to lose some weight. Skinny, sexy Solomon, remember? Get some confidence back. Maybe get that sun damage around your eyes seen to? You need to forget about opera and fall in love with your own music again, rediscover your inner rock god. I can still help you with the songs, God knows I've tried in the past…'

'Fran, stop. Are you suggesting I write songs with a dead person?'

'Happens all the time. The last Robbie Williams album? I wrote that. Well, a couple of tracks…not that I got any credit; that's what happens when you're a ghost-writer.'

'Ugh…'

'Look, you still have the voice. You're twenty years younger than Mick Jagger, and a better dancer. Make another record, do a live album, do something. What about reworking some of the Fortune Favours classics, get some hip rap artist to do an interpolation?'

I am humbled, I confess, by Fran's concern from beyond the grave. I scrunch up my chin in humility as he tells me how much a fan Tupac is. 'Do you mind if I just do this last line?' I ask when he starts lecturing me about God-given talent.

'Just like old times,' he replies.

I do the line and by the time I look up again, Fran has gone.

It's four a.m. I haven't had a wink of sleep, been tossing – literally – and turning since I went to bed at two, running over in my mind what Consuelo said and has been saying for the last few days:

'Why are you pretending? You're so good at pretending.'

What if it's true? If, indeed, it was Consuelo and not Jenny, or some emanation of spirit, that I had semi-conscious sex with, then I am in deep shit, and, much worse, Consuelo's behaviour becomes understandable, perhaps even forgivable. Three kids, Fran said. Then she could well be pregnant. Fuck, why didn't I ask him to look at that?

I'm trying desperately not to resort to the sleeping pills, but at four-thirty, I relent. Bliss, no dreams of great significance. Eight o'clock, I am disturbed by the sound of heavy machinery and the raised voices of workmen. Shit, they're draining and lining the pool, I completely forgot. I drift in and out of sleep for a couple of hours until my phone, which is next to me on the bedside table, vibrates against the wood. It's a text from Lexi.

'Calmed down. Won't go to police so quit worrying. Not done with psycho-bitch though. I know where she works and I know the owner of the salon. Watch this space. You owe me. Nice cock, by the way.'

Like a castrated idiot, I text back, 'Thank you! Xxx.'

CHAPTER 20

Rosa's being very funny with me this morning. She tries the occasional smile, but it hangs on her face as successfully as runny custard. I assume Consuelo has said something. Even if it was just about Lexi and the coke, I would have plummeted in Rosa's estimation, my prefect's badge torn from my lapel, my halo exploded into a cloud of gold glitter. And if she mentioned the V word to her parents then I expect Ernesto to appear any minute with a shotgun and some orange plastic rope demanding I make a decent woman of his daughter, despite the fact that I'm already married. Part of me wonders whether it was all part of some weird Velasquez family plan.

Conversation is cagey, but I eventually glean that Dr Sparks was knocking on the gatehouse cottage door at seven this morning, enquiring about breakfast, and that, when Rosa went into the studio to prepare it, she thought an animal had been in because of the smell, then had to leave the doors and windows open for fifteen minutes. Maybe that's all it is – housekeeper's pride. Maybe Consuelo is keeping everything to herself to exact further revenge.

This morning I decide to shave off the goatee. I look a complete mess after my night of debauchery and the stray bits of facial hair really aren't helping, nor is the grey that's starting to poke through. I keep thinking back to my conversation with Fran – not that I really believe in ghosts – and I begin to view it in a serious and sober light. Perhaps they were words of wisdom from somewhere deep within. I should forget about this opera stuff and try and resurrect my enthusiasm for the thing I do best; not-so sexy, not so skinny Solomon, front man of Fortune Favours The Brave.

I'm not quite sure how I'm going to tell Dr Sparks. I might just go along with the lessons for a couple of days and, once his bilges are cleaned, and he's back in the barge, slowly extricate myself from the relationship. I'll make excuses, a cold, the flu, strep throat, then start thinking about a new FFTB album.

Ten minutes in the bathroom tweaking my hair, moisturising and applying concealer, and I'm starting to look a little more human. In the bedroom, I pick out something a lot smarter than I'd usually wear at home in the winter; a black cashmere sweater over a plain black t-shirt, smart, slimming black jeans, black ankle boots, and a charcoal-grey and crimson scarf worn like a cravat around my neck – all designed to provide a smokescreen for how I feel inside.

It's a dry, bright day, just as forecasted, and as I walk out the front door, I can really sense the death throes of winter. As I head down to the studio, I clock Martin, our architect, walking nonchalantly up the drive towards me. He's obviously here to check on the builders.

'Solomon,' he says as we near, 'finally. I'm so sorry about all this palaver. But here we are, not long now. You're looking well, have you lost weight?'

Martin is in his early forties, has blonde thinning hair and wears thick, rectangular frameless glasses. He's dressed in a green wax jacket and hiking boots, and is carrying a sturdy but extremely worn briefcase.

'An illusion caused by black,' I reply. 'You know Jenny's skiing at the moment?'

'Yes, we've been chatting on Facebook.'

'You're on Facebook?'

'Yes, you friended me a month ago.'

'That wasn't me, that was one of five imposters.'

'Really? Oh. Anyway…great idea about the helipad.'

'What?'

'The helipad. I've got the drawings if you want to see them.'

Martin can see I haven't a clue what he's talking about.

'I…I'm sorry,' he says, 'you don't know anything about it, do you?'

'Where the hell is a helipad going?'

'In the field beyond the pool. We'll have to cut back some trees, but it's a simple procedure.'

'OK, Martin, let me talk to Jenny about it and I'll email you, yeah?'

'Of course. Sorry, I assumed you knew.'

What the hell does she think she's playing at? A helipad? I suppose that Andreas is a qualified helicopter pilot, has his own helicopter, and is going to fly her back all the way from Switzerland? Why don't we just build a runway for a private jet? This is not what I want to hear right now. In a foul mood, I stamp my way into the studio courtyard. There's a green Volkswagen Polo parked there and I'm reminded that Sparks has another lesson, another client. Am I early, or are they running late?

I take a deep breath, try and look a bit cheerful, and go through to the studio kitchen. Dr Sparks is sitting at the island drinking a cup of coffee, but there's no sign of – what was her name? – Samantha.

'Ah, my budding protégé,' he says, 'I trust you had a good night's rest?'

So much for looking a bit cheerful; I can't keep it up and for some reason I can't speak. I can't look at Sparks either.

'What's wrong, Solomon, cat got your tongue? I see you've had a shave. Why does this seem significant, I wonder?'

I'm done with the pretence. There is far too much to worry about at the moment. Eyes to the ground, I mumble, 'I can't do this any more.'

Sparks looks at me with a mixture of amusement and pity. 'Why?'

'I don't think either show is gonna work out for me. It's all just pie in the sky.'

The old man sniffs incredulously. 'Have you just heard from your agent?'

'No, it's…'

'Then how do you know?'

I hesitate; I realise in advance how stupid it sounds. 'A ghost told me,' I say, under my breath.

'Pardon?'

'A ghost told me.'

'Ah, I see, and is this ghost a busty woman in high heels wearing a dark blue overcoat?'

So much for the smuggling. I feel myself cringe with embarrassment. 'Oh, no, that was a friend of Jenny's…popped in to borrow a cup of sugar. No, the ghost was my dead guitarist, Fran.'

'The one we were talking about while we were halfway through our second spliff?'

'Yes.'

'How often does he turn up?'

'That's the first time.'

'Right, well if he shows up again any time soon can you ask him who wins the Grand National this year? I could make a fortune.'

I hear the flush go in the nearest loo, the sound of the sink running. I turn and watch the loo door open and a woman emerge. She seems as surprised to see me as I am to see her, probably because she didn't hear me come in. I recognise her instantly as the classical-singing busker in Bath. My interest is suddenly and hugely aroused.

Samantha is a woman in her forties who clearly looks after herself. She has the cheekbones of an Eskimo, white-blonde, possibly even white-grey hair, and skin that has been carefully shielded from the sun. She's wearing very little make-up, dressed in a tight, white polar-neck sweater, belted at the waist, and grey, checked trousers which flare at the knee to cover the tops of her shoes or boots or ice skates, whatever she has on her feet. She's curvy, not heavy, not thin, just womanly. She's not too tall, not too short, and when she smiles to greet me, she instantly elevates my mood. For a brief second, I study her to see if she's got any prosthetic limbs, examine her eyes for cataracts. There must be something wrong with her, I think. She can't possibly be normal. Maybe there's some kind of personality defect or something simple like bad breath, or even herpes; there has to be something, because right now, in the state I'm in, it feels as though the angel that sang on the streets of Bath has flown gloriously into my life.

'Samantha,' she says, holding out her hand, 'pleased to meet you. Thanks for letting me have a lesson here. Fantastic place.'

I take hold of her hand lightly. 'Solomon,' I reply, and don't let go. I'm looking at her with far more fascination than I should. She doesn't look away, she just smiles. Does she know how handsome she is? Is there a wedding ring? Yes. Damn.

'You were busking,' I say, 'in Bath for the stroke charity.'

'Yes, and you rather generously put a fifty pound note in the box. I would have thanked you but I was mid-phrase.'

'Really...not a problem.'

'Eugene was telling me how easily you've taken to singing opera.'

Sparks looks away. I let go of her hand. 'Did he?'

'Says you're a natural. High praise indeed. Have you ever sung classical before?'

'When I was a teenager.'

'I'm so excited about the recital,' she continues, 'have you decided on our duet yet?'

I glance at Sparks who is consciously avoiding my gaze. 'Er... no, not yet. I'm, er, still toying with a few ideas.'

'Well, let me know soon so I can start practising. I don't want to let you down.' Samantha looks at her watch. 'Oops, better go; have to pick my son up from the train station in Bath. Good luck with the lesson.' She crosses to the table where a beige mac is folded over a chair, grabs it, waves as she walks past us both and then exits the studio.

Dr Sparks, the sly dog, is chuckling to himself. It's obvious that I'm smitten.

'Quick,' I say, in a fluster, 'tell me the name of a really famous duet...'

He hesitates. 'Oh, er...*Là ci darem la mano* from Don Giovanni?'

I repeat it over and over in my head as I rush out after Samantha. She's just getting in her car when I shout, '*Là ci darem la mano*... from Don Giovanni, that's what we should do!'

Samantha stops for a second, looks at me with a pained and puzzled expression, then that look changes to one of sorrow and regret. With tears rolling down her face, she gets in the car and drives off.

'I can't believe it,' I say to Dr Sparks as I head back into the kitchen, 'she just burst out crying.'

'Mmm,' says Sparks who seems to have suddenly descended into a mournful mood. 'Tilda and I sang that duet at Samantha's wedding; it was also played at her husband's funeral.'

'Christ! Then why did you suggest it?'

'She needs to move on; we all need to move on.'

'When was the funeral?'

'2005.'

'Six years ago? What did he die of, if you don't mind me asking?'

'Sadly, he was in London on July 7th of that year and got on the wrong bus.'

And then the penny drops; I feel such great sorrow for the old man. 'The recital isn't for my benefit, is it?' I ask, trying not to sound too accusatorial. Sparks remains silent, hunched over his coffee. 'It's for her...and you. She's your daughter-in-law, he was your son.'

CHAPTER 21

I guess a lot of people would feel used by this, but I don't. I am humbled by the pain that other people have to deal with in their lives; my problems are nothing compared to the loss that Eugene, Tilda and Samantha have had to endure because of the 7/7 bombings. I was in Brazil when it happened, playing some two thousand-seat echoey hall in Porto Alegre or Belo Horizonte, opening for some blue-eyed soul act from the States, I can't quite recall. But it didn't register the way it would have done had I been in England. Plus, it seemed so minor compared to 9/11. Not now.

I wonder when Dr Sparks decided that I should be part of Samantha's recuperation; six years is a long time to carry around such immense grief. He told me about his grandson, also called Eugene, Samantha's son, who is now at a military academy as though he's seeking to somehow avenge his father's death. By this time I'm no longer angry about the helipad; I'm not even concerned that I may have unknowingly impregnated my housekeeper's daughter, at least for the moment. That's life. My relationship problems, my stupidity; that's life. It's not death.

The piano arrived and was duly installed in the conservatory, and painstakingly tuned by a man with a beard, who refused any offer of refreshment, and who told me it would need tuning again in a week's time once it had stabilised. I told him that if he could take away the brown three-piece suite, he could have it for nothing, but he politely refused that as well. The whole episode had interrupted my lesson; but neither I nor Sparks particularly cared. Since his confession, he'd been incredibly subdued. I, on the other hand, had begun singing with increased emotion, more freely, less self-consciously, perhaps, with a sound and fresh purpose that had little to do with glory or fame.

The next day, as promised in an email to Petra, I travel to London, this time by car – the same big black Mercedes that took Jenny and me to the Savoy, with the same driver, Mo. By the time I get there, there are already several big black Mercedes parked up and down the street. There's also a white stretch Limo, several Aston Martins, a Bentley, and one of those preposterous yellow Lamborghinis. It looks like the car park at Stamford Bridge. Mo manages to find a space about six feet from the zigzags painted either side of that iconic zebra crossing featured on The Beatles' album, *Abbey Road*. I get out the car and am immediately accosted by a cute Japanese tourist, who wants me to take a picture of her and her three friends on the crossing, one of whom has already taken her shoes off in homage to Paul. It's a bright morning, the girls have smiles like laser beams; I take a snap of them on my iPhone too, to keep for myself. They've already made my day.

After this brief photo session, I walk down the road, up the steps, through the doors and into Abbey Road Studios' reception with its blue carpet and white walls. I'm expecting to see an ageing, familiar face or two, but it's full of young, hip people, some with hooded sweatshirts, some with baseball caps, all of them texting on their phones. I don't recognise any of them, they probably think I'm the janitor. There's a placard here which points to where the Malachi Jones programme is being filmed. It's in studio one, the infamous studio with the huge orchestral room.

I know studio one; I was lucky enough to work there for a few weeks while making the second Fortune Favours album. It was an incredibly inspiring and humbling experience, a constant reminder of the epoch-making albums that the Beatles recorded there. Some of the tech staff were still around from the sixties and we used to badger them constantly for stories about the Fab Four, the arguments between Paul and John, or when George invited Clapton to guest on a recording.

As I head down the hall though, past pictures celebrating Abbey Road's glorious heritage, I spot an area that looks uncannily like airport security. There are two people at a table taking everyone's name, making them sign release forms, taking their phone from them, writing the owner's name on a yellow envelope, placing the phone inside and storing it in a massive block of numbered cubby holes, then handing over a ticket with a matching number. I see two signs on the wall: 'THIS IS A TWEET-FREE ZONE', 'NO SECRET FILMING ALLOWED'. No wonder all those kids were hanging out in reception. There's also an x-ray machine for bags and an x-ray frame we all have to walk through. What did Petra say? 'We rely on trust, goodwill, spontaneity.' Yeah, right. 'In some ways, it's no different to filming kids from a rough council estate.' Yeah, that's more like it. If I didn't know Petra, if I didn't feel such a strong connection, I would walk straight out, right now. But I don't; I give them my name, sign the form, hand my phone over and get given the number fifty-two. Christ, how many people are doing this show? I'm then instructed by a security guard to remove my coat and place it in a plastic tray, any metallic objects including my watch. It all then goes through the x-ray machine. I pass through the frame without setting anything off.

There are a series of yellow tape arrows on the floor, which lead you up to the doors, doors that are opened by two burly security guards. I enter the monolithic recording room of studio one and grow suddenly nervous. I count about four cameramen with cameras on stands, and a couple with handhelds. The whole studio is lit very brightly. The walls are half-wood, half-soundproofing, which stretches all the way up to a high ceiling containing hundreds of hanging baffles. There are God knows how many red, plastic, padded chairs – the chairs an orchestra would normally sit on – set out in rows before a small raised plinth, on which is placed a music stand; above which is a giant projection screen. An upright piano and a piano player are set back and to the right of the plinth, and there are microphones on tall stands seemingly everywhere. There are already around forty people here, but no one wants to sit at the front. It reminds me of a parent-teacher meeting – the first five rows are entirely empty. I look around for any people from the past I might recognise and see quite a few. Peter Duffy from Irish folk-rockers, *Ivy Moon* is there along with Eddie Corn from the brilliant *Deccan Traps*. Like all of my peers, they are sitting right at the back. About five rows in front of them, I recognise a few guys who were big in the nineties. There's Richard Crawley from nineties House music outfit, *Hausmuzic*. It's like the whole thing is organising itself by decade. And you can see that all those young guys and girls in reception, if they can be bothered to hand in their phones, will end up down the front. Bizarre.

At this point, I am heartened to see Petra. She must have noticed me come in and has made an instant beeline for me.

'Hi, gorgeous,' she says, and then gives me a big hug. 'Thanks for coming all this way at such short notice.'

'No problem,' I reply. 'You look well,' I add. She does, a lot better than she did two days ago. There's a wig, for a start, a high-quality dark-blonde wig, a little more make-up – perhaps for the cameras – and attention to her clothing: a long, brown, woollen dress with grey, stripy sleeves and similar stripes below the knees; lots of heavy, wooden bracelets.

'Thanks. So, how have you been since I last saw you? Do anything exciting?'

God, I think. My mind darts back to my altercation with Andreas, to Consuelo riding on Lexi's back, nails digging into her skull, then to Fran's ghost telling me I should give up on this whole opera idea. 'No, not really,' I reply, 'How about you?'

'Well, Jez Butterworth, the author of *Jerusalem*, has given us permission to turn it into an opera and wants to help with the libretto, plus Jean Luc Hazard has started working on the score.'

'That's great news,' I say.

'Yes, we're all very excited.'

Petra is all smiles, but I'm curious about something. 'Um...can I ask you a question?'

'Sure.'

'Why all this heavy security?'

Petra leans close. 'Captain Scarlet has been receiving death threats. His management paid and arranged for it, what can I do?'

'I see,' I reply. I'm guessing Captain Scarlet is the pseudonym of some young rap-artist who borrowed it from the lead character of the iconic sixties puppet show *Captain Scarlet and the Mysterons*. Is nothing sacred anymore?

'And the phones, of course,' she continues, 'bloody nuisance. I'm sorry, I should have warned you. Anyway, I better go and get ready.'

'You look pretty ready to me.'

'Thanks,' she curtsies, 'I'm going to say a few words then introduce Malachi.'

I watch Petra walk off and join a pair of rather attractive female assistants. I then go and sit down, avoiding eye contact with absolutely everybody, on the end of a row, three from the back, with at least four empty chairs between me and...is that the guy from *Tears For Fears*? Five minutes later, the younger artists arrive in dribs and drabs, some with hoods covering their heads. I notice one has managed to smuggle his phone in and he's texting or tweeting for all the world to see. Once the room settles, Petra takes to the plinth and introduces herself.

'Thank you all for coming,' she says. 'I realise most of you have busy schedules and that, for some, news of this programme has come at the last minute.' She pauses. 'In six months from now, a new opera will be performed at the Royal Opera House by people who are far more used to shouting down a microphone in front of thousands of screaming fans...' This gets a chuckle. '... The profits from ticket sales will be split between four homeless charities in the UK. Six months is a long time, so we are looking for commitment, especially during the last month of intense rehearsal. So if some of you are not sure, if some of you turned up because you were told to; if some of you have any doubt about your availability – despite what your agents or managers may have said, we will not be working around your schedule – you may as well leave now.'

Despite ceding to the security request, Petra clearly has balls. The guy with the mobile phone gets up and walks out, still texting or tweeting. He is followed by two hoodies – a girl and a boy – from the front. I notice a striking, blonde young lady to my right making her way out as well, plus one guy from the back row. Keep talking Petra, I think to myself, keep saying how tough it's going to be, keep clearing the room 'til there's only one person left: me.

The room settles once more and when it falls completely silent, Petra introduces Malachi. There's a respectful round of applause, at least from those who don't have their arms folded. Malachi takes to the plinth as Petra leaves it. He modestly acknowledges the audience and speaks.

'The last time I stood in front of so many familiar faces, I was best man at my brother's wedding,' he says in that silky Welsh accent of his. 'I feel like I know you all already. Thank you for coming and welcome to Abbey Road Studios.' He makes a welcoming gesture and there's another modest ripple of applause. 'Opera for so many years,' he continues, 'has been an art form for the privileged. The same operas have been performed by the same companies for centuries. But there is a sea change occurring at the moment with a new generation of operatic composers telling stories with modern relevant themes. Has anyone here seen *Jerry Springer: The Opera*?'

'Yeah, it was shit,' yells somebody from the nineties.

'An acquired taste,' argues Malachi. 'What about *Anna Nicole*?'

My wife and her lovers, I think to myself. I see a few hands go up.

'Well,' continues Malachi, 'that is just the tip of the iceberg.'

It's quite amusing; Malachi Jones comes across, just as he does on TV, as something between a schoolteacher and a vicar. He has colourless, teacher-like hair and hollow cheeks. He speaks very softly with a beautifully restrained wit. And yet, look him up on Wikipedia, and it will tell you he came from a family of travellers in North Wales, was illiterate until the age of fifteen, and led a life of petty crime before eventually winning a music scholarship to King's College, Cambridge. I must ask Petra whether any of this is true.

And he gets very animated when he tells us what the new opera is about. He gushes about the central figure, a drug-dealing gypsy who lives illegally in a mobile home in a forest. He tells us how the residents of the nearby estate, and the council, are determined to get rid of him. He talks for ages about the mythology of gypsies, pikeys, travellers, that in many ways they are the true inheritors of the land. Maybe all that stuff on Wikipedia is true; maybe this is a story he deeply identifies with. So far, so good. He's won the audience, convinced us we can do it, convinced us that the story has a strong, moral point and is socially relevant. But now he does something which I'm sure he realises will lose more than a few of those in the undecided camp. I see the words go up on the projection screen: ALL THINGS BRIGHT AND BEAUTIFUL...

'And now, let's do some singing,' he says with a mischievous smile. 'I thought we'd start off with something simple. Would you all please stand?'

Now, anyone here with small children would have to endure this kind of thing on a regular basis, but clearly a lot of people don't because by the time we've completed a dismal and self-conscious attempt at this hymn, there are at least ten less people in the room. I'm also guessing they haven't watched many of

Malachi's programmes before, because this is what he does. He plays with you, he breaks down invisible walls, he'll drag anyone on a high horse off it by the short and curlies.

'Well, that got rid of the stragglers,' says Malachi to a chorus of chuckles from the audience. 'Now for the serious business...'

There's no real surprise, at least to me, when the words, 'Stand up and fight until you hear the bell...' appear on the screen: *Toréador* is a commonly known aria that I was singing in French only two days ago. But once again, although the pianist is banging away loudly, and Malachi is trying to rouse us by singing it himself, swinging his arms about like the mad choir master he is, the audience is so self-conscious that it seems as though no one here has sung before in their life, let alone earned a fortune from it. I've had enough. I think about what Dr Sparks and Samantha have been through, and let rip. I sing as loudly and as operatically as I possibly can. Heads are turning and looking at me. I don't care. Even Malachi notices and peers quizzically in my direction for a few seconds.

When the aria finishes, and with young heads still turning, trying to work out who the hell I am, Malachi makes a joke, 'I thought for a moment there Russell Watson had turned up.' People laugh. I feel and look embarrassed. Have I just been dragged off my high horse by the short and curlies? What if that's not what he's looking for? Maybe he doesn't want an operatic tone, but something more idiosyncratic? But then he adds, 'Well done, whoever you are, that's what we need more of,' and I breathe a sigh of relief.

CHAPTER 22

After the recording, we are shepherded towards a corner of the studio where we are given a chance to mingle with each other and meet the man himself. There is some cheap wine in plastic glasses, some orange juice, and a few snacks put out on a table. I guess this is also part of the test for Malachi to see whether there are any odious prima donnas in the group that could make his life difficult. I look around for Petra, but she's playing the professional aide and won't leave his side. The two female assistants, however, are moving in and about us, taking everyone's name, those of us who braved the storm. I count about thirty.

One such assistant – a young and attractive brunette with wavy, shoulder length hair, hazel eyes and thick, made-for-kissing lips – notices I'm not mingling very well. She approaches me, smiles politely and asks me who I am.

'Solomon,' I reply, 'Solomon Capri.'

'Ah,' she says with a cheeky look, 'so you're Solomon. Mum was telling us about you.'

'Mum?' I ask.

'Petra,' she says.

'God, wow, you're her daughter?'

'Yes, and that's my sister,' she says, nodding in the direction of the other assistant. 'Mia's actually three years younger than me, but people don't realise because she's so tall. Sorry, I'm Eva.' Eva gives me her hand, which I shake gently. 'Yes, she told me she was one of your groupies in the eighties.'

'That was a long time ago,' I reply, wincing, as I taste the cheap white wine.

'She told me about some of the things you used to get up to.'

'Really? Should a mother be that candid with her daughters?'

'You know Mum, she's very liberal. She still walks around the house naked, even now. Oh look, here she comes. Bye.'

Eva leaves, soon to be replaced by a fully clothed Petra and a smaller-than-he-looks-on-TV Malachi.

'Hi Malachi,' I say, 'very pleased to meet you. I'm a big fan of your programmes. Solomon, Solomon Capri.' I offer my hand. He takes it and studies me momentarily.

'Ah, the man with the lungs,' he says.

'Yeah, sorry about that. I didn't mean to show off, I was just surprised by everyone's lack of enthusiasm.'

'Yes, I was a little bit disappointed by that too. I've heard more guts and gusto from a bunch of five-year olds. But you must have sung classically before?' He pauses and squints. 'You weren't on Popstar to Operastar last year, were you?'

'No,' I reply, 'not guilty.'

'Good,' he says, 'I hate that show.'

I look at Petra, hoping she hasn't said anything. 'Well,' I explain, 'I sang a bit when I was a teenager. We had this amazing music teacher who got us together with a local girls school and we put on a performance of *The Pirates of Penzance*. I played the Pirate King...'

'Hoorah!' interjects Malachi, quoting from the libretto.

'Yes, hoorah! The guy who directed us was also the musical director for a local operatic and dramatic society, and he invited me to audition. I passed and landed a part immediately: Lieutenant Tranisch in Noel Coward's *Bitter Sweet*...'

'I hate Noel Coward,' says Malachi.

'Me too. I was then spotted by a local opera coach and offered free lessons, which I took for about six months. That was my brief flirtation with opera.'

'I see,' he replies. 'And have you seen the play, *Jerusalem*?'

'Yes, I saw it the other day.' (Well...a third of it before I was escorted out.)

'And what do you think?'

'I think it will be an amazing opera,' I reply. Petra looks very pleased, so does Malachi.

'Good to have you on board,' says Malachi, and once again shakes my hand.

Following this positive interaction with Malachi, I say my goodbyes to Petra, retrieve my phone, and, in a buoyant mood, head back to the car. It's around one-thirty. I'm hungry, but I can probably pick up a sandwich in a service station, because I'm keen to return to Sunnymore, to see how Dr Sparks is getting on, and to share with him the day's events.

Thanks to Mo's satnav, we avoid the traffic at Hammersmith and make excellent progress along the M3. After an hour or so, I realise I haven't switched my phone back on. When I finally do, I receive a couple of predictably lewd texts from Lexi relating to a certain body part of mine, which seems to be growing in girth, length and reputation, at least in her mind anyway. But the third text that pops up a few minutes later is a little more cryptic, it reads, 'Revenge is mine.'

By four, I'm back at Sunnymore. I briefly swing by the studio to say hi to Dr Sparks and tell him how well it went in London. He seems pleased for me, though a little preoccupied. He then explains that he's waiting for his daughter-in-law to call him back, so I walk up the drive to the house. Once inside, I take off my coat and go upstairs to put on something a little warmer and a little less formal than what I've been wearing all day.

Up in my bedroom, everything looks perfectly normal until I go into the bathroom to take a pee. That's when I notice one of the drawers has been left slightly ajar. It's the one with Rosa and Ernesto's rings in, and my immediate thought is that Rosa has been rooting around and having a quick, excited peek, especially as I haven't mentioned anything about the rings since I bought them. But when I examine the drawer and see that several blister packs of sleeping pills have gone missing, I realise it wasn't Rosa at all. My mind immediately jumps to Consuelo, to the text from Lexi threatening to get her the sack, to the one that came in today, to my abusive dismissal of Consuelo the other night. I don't care if it's paranoia but I charge down the stairs, hurtle down the drive, and barge into the gatehouse cottage.

Rosa and Ernesto are sitting at the kitchen table in close conspiracy, holding hands and whispering in Spanish. Several candles have been lit and the atmosphere is akin to a séance. They look up, but my presence barely changes their expressions or their mood.

'Is Consuelo home?' I ask, still trying to catch my breath.

This is the stoniest reception I have received from this couple since the day we interviewed them for the job. Rosa whispers to Ernesto in Spanish before she replies to me in English. 'She has been fired, Mr Solomon, told to leave the salon. She is in her room and doesn't want to see anyone.' There are no smiles. I'm not sure how much they know about what happened between their daughter and me.

'How long? How long has she been in her room?' I cry, but they show no concern for my sense of urgency.

'Please, Mr Solomon, she doesn't wish to see anybody,' says Ernesto. He's not angry but he's firm and clearly bitter.

I pay them no more heed. I rush up the small staircase and burst into her bedroom. Then, my head really starts to spin. Consuelo is lying fully clothed on her bed, belly down, a duvet pulled half across her, hair draped over her face, left arm hanging lifelessly off the bed.

'Consuelo!' I yell, rushing up to her and trying to shake her from sleep. I shout her name again and she stirs briefly, opens her mouth almost into a smile and whispers, 'I was just dreaming about you, Mr Solomon.'

I look at the walls, at all the posters of myself. I look at the youth, the health, the naivety, the vanity. I want to tear those pictures down – that's not me, that's not me anymore. 'Fran,' I plead, 'please, for fuck's sake, help me now. Help me now from beyond the fucking grave.' I hear Rosa and Ernesto clomp their way up the stairs, roused by my voice. I notice the glass of water by the bed, then look under the bed and see the blister packs but have no time to work out how many pills are gone. I plead with God, curse and curse, and shake Consuelo again. This time, her eyes open slightly. I glimpse a flicker of white.

'Call a fucking ambulance!' I scream, 'Call a fucking ambulance!'

At least Ernesto reacts positively. Although everything now appears in some kind of sick slow motion, he moves like I've never seen him move, as he finally realises what his daughter might have done. But Rosa becomes hysterical. She barges me out of the way and starts shaking Consuelo; screaming and sobbing and turning her over, holding her to her chest, squeezing her sleeping body so tightly, I'm worried she's going to do her physical harm. I literally have to grab Rosa from behind and wrestle her off. In less than ten minutes we hear the sound of a distant siren.

Thank God for the Great Western Ambulance Service, it's just unfortunate that the ambulance's arrival coincides with Consuelo's sisters coming home from their schools. There are tears, confusion, and so much fear in the younger girls' eyes. They really don't understand, it's simply heartbreaking. Dr Sparks appears, alerted by the commotion and the flashing lights on top of the ambulance, and once he realises what is going on, he shepherds the three girls into the cottage so that Rosa, Ernesto and I can follow the ambulance to the hospital.

Rosa hasn't stopped crying since we left. At the hospital, we are led to a private room where our names are taken, forms are filled in, and questions are posed to us by a softly-spoken nurse about the possible period between ingestion and discovery. She enquires about the brand of sleeping pill, whether there was any alcohol involved etc, even though all this information was already given to the paramedics who arrived on the scene. There is no hint of accusation or interrogation in the nurse's voice. So far, no one has asked us why.

Rosa, Ernesto and I sit together in morbid silence. Rosa occasionally crosses herself while Ernesto mouths inaudible prayers. There's an old guy attached to a mobile drip who keeps opening the door and making faces at us until some ward nurse finally ushers him away. On a table are magazines you don't want to read; on the wall is a poster advertising job opportunities for the NHS and a sign requesting that mobile phones be switched off. Mine isn't. It's on silent. At one point, I feel the vibration of an incoming text. I stand up and walk into a corner with my back to Rosa and Ernesto to see who it's from.

'In the bar of the White Hart Hotel,' it reads, 'plenty of rooms available. Xxx.' It's Lexi.

The gall, the timing. 'Sorry Lexi,' I reply, 'I'm in the hospital. Consuelo took an overdose. Well done for getting her fired.'

A minute passes before she answers. 'You're fucking kidding me!'

'NOT FUCKING KIDDING!!!!' is what I type.

I've been watching the clock and it's now more than an hour since we arrived. Finally a man comes in who introduces himself as Dr Levine. He apologises for the wait, sputters some medical jargon about 'gastric lavage' and 'activated charcoal' and then informs us that Consuelo is being closely monitored, but all the signs indicate she is not in mortal danger. In a nutshell, he tells us we just have to let her sleep it off. The joy shared between Rosa, Ernesto and me completely obliterates any sense of boundaries or formality. In tears, they hug each other so tightly, both thanking their Catholic God. I put my arms around them both and experience such immense, existential relief, the scale of which I haven't felt since Raffy and Mili were born. When we finally break away, Dr Levine warns us there will have to be a psychological evaluation before she can be discharged. Rosa and Ernesto don't understand what he means, so I explain that it's just procedure.

Back at Sunnymore, I drop Rosa and Ernesto at the gatehouse cottage and leave them to tell their family, and Dr Sparks, that Consuelo is going to be OK. I park the Range Rover in the garage, go into the house and head straight for the sanctuary of my study. I throw my coat onto the sofa and slump down next to it. Any moderate or careless thoughts are put on hold while my mind tries frantically to take stock of what just happened. I'm almost expecting Fran to materialise in the chair opposite, but I'm just as startled by my phone vibrating repeatedly. Someone's trying to call me. I only hope it's not the hospital with some bad news. I fumble to get my phone out of my coat pocket in time, but I do. It's Jenny.

'Solomon? Lexi left a garbled message on my voicemail. She said I need to talk to you urgently. What's going on?'

I can hear a crowd of people laughing and talking in the background, the clinking of glasses, the whine of an accordion. She must be in a restaurant or a bar.

'Consuelo took an overdose of sleeping pills,' I say, trying to sound calm.

'Where did she get them?' asks Jenny. I hear the shock in her voice.

'From the drawer in our bathroom.'

'Fuck! Why? She was always so happy.'

And then it all comes pouring out; I'm overcome, overwhelmed. It's hard to speak through the sobs, through the waves of guilt and grief. I explain with remorse about the events of the other evening. I confess to her about the spliff, the coke, the blowjob, the catfight, and how Lexi got Consuelo fired. I tell her about Samantha, and that Dr Sparks lost his son in the July 7 bombings. I tell her about finding Consuelo and all the posters on her wall, about the hospital and the doctor but not about what happened between Consuelo and me. I'm not sure how Jenny is going to take it, how she will react, but when I finally run out of things to say, all I hear is the background noise from her phone of a crowd singing someone happy birthday.

'Jenny? Did you hear me?'

There's a lull in the background noise as Jenny moves away.

'It's a full moon,' she replies dreamily, 'the piste looks amazing from up here; the snow is almost blue. Why don't you go on holiday, Solomon, go lie on a beach somewhere, get away from all the pain?'

She's not upset; she's not even concerned about my indiscretion with Lexi. Is she so removed she can forgive everything?

'I can't, Jenny,' I cry, 'I can't leave these people. Not now. They need me. Come home. Please come home.'

CHAPTER 23

I've no idea how long I've been asleep. I went upstairs after speaking to Jenny and just crashed, exhausted from the day's events. It's pitch black outside the windows and the only light inside is coming from the hall through the gap in the bedroom door. Something stirred me from sleep, something I'm not used to hearing in this house, the sound of a distant piano. Someone must be playing the one downstairs. Is that Fran? I wonder. Has Fran's ghost returned, or is it Dr Sparks? I sit up, swivel round, put on my shoes, stand up, go to the door, open it fully, and realise it couldn't be anyone else.

I head downstairs and into the sitting room; the frosted doors to the conservatory are closed. I open one and look inside. The old man seems very sullen, sitting there at the piano in semi-darkness. He looks at me, but doesn't stop playing. I'm beginning to feel guilty, wondering if I'm in his bad books too, whether word has spread about my night, or nights, with Consuelo.

'That sounds beautiful, what you're playing. What is it?' I ask, as I tentatively approach.

'*Là ci darem la mano*,' he replies, 'I found the sheet music, just trying to reacquaint myself...' No wonder he's sullen. He stops suddenly and stares straight at me. 'I suppose you blame yourself for what Consuelo tried to do.'

'Just a lot,' I reply.

'I suppose you've been going over and over in your mind what you could have done to avert it?'

Well, I think to myself, I could have hidden those bloody pills a lot better. 'Yes,' I admit.

He begins playing again. 'It's natural,' he says, 'gives us back a spurious sense of control, puts us at the centre of things, makes us feel our lives are not spiralling out of control when they truly are.'

I've just woken up and don't have the stomach for philosophy. 'You know she's gonna be OK?' I say.

'Yes,' he replies as he pauses once more. 'You may have saved her life, that's how Rosa and Ernesto see it. Another saintly act from Saint Solomon, psychic in his ability to know when someone close to him is in mortal danger.' I feel some relief when I hear this, yet Sparks' tone doesn't convince me he sees it that way at all. 'The piano sounds wonderful in this room, doesn't it?' he adds.

'Majestic.'

'Majestic, yes, that's the word. I spoke to Samantha earlier,' he continues, 'actually, I spoke to her a few times; she apologises for driving off like that the other day.'

'Actually, I was hoping to apologise to your daughter-in-law, if I ever see her again, if I haven't frightened her off.'

There's a slight smile at the corners of Sparks' lips. 'Have you spoken to your wife?' he asks.

'Yes.'

'I suppose she's rushing back to be with you now, as we speak, rushing back to be with her husband at this difficult time.'

Is that sarcasm, I wonder, or does he know something I don't?

'I doubt that somehow,' I confess.

Sparks shakes his head disapprovingly. 'I hope you don't mind but I told Samantha about Consuelo. She's very concerned…'

'That's good of her…'

'…about you. You need people around you right now, Solomon, to keep you from slipping into that black hole of regret and self-blame, people who know a thing or two about…' He strikes a loud and sombre chord on the piano. 'I hope you don't mind, but I've taken the liberty of inviting Samantha over for dinner this evening.'

'I don't mind at all. What time is it now?'

'Five minutes past eight.'

'Is Rosa cooking?'

'No, I thought you might like to venture out of your estate, and let us take you somewhere where you're not lord and master, where someone can look after you.'

Sounds like hell. 'Well, the nearest restaurant is the Indian in Burton Marsh. Do you like Indian?'

'I don't mind, as long as you promise not to pick up the bill.'

'Fine. What about Samantha, does she like Indian?'

'What about you, do you like Indian?' asks Sparks, imitating me, clearly irritated.

'Yes.'

'Then stop worrying about everyone else.'

'What about Tilda?'

'Tilda is happily stuck in front of the TV, watching repeat after repeat of Antiques Roadshow. We'll bring her back a take-away. Ernesto said he would pop in and check on her every now and then. Anything else?'

At least Sparks allows me a moment to freshen up. When I eventually come back downstairs, Samantha is already waiting for me in her coat, in the kitchen. Sparks, however, is not. The moment she sees me, she rushes up and puts her arms round me. 'I'm so sorry,' she says, 'what a day; you must be feeling awful.' She pulls away and looks at me. 'And I'm sorry about the other morning too; you just caught me off guard, that's all.'

'No, no, I fully understand. Eugene told me everything. I didn't have the faintest idea. You must have been through hell and back, both of you.'

'It's been tough, let's just say that. So how's the girl doing? Have you had any more news?'

'No, but the doctor said she'll be fine – she just needs to sleep it off. I'll go in and check on her in the morning.'

'And you're OK with this tonight? I mean, it was Eugene's idea. Having said that, I didn't need much persuading.'

'Absolutely,' I reply, 'it's very kind of him, and you.'

I feel like a fraud. I'm getting sympathy, attention, for something I undoubtedly caused.

'I love this kitchen,' says Samantha, interrupting my train of thought. She wanders from cabinet to cabinet, studying it in more detail. 'Your guesthouse is fabulous, but this is more my style; this is a real cook's kitchen.'

'You like to cook?'

'I love to cook…and eat…possibly more than I should.'

'You look fine to me,' I say, and then realise how much like a cheap chat-up line it sounds. Samantha simply smiles. 'So where's the old man?' I ask.

'He went to get his coat. Look, if you want, I'm happy to drive. It's just a Polo, but we'll all squeeze in. And it means you can have a drink as well; I have to drive back to Bath, anyway.'

I'm tempted to say, 'No you don't, you can stay the night,' but then I remind myself I am supposed to be in a black hole of regret and self-blame. 'That'd be great,' I say, instead.

Twenty minutes later, we are sat in the Rajdoot, pride of Burton Marsh. 'Is there anything you recommend, Solomon?' asks Sparks, as he peruses the menu.

'Well, it's a pretty standard Indian menu, it depends on how spicy you like your food,' I reply. 'Me, I usually go for the lamb madras, but you might prefer a korma or something. How about you, Samantha?'

'Oh, I'll probably have something simple like a vegetable biryani.'

A couple of men across from us are asking for the bill. I recognise one of them – Reverend James Walker, the vicar of this fine parish, dressed in his civvies. I put my hand up to say hello; he nods but doesn't make much of an effort to acknowledge me. Some might take it as a snub.

'Who was that?' asks Samantha, after they've left.

'The vicar of St Thomas, the church across the road. When Jenny and I first moved down here, and I was still a youngish pop star, he asked me to open the village fête. Which I did. I must have seen him in this restaurant at least twenty times, yet the only person he seems to recognise is my wife. Bizarre.'

My wife, I think to myself, is she my wife, or my ex-wife?

The waiter comes and takes our order. To my surprise, Dr Sparks asks for a lamb vindaloo. 'That's probably the hottest thing on the menu, you know,' I say to him.

He fixes me with a wolfish stare. 'Do you think I live on a diet of Hobnobs and cup-a-soup? Do you think I got to this grand old age eating nothing but grain and seeds?'

'Just warning you.'

Once the order is taken, Dr Sparks excuses himself and pops off to the Gents.

'Is he always this grumpy?' I ask Samantha, once he's no longer in earshot.

'He doesn't know how to deal with your generosity,' she replies, 'and, in some ways, your wealth and success.' A waiter arrives with a bottle of white wine and asks if I'd like to taste it. 'He was a bit of a star once, you know,' she continues, 'albeit a long time ago. He was still singing professionally until 2005. It tore him apart…' she pauses. It's obvious it did the same to her. '…but he got back on track, eventually; he settled into a very simple life on the barge until last November when Tilda had her stroke. It came out of the blue. She was so active as well, they both were – walking every day, up in the hills, down the canal, shopping together, leading a normal, healthy life. It's like he's lost his wife, you know, his best friend, his partner, and I think he feels that you have too.'

I can't look at Samantha at this point; she's touched a nerve. Her knowing about Jenny accentuates how I feel – sick, lost, scared. A different waiter plants a pile of poppadoms on the table along with a selection of chutneys, and I stare into them; the dirty green pickled limes, the red of the chilli sauce, the off-white flecked yogurt.

'I'm sorry,' she says, 'I keep saying I'm sorry, but I am. And all the stuff going on with the girl must make things doubly bad.'

Finally, I look at her and she can see my vulnerability. 'Carry on and you'll have me in tears,' I say. She simply nods her head. 'So what do you do for a living?' I ask, 'Are you some kind of therapist?'

She pulls a playful, noble face. 'Have a guess.'

'I just did. Something in the caring or medical profession, I reckon. Am I close?'

'Go on.'

'Social worker, doctor, nurse, counsellor...sex therapist?'

'He told you.' She's completely deadpan. I was only joking, trying to lighten the mood.

'What do you mean?' I ask.

'He told you I'm a sex therapist.'

'Honestly, that was a stab in the dark.'

'Do I look like a sex therapist? Is it that obvious?' She seems mortified, either that or she has excellent acting skills.

'Well...I...don't know...'

'I'm a dental hygienist,' she replies, with a wink, 'if you ever need your teeth cleaned, I'm your girl.' She pauses, sensing a faux pas. 'Not that I'm saying you need your teeth cleaned...in fact, they look very white to me.'

Sparks returns and the flirtatious banter stops dead. I tell Samantha about the TV shows I'm hoping to do. She seems to like Malachi Jones as well – that's another person. She then tells me about Bath Opera, of which she is a member, and the opera they performed last year, *Così fan tutte*. I'm probably not in a fit state to judge, but I'm getting mixed messages from her. She keeps playing with her hair when she talks to me, there's the occasional intimate eye contact, but then she suddenly becomes cold and professional as though I'm in the hygienist's chair and she's discovered I haven't been flossing my teeth regularly. I'm confused.

We've been drinking, talking and picking at poppadoms for around twenty minutes when our main courses arrive, and regardless of what Sparks was saying about his iron stomach, after a few mouthfuls he begins to sweat.

'How's the vindaloo?' I ask, trying not to sound like I told him so.

'Delicious,' he replies, as stubborn as ever. Ten seconds later, he asks the waiter for a glass of water.

'If it's a little too spicy,' I say, 'you can always have some of mine.'

'And mine,' offers Samantha, who, I can see, is also growing concerned.

Sparks doesn't reply, but just speeds up his intake as though he's trying to get it over and done with as quickly as possible. When the water arrives, he gulps it down. Now, I know for a fact he should be drinking yogurt, not water, and I'm surprised he doesn't know that too. I can hear his stomach trying to digest what he's thrown at it, even from where I'm sitting. Defeated, he finally gets up, excuses himself and heads back to the Gents.

I shake my head and laugh and Samantha laughs too. I know we shouldn't. In Sparks' absence the conversation becomes personal again.

'Eugene mentioned that the girl...'

'Consuelo.'

'...Consuelo, has some kind of shrine to you and your band, in her bedroom. It must be so strange being worshipped like that.'

'At my age, more than a little weird.'

'But I suppose it was fun when you were younger, right? I bet it was all sex, drugs and rock and roll?'

'Yeah,' I reply, 'now it's all sex, drugs and opera.'

'Pardon?'

'I mean, now it's opera…not the sex and drugs bit.'

'I'm glad to hear it,' she says, 'at least about the drugs.'

Damn, and I was hoping she had a wild side. 'I don't mean to pry,' I say, 'but I see you're still wearing your wedding ring…' Samantha glances down at her ring finger, and gives a little emotional shrug. 'Have there been no men since 2005, men with incredibly clean teeth?'

'Two or three,' she replies, distantly, 'but my son can't abide it. He makes it very uncomfortable for them, and me.'

'It shouldn't be up to him though, should it?'

'No, but just like his father and grandfather, he can be very forceful without actually saying anything.'

'Isn't he at the academy most of the time?'

'Yes, but he has a sixth sense about me. Then when he comes home, it's like he can smell any man who's been there.'

Personally, I find it quite abhorrent that a child can control a parent like that, but I keep it to myself, at least for the time being. 'What about women?' I enquire callously, 'Can he smell them too?'

Samantha looks away. She doesn't answer. I think I may have just stumbled upon a little secret.

Ten minutes pass and still Dr Sparks hasn't returned from the loo. Both Samantha and I decide I should go and check on him.

I open the thick black door to the Gents, then half-open the next, thinner, white one. I can't see the old man, but I can certainly hear him and, much worse, smell him. It's awful – sulphurous, poisonous, like rotten meat and rotten fruit combined. My heart goes out to him but my nose shows no sympathy at all. 'Eugene,' I yell, some distance from the cubicle, 'are you alright?'

'What does it look like?' he yells back. There's another diabolical outpouring followed by a cry of anguish. 'I may be some time,' he adds.

'OK,' I reply, 'I'll leave you to it. Do you want me to order a take away for Tilda?'

'Yes, but make damn sure it's not spicy!'

Driving back in the car, it's clear Dr Sparks has entirely lost his sense of humour. At one point the car fills up with the same stench and Samantha quickly opens the windows. 'Eugene,' she shouts, 'that's disgusting!' We can't help but fall into fits of giggles. But not the old man, he's clutching the bag that contains Tilda's supper, and staring at the road ahead.

When we arrive back at the studio courtyard, he manages a polite and brief goodnight and then makes a dash to the studio door before disappearing inside.

'He'll be alright,' says Samantha, who doesn't make any attempt to get out the car. I remain where I am and there's an awkward moment; it's like she doesn't want to turn and look at me, or even glance in the mirror. I get the sense that she really is in two minds. But then, so am I.

'Nightcap?'

There's a moment's indecision before she answers. 'I probably should be heading back; I have a nine a.m. scaling and root planing to do on some poor student from the University. He's only twenty-one, you wouldn't believe the state of his gums.'

'Sounds like fun,' I reply. I hear Samantha take a deep breath. It sounds like a breath of frustration. I smell blood. 'We haven't talked about the recital,' I add, very quietly, seductively even, 'about our duet, or has the idea lost its appeal?'

Again, a pause followed by another deep breath. 'I don't suppose you have any chamomile tea, do you?' she replies.

'Of course.'

CHAPTER 24

Samantha is perched on a stool at the island in the main kitchen. She watches me as I pour boiling water from the kettle into a mug bearing the words, *World's Greatest Dad*. It was a present from Mili and, unfortunately, the mug closest to hand. Following recent events, it seems incredibly hypocritical.

'Just leave the teabag in,' says Samantha, after I dunk it several times, trying to get some colour into the brew. I do as requested and hand her the cup. I then pick up my glass of wine and take a sip.

'So, did you not sing before 2005?' I ask, 'Eugene told me you've been having lessons for six years. What happened, did you start from scratch?'

'No, I always sang, folk music mainly. I do a very good impersonation of Joan Baez.'

'Kumbaya! I want to hear it.'

'Really?'

'Absolutely.'

'Do you have a guitar?'

'In my bedroom.'

Samantha looks to the heavens. 'You really are intolerable.'

'No, I'm serious, it's in the bedroom. Don't worry I'll go and get it. Take a seat on the sofa, bring your tea.'

A minute later I return with my Gibson acoustic. I hand it to Samantha, sit beside her and listen as she starts to pick at it.

'I normally play a Spanish guitar,' she says, 'you'd laugh if you saw it. I'm not used to steel strings.'

I can see she's a pretty good guitarist simply from the way she adjusts the tuning according to the harmonics.

'Alright,' she says, 'do you know this one? I usually play it with a capo on the first fret. I don't suppose you have a capo?'

'Somewhere, probably in a box in the attic.'

'Never mind.' She plays the introduction and I recognise the song immediately; it's a song my father used to listen to over and over again until the record was scratched beyond use – *Diamonds and Rust* by Joan Baez. Samantha opens her mouth and starts to sing just like the American with that pronounced, rapid vibrato. I know the lyric so well; I know that Joan Baez wrote it about her ex-lover, Bob Dylan. I can't help but join in, part in unison, part in harmony. Samantha seems impressed, even delighted. I even try and imitate Dylan for a couple of phrases. God, I've missed this feeling so much, the coming together of voices purely for the simple pleasure it gives. I guess Jenny was right; I barely make music any more. I don't pick up the guitar or sit at the piano anywhere near as much as I used to. It's as though the mystery, the sparkle has gone, but in this brief exchange, I catch a glimpse of it again. When the song finishes, both Samantha and I look at each other in disbelief.

'That was amazing,' says Samantha.

'Sounded really good. We could get a gig down the local pub.'

'Do you want to try something else?'

'I'm not sure if we can top that, maybe we should just savour the moment.'

'I think you're right. How do you know that song so well, all the lyrics, everything?' she asks.

'My father was into Joan Baez, especially the early stuff. He was also big into the civil rights movement, the anti-war campaign, CND. He was in the Second World War. I think he felt so humiliated and traumatised by the whole experience, he just had to tell the world. She was one of his heroes, all that stuff she did to get soldiers not to join the draft.'

'He must have been quite old when you were born?'

'Forty-five.' Samantha puts the guitar to one side and leans back against the sofa. 'You really do have two different voices, both beautiful,' I continue. 'So tell me: there you are singing like Joan Baez, playing the guitar...how did you get into opera?'

'Osmosis...and my husband's death.'

'Of course. I'm sorry. You know, when I got back from the hospital earlier today, I completely crashed for an hour or two, got woken up by Eugene playing the piano in the conservatory. I'd forgotten it was there, it sounded so ghostly for a minute. *Là ci darem la mano*, that's what he was playing. He said he was reacquainting himself with it. It's a terrible reminder for both of you, isn't it?'

'Taboo,' says Samantha, with a touchingly sad smile.

'You've never sung it in public?'

'No,' she replies, 'I sing along to the recording at home when I feel a bit sorry for myself. I know it off by heart. I'm just very nervous about singing it in front of Eugene. But, as he keeps saying, we have to move on.' She leans forward, takes a sip of tea, then looks at the words on the mug. 'So what was played at your wedding, world's greatest dad? Do you have a special song? I'm sure it was a grand affair.'

I chuckle as I think back. 'Funnily enough, we didn't have any music. We got married at Chelsea registry office at eleven-thirty in the morning. I wore a sleeveless denim jacket. Jenny was in a stunning, shimmering, silver-purple dress and I was back rehearsing with the band in the afternoon.'

'Was there no reception?'

'A bottle of champagne in The Cadogan Arms.'

'Honeymoon?'

'About eight months later, when there was a break in the schedule.'

'Must have been tough,' says Samantha, 'but it brought you all this.'

There's absolutely no way I'm going to tell her about the tampon applicator.

'Yes,' I reply, 'I really should be more grateful.'

'Do you mind if I use your loo for a minute?' she asks, slightly spoiling the intimate mood.

'Not at all, it's just out there in the hall, on the right.'

While Samantha is in the loo, I quickly fetch my phone and place it on the iDock. I'm so enjoying her company, loving her voice, shocked that she plays guitar so well. There's a real rapport; I don't want this to end. I browse the albums on my iPhone until I spot *Seasons Of My Soul* by Rumer. The song I'm looking for is a ballad called *Slow*. It's about as seductive a piece of music as I've ever heard. I hear the flush go and wait until Samantha returns to the kitchen.

'I was gonna put some music on just in the background, if that's OK?' I ask her.

She looks at her watch. 'I should probably be heading home.'

'You wanted us to sing another song just a minute ago,' I protest.

'Go on then. Is it something by Joan?' she replies, as she sits back down.

'Just listen,' I say. I press play, and out from the speakers comes the richest, creamiest, most sexy female voice I've heard in recent times. Rumer sings, 'You make me want to sing about love, every time I raise my head...' It's crushingly beautiful. The words are unashamedly romantic.

'Who is this?' asks Samantha.

'Her name is Rumer, R-U-M-E-R. It was released in 2010. Like it?'

'Yes I do, she sounds a little like Karen Carpenter.'

'She does. I think she's worked with Burt Bacharach, it has all his dreamy chords.'

I turn the volume up and return to sit beside Samantha where I just study her for a while as she listens to the music, music which is so honest and haunting it slips through the pores of your skin, into your veins and threatens to root out the secrets of your heart.

I can see her paying attention to the lyric, her eyes constantly moving as though she's reading the words off a page. But then, to my dismay, her body language changes. She crosses one leg over the other, away from me, puts her arms around her waist as though she's protecting her most vulnerable organs. It's like suddenly I'm the Big Bad Wolf threatening to blow her fragile house down. She doesn't want to look at me, I guess, because the song is a love song, one might argue, in its purest form. It's not cynical, it doesn't possess the clever words of a spurned lover as in *Diamonds and Rust*. The chorus floats in like a wave of longing. 'Slow, slow this right down, don't burn it out, don't let it show. Slow, oh how my heart is racing, to hold your gaze and let it go…'

And then Samantha starts to fidget. She has a troubled look on her face, a visible lump in her throat.

'What's going on?' I ask her.

'It's very nice, Solomon,' she says, finally turning to face me, 'the romantic, seductive music, but it's not what I came here for.'

Her sudden mood swing is so frustrating. 'What's gone wrong?' I ask, trying not to sound too confrontational. 'We were having such a great time. We were singing together, I put on some background music…It's only a love song,' I add, 'a beautiful…ok, maybe a seductive love song. You just need to let it wash over you, surrender to it, open your heart a little. I'm not gonna hurt you, I'm not a ghost, or a memory, I'm real, I'm here. I'm not gonna suddenly disappear.'

I don't know where that came from and I guess it was completely the wrong thing to say, because Samantha begins to weep, her head in her hands. I've fucking done it again, this has completely backfired. I put my arm around her but she's inconsolable. Six years and there's still so much grief.

Eventually, the sobs recede. 'Let me get you some tissues,' I say, heading off to the bathroom and returning with some Kleenex. 'I'm sorry,' I say, when I return, 'this is the second time I've seen you and the second time I've reduced you to tears. Not doing very well am I?'

'It's not your fault,' she replies, blowing her nose repeatedly. 'I just can't seem to get over it.' It sounds like an honest admission, but now she really does want to leave. There's nothing I can say. She quickly gathers her coat from the stool at the kitchen island and I escort her to the door.

'Let me at least walk you back up to the studio,' I offer.

'No, it's OK,' she replies, 'you stay in the warm.' There's a formal hug from her as we say goodnight. There's so much confusion, so many questions rattling through my brain, as I watch Samantha walking at pace up the drive back to her car.

The next morning I wake around ten-thirty, with that Rumer song still going round and round my head. I wonder when I'll see Samantha again. I wonder if she even wants to see me. I go down to the kitchen to find Rosa changing the fruit in the fruit bowl. She's wearing the broadest smile ever.

'Morning Rosa, you seem happy, what's going on?'

'We went to see Consuelo this morning.'

'How is she?' I ask, 'Is she still groggy?'

'She is fantastic, Mr Solomon,' she gushes. 'She has seen Our Lady, Mother of God, the Blessed Virgin Mary. It is a miracle. She spoke to Consuelo; she came to her in a dream. She said she would be blessed with child.'

CHAPTER 25

My mind has been a blur since I left the house. At the hospital, I see three middle-aged women manning the counter and neither is dressed like a nurse. I approach the only lady who isn't dealing with someone else and I explain my visit.

'Consuelo Velasquez,' she repeats, looking at her register. She then picks up the phone beside her. There's a brief conversation before she puts it down. 'She's with the counsellor at the moment. Could you possibly wait for fifteen minutes? Oh, and you are a relative?'

'I'm her godfather,' I lie, 'the person who found Consuelo and called the ambulance.'

'I see. Please take a seat.'

I'm sweating – wave upon wave of panic. I now realise if the truth came out, it would destroy me in the eyes of my children. Mili hates Consuelo; Raffy loves Consuelo, either way it would be impossible for them to understand or forgive, or even believe my version of events. What about Jenny…or Samantha? I suppose I could always deny it. After all, Consuelo has been a bit crazy lately, she took an overdose and she has pictures of me all over her bedroom wall. No one would believe her. Unless, of course, she really was pregnant. There would be a DNA test and then…a quarter Jewish, quarter English, half El Salvadorian Solomon or Solomonita would become my third born child. I dread to think. At least Fran's ghostly prediction means it won't be twins.

Half an hour passes before I'm led to the ward where Consuelo is recuperating, her bed lying between that of a large Afro-Caribbean woman, who is singing quietly and nonsensically in a high-pitched voice, and that of a rough, clearly violent, teenage girl who is handcuffed to her bed and keeps telling everyone, including me when I walk in, to fuck off. Curtains are drawn to allow some privacy.

I assumed she'd be awake, because she just saw the counsellor. But she's not; she's fallen asleep again. Not even the cursing of the girl in the next bed is making an impression. I study Consuelo for a few minutes and appreciate, in the calmness of sleep, just how young and beautiful she is. Did we really make love? I still can't believe it.

I really shouldn't disturb her, but selfishly, I need to know if she's said anything to anyone about us. I try blowing on her eyelids to wake her up. I shake her gently, but it's all to no avail. But then I have an idea. I don't know where it came from, but in this present situation, with the cursing to my right and the strange warbling to my left, it seems relatively sane. I lean close to Consuelo, my mouth right next to her ear, so no one else can hear me. I sing, very quietly, 'Dust in the attic, there is dust in the attic, well there's no need to panic, cos we can't hear the traffic…'

Consuelo starts to stir. And then her eyelids flicker. She opens her eyes, yawns, looks at me and says, 'Mr Solomon, was that you singing?'

I can't express my joy enough at seeing the girl awake and talking. 'Yes, Consuelo, it was me. I'm so glad you're alright,' I say, planting a kiss on her forehead. 'I was so worried about you.' I sit down on a chair next to her bed, and take her hand.

'Please don't worry,' says Consuelo, 'everything will be fine. I know it. I saw Mama and Papa this morning…they are so happy.'

'Yes, I spoke to Rosa. She mentioned something about The Blessed Virgin?'

Consuelo appears coy for a moment but then proudly shakes that look away.

'She came to me in a dream,' she explains, 'she told me I was a good girl like her, and that God would bless me with a child.'

Just like Rosa said. Fuck. What if it's true? Does that make me Joseph? Have I unknowingly provided the seed for the Second Coming? Is that why I have trouble remembering the whole thing, because it was erased from my memory by Divine Command? It's funny, when I was six I was asked to play Joseph in a nativity play. I told them I couldn't because I was Jewish. They told me Joseph was Jewish too. I couldn't wait to tell my father.

'Did the counsellor talk to you,' I ask Consuelo, 'about why you did what you did?'

'Yes. I told her it was because I lost my job. I didn't say anything else.'

'Did you tell them about your dream?'

'Yes.' So much for the psychological assessment.

'And what was their reaction?'

'The lady was very happy for me, she is a Catholic and loves the Blessed Virgin.'

Phew, I can see how that would work in her favour. 'Have you...told anyone about...mentioned anything about...giving up your virginity, or anything along those lines?'

'What do you mean, Mr Solomon?' she asks, almost offended that I would mention such a thing. She's either pretending or has suffered some kind of memory loss. 'I am a good girl,' she continues, 'like our Holy Mother.'

'Of course you are, Consuelo,' I say, 'of course you are.' I just hope she sticks to that story.

'I had another dream, Mr Solomon...'

Uh-oh.

'I dreamed you were singing opera in front of thousands of people.'

I'm trying to work out if this fantasy is as crazy as the one about The Blessed Virgin. Maybe I shouldn't be so cynical?

'It's your parents' anniversary soon, isn't it?' I ask.

'Yes, Sunday. Have you given them the rings yet?'

'No, but I have an idea.'

Fifteen minutes later I'm speeding back to Sunnymore. I almost miss the Burton Marsh turn off but, just at the last minute, manage a sharp turn. I drive into the village to see if I can find Reverend Walker, to remind him who I am, then ask him to repay a favour.

As I arrive in the village, I see a few elderly people spilling out of the entrance to St Thomas. This must be the end of the morning service, I assume. And then I see the man himself in his dog collar exchanging pleasantries with a few members of the parish. I park the car, head up the steps, approach Walker and offer my hand, 'Solomon Capri,' I say, 'I don't know if you remember me?'

Now, Walker, at least on the surface, is a very considered and philosophical man. He tends to peer through his specs at you as though you are a specimen under his microscope, especially if you're a woman. Despite his age, he still has very dark hair, which has receded into dramatic widow's peaks. He could play Dracula very easily. Uncertain, he takes my hand. 'Remind me,' he says.

'I saw you in the Indian last night. In fact, I've seen you in there about twenty times.'

'Really?' he says.

'Yes, more importantly, I opened the fête for you once. Long time ago – pop star, Fortune Favours The Brave, just moved to the area? Blonde wife. We had a good turn out, I recall.'

'What year was that?'

'Christ...I mean...not Christ...sorry. Must have been...1993.'

'Blonde wife.' He thinks for a second. 'An attractive blonde wife?'

'Yes.'

'A very attractive woman with a wonderfully slim figure?'

'Yeah.' OK, don't go on about it.

'Does she eat in the Indian occasionally?'

'Yes, with me, her husband.'

'Mmm, I remember now. You were the half-Jewish young man who could only come to church half the time.'

Now he's got me thinking. 'Really, I said that?'

'It was amusing...back then. So, what can I do for you?'

'Um, we have a couple who work for us, Rosa and Ernesto Velasquez, they've been married for years. They have an anniversary coming up and I'm trying to arrange a small ceremony for them to renew their vows. It would be low-key, at our house, Sunnymore. They are good Christian people, devoted to each other, and have three, I mean, four fantastic daughters. Is this something you would consider?'

Walker frowns. 'I assume these people, by their names, are Catholic. You do know there are plenty of Catholic priests in Wells. Wouldn't they be happier with a Catholic priest?'

I didn't even think of that.

'I've already considered this,' I lie, 'but there will be all denominations at the ceremony and our house does fall under the St Thomas parish boundaries.' I doubt even that is true.

'Very well, as long as it's not on Sunday, that is my busiest day, as you can imagine.'

'Ah,' I reply, 'it wouldn't take long...you could be in and out in ten minutes.'

Walker shoots me a look of exasperation and fatigue. 'I have two services and a lunch with the W.I. on Sunday.'

'I appreciate that, but it's their anniversary and their daughter is in hospital. It's been a difficult time for them. It would be incredible if you could just find a small window in your busy day.'

The reverend pauses to consider. 'Very well. What time were you thinking of holding this ceremony?'

'Around four in the afternoon?'

'Promise me we'll keep it short.'

'Promise. Er, can I call you when things are a little more solid?'

'My number's in the book. Not the good book, that is, the phone book.'

That was easier than I thought. Back in my study, I open my laptop and read the two emails that popped up on my phone while I was driving back. They're both from Petra. One is from her usual business email address and the second from some sort of junk alias.

The first email – again, so last minute – is to inform me that Malachi will be filming tomorrow in the field where he was born. That field has now been successfully subsumed into the fairway of the fifteenth hole at the Underwood and Crickley Golf Club. She makes a joke about me bringing my golf clubs. She also says there is a coach driving up from London with the talent, but given where I live, I might prefer to fly from Bristol to Liverpool, or drive myself even, which I'll probably do, in the R8.

The second email is a lot sneakier, and she warns me it would be very embarrassing for her if anyone found out. And here's why – she's attached two MP3s, both rough piano and voice renditions of Jean Luc's first, embryonic, newly-written pieces of music for *Jerusalem: The Opera*. I listen to them both. The first piece begins very jauntily, like an old English folk song, which, I discover later, is exactly what it is. I find it bland and a little bit silly. I vaguely remember it being sung offstage pretty much near the beginning of the play.

With the merry ring, adieu the merry spring,
For summer is a-come unto day,
How happy is the little bird that merrily doth sing,
In the merry morning of May.

I suspect that Malachi will start with this when we're all assembled in some function room at the golf club. It's a simple melody and I'm sure most people will pick it up in five minutes. The second piece, however, is very aggressive, intentionally discordant. There are diminished chords, augmented chords, minor 13ths, major 9ths, and chords the like of which I've never heard before in the same sequence, except, perhaps, when our music teacher forced the class to listen to Stockhausen. And the lyric is one long list of largely unfamiliar, mythical names punctuated by, what sounds like, someone slamming down the lid of the piano or, perhaps, thumping it on top. I guess this must be from the second or third act, because it certainly doesn't ring a bell. (I am yet to receive the script, which I ordered from Wright's Books two days ago.) Nevertheless, I listen to it repeatedly. I've pretty much memorised that list as well, and looked up all the names of the mythical entities on the internet, just in case. I feel a bit guilty being helped like this by Petra. It feels like I'm cheating in an exam. But, as she said, she's doing it for Anke. Who am I to deny her that?

CHAPTER 26

The next day I find myself driving up the M6 towards an area in North Wales, west of Wrexham, the postcode, thankfully, plugged into the R8's satnav. So far, it's taken more than three hours but finally, having driven a mile down a long gravel drive, I see a large white sign that reads, Underwood and Crickley Golf Club. There's also a makeshift orange arrow on a pole stuck into the ground. It's pointing to the right. I follow it and park in the designated car park, which I find surprisingly empty. I count maybe four un-pop-star-like cars, two big black Mercedes and a couple of grey equipment vans, certainly no coach.

I get out the car and, in a fairly strong breeze and blinding winter sunshine, walk towards the clubhouse – a large, though unremarkable, white painted building. As I near the entrance, I stop for a second, shield my eyes, and look down across the undulated land, at the bunkers, the vast fairways, the shivering flags, and see no one on the golf course, except in the distance, what must be, Malachi with a crew composed of one cameraman and a sound guy holding a long, wind-shielded microphone. There's a woman there too, who could easily be Petra. They must have hired the whole course and clubhouse for the day. I bet that cost a bob or two.

Inside the clubhouse reception, I spot the younger of Petra's daughters sitting on a chair and typing away at a laptop. She sees me, puts her hand up, closes the laptop, and stands up. Now, I can't for the life of me remember her name. Luckily, she introduces herself, 'Hi, I'm Mia.' A few inches taller than her older sister, with dark blonde hair pinned back from her face, acutely square shoulders and a broad nose, Mia has clearly inherited more of her mother's Dutch genes.

'Oh, hi. Solomon,' I say, 'I spoke to your sister at Abbey Road.'

'Yes, she told me. You're the guy who used to have wild sex with Mum and her best friend.'

Why do they have to mention it? I hope no one's listening. Actually no one is. There's no one here except an old, white-whiskered gentleman behind the reception desk.

'I hope you're both keeping it to yourselves,' I say.

'Promise you, it won't go any further.'

'Good. Where is everyone?' I ask, somewhat dismayed.

'Oh,' she says, 'the bloody coach broke down just outside Birmingham. Those who made their own way here – about six of them – are in the bar.'

'I see. What time are the rest due to get here?'

'Well, the coach managed to crawl to the nearest service station and they're changing it over as we speak.'

'Right. Guess I'll just have to wait then.'

'The bar's through there,' says Mia pointing at a glass panel door above which is written, Members' Bar. 'There's food in there as well. And Eva. I've got to stay here and wait for anyone else who turns up.'

The members' bar is a large, square room with white walls and a dull pinkish carpet. There are numerous photographs hanging up – wooded areas of the golf course in various seasons, pictures of a few famous golfers shaking hands with someone who I assume is the club's owner. The bar itself is to my right and is unmanned. To my left are patio doors, which open onto a large glass-enclosed patio with a pretty spectacular view of the course. Eva is sitting at one of the bar's many square tables. She sees me, stands up, comes over and kisses me on the cheek. 'You've heard about the coach?' she asks.

'Yeah, Mia just told me.'

'They're gonna be so pissed off when they get here.'

'I can imagine,' I reply.

'That's all we need, pissed off pop stars. Mum will be back in twenty, by the way,' she adds, 'they're filming at the fifteenth hole at the moment. It's where Malachi's family used to live in their caravan.'

'I think I saw them on my way in, Malachi and your mum, that is,' I say. I look around at the pop stars who are gathered here, most of whom are thumbing their phones, none of whom I recognise. I feel old and out of place. 'No security this time then?' I ask, 'No signs up about tweeting or filming?'

Eva shrugs. 'No, Captain Scarlet dropped out.'

Ah, I think, so the Mysterons finally got him.

'Besides, there's not much of a signal here,' she continues.

'Why are they on their phones then?'

'Playing games,' she replies as though it's strikingly obvious. 'Can I get you a drink?' she adds, 'Something to eat?'

'Please, it's been a long drive.'

Eva kindly fetches me a lite beer from the bar and a couple of cheese salad sandwiches from a plate on the counter. She then grabs herself a diet coke and comes and sits with me, one leg resting on an adjacent chair.

'So, how old were you when you used to hang out with Mum and Anke?' she asks.

'God, I must have been twenty-one, twenty-two.'

'What year was that?'

'Eighty-three, eighty-four. Not quite sure when it fizzled out.'

Eva looks away briefly as though she's trying to work something out – probably my age. 'You heard what happened to Anke?' she says.

'Yeah, your mum told me. Tragic. Did you know Anke's daughter?'

'We still do, still keep in touch. She lives in New York now.' For a moment, Eva studies my face so intensely, it feels as though she's about to pull out a pencil and pad and sketch it. 'Heaven in your eyes,' she says, 'that was one of your songs, wasn't it?'

'Yes,' I reply, 'not one I'm particularly proud of. Do you know it?'

'I remember Mum singing it when I was small, when I couldn't sleep. I always thought it was by some old crooner.'

'That's probably not far from the truth,' I reply.

It strikes me that Eva has her mother's openness and natural charm. Every now and then, she gets up to check on the others, to offer them another drink or some food. She goes out every few minutes to talk to Mia and then returns to sit with me. Time passes very quickly in her company, I must admit, and it's not long before Petra appears. She walks in through the patio doors, makes a huge apology to everyone in the bar, then informs us the replacement coach is less than an hour away. There are a few sarcastic cheers, or maybe they're jeers, then she walks straight past me and approaches a tiny, beautiful, young, coffee-coloured girl with long, painted nails. She talks to her for a second and then leads the girl out through the patio doors and off somewhere to the right. Petra's wearing her headscarf again and doesn't even say hello. She seems stressed.

'Who's the girl?' I ask Eva.

'Silky Swann?' she replies, looking at me like I've been living in a cave for the last year. 'She's had three number ones in a row.' Now I don't just feel old, but completely out of touch. 'Don't worry,' she adds, 'they all think you're Bob Geldof.'

'Thanks,' I reply, 'he's considerably older than me. Anyway, so what are they doing in there?'

'Killing time by getting a few solo shots and performances. They were gonna do it after, and single out people as they go along, but now we're running late...'

Fifteen minutes later or so, Silky returns on her own. A couple of young guys applaud her, although I'm not sure why. Petra briefly appears outside the patio doors and signals to Eva, who stands up and says, 'your presence is required, follow me.' Just like that. Not even a chance to warm up. We walk though the doors, hang a right and enter, what a proud plaque tells me is, the Wrexham Lounge.

I'm sure this room has hosted many a wedding reception, but the tables are gone, and, similar to Abbey Road, the chairs are arranged in rows, though this time they're in a wide arc about three deep. Malachi is sat at the piano in conversation with the cameraman and the sound guy. Another man whom I recognise as the piano player from Abbey Road, is sitting in the back row with his eyes closed. Petra is on her phone, standing at the window, trying to get a signal, it seems. She briefly waves.

'Ah, the man with the lungs, the Pirate King, hoorah!' says Malachi once he sees me. 'What a fuck up,' he adds, 'sorry about the wait. Did you fly or drive?'

'Drove…from the West Country.'

'Did it take you long?'

'Three and a half hours,' I reply.

'See you later,' whispers Eva before she disappears, soon to be followed by her mother.

'Blimey,' says Malachi. 'Well…welcome to my part of the world, changed a bit since I was a lad. Are you a golfer?'

'No. Tennis.'

'I can't stand golf,' he admits, 'a good walk spoiled, as they say. I can't stand rugby either, and I'm Welsh. Anyway, while we're sat here twiddling our thumbs, I thought we'd do a bit of filming, try out some of the new music, get a few people singing on their own so I can get to know them a bit better, get to know their voices. So, if it's alright with you, that's exactly what we'll do. Er…don't feel nervous, if it doesn't work, we won't use it, you have my word.'

'Thanks.'

'Now…do you read music?' he asks, 'doesn't matter if you don't, there are only about three or four notes in this aria.'

'I do,' I reply, remembering not to slouch, 'I actually have a grade A O-level in music – one of the few qualifications to my name.'

'A real bona fide musician then. I suppose you were in the school orchestra?'

'Indeed.'

'Trumpet?'

'How did you guess?'

'The lips,' he says, 'always a dead giveaway.'

I notice that the camera is already rolling. Malachi hands me a piece of sheet music and I recognise the lyric immediately.

'Now,' he continues, 'this is something the composer has just written for us to try out. I don't know if you remember, but it's the scene at the end of the play where Rooster Byron is banging a drum and invoking the giants to come to his aid and defeat the army of police who are poised ready to remove him from his home.'

'Yeah,' I lie, nodding sagely, 'I remember. Very powerful.'

'Have a look at the words. They're a bit of a mouthful and although the vocal melody barely shifts, the chords around it are quite complicated and dark. You have to imagine the double basses, the cellos and the bassoons moving around like sharks in the deep, the bass drum and tympani banging before and after every word like giants stamping their feet as they march across our sacred land, the high strings circling around the top like vultures eyeing their prey. Right now, it's just me at the piano though. Have a look at the words. That tricky one is pronounced IG-DRA-SIL. It looks Welsh, but it's not.'

'Norse...the tree,' I say, 'its branches extend out all over the world. I have an old ink drawing of Yggdrasil in my study at home.'

'Really?' Malachi asks. 'Are you winding me up or is someone trying to make my job a little easier?' He laughs.

I could say something about destiny, but I don't, I just shrug. 'Do you want to sing it through for me once?' I ask. Malachi complies and I have to stop myself from smirking. His voice is so overly dramatic, his arm movements as he hits the piano, so jerky and flamboyant. But I take this opportunity to sing very quietly along, get a sense of the pitch, and warm up at least a little.

'So,' he says, when the aria comes to a halt, 'ready to have a go? You don't have to go mad, just feel your way into it.'

'Let's give it a try,' I reply.

Malachi hits a sequence of complex chords and then I sing, 'Rise up! Rise up!' with as much power as I can muster. The first thing I notice is the sound guy wincing. He pulls the microphone away about a foot. Malachi stops playing.

'Jesus Christ man, are you trying to deafen me?' he jokes. 'Fantastic for a concert hall,' he adds, 'but let's just rein it in a bit for the run through, shall we. We need to show the public that you're learning, we need to show that you're on a journey, not already parked at your destination.'

'Sorry,' I say, 'let's try it again.'

I do, and this time I nail it.

'Sounds great,' says the sound guy once I've finished. I notice the cameraman nod in agreement.

'It does, doesn't it?' adds Malachi, turning to his crew with a great big smile. He then turns to me. 'Not much of a struggle for you, is it? I mean, your enunciation is perfect, and I like the way you introduced a little of that West Country twang. Almost sounded like the Pirate King there.'

'Yeah,' I say, 'I wasn't sure if that was the right thing to do or not. I mean, the play is based in Wiltshire.'

'Absolutely,' he replies, 'I think that's definitely the way forward. Now, this character, Rooster Byron, is a bit of a roughneck. I don't mean to insult you, but you look like you've been wrapped in cotton wool for the past few years...'

And yet here I am feeling as raw as the skin beneath a picked-off scab.

'Do you think you could bulk up?' he continues, 'Grow a bit of facial hair, work on those biceps?'

'I'm pretty sure I could.'

'Good man.'

'I can't believe you're going to drive all the way back, now,' says Petra, once all the filming is over. The bar is packed with pop stars, all downing drinks and grabbing pieces of recently-delivered pizza before they have to get back on the coach. Petra and I, however, have managed to find a quiet corner. 'You know, we're staying at a fairly decent hotel in Wrexham,' she continues, 'I'm sure we could find you a room. Have dinner with us. You made a big impression today on Malachi. It might be a good idea.'

'I would love to but…'

'It's OK,' says Petra, interrupting, 'I know, you have to get back to your wife.'

What should I say? Should I tell her? It would be easy just to lie, much harder to explain that Jenny is talking about divorce, or that an eighteen-year old girl I just slept with is in hospital recovering from a suicide attempt, or the fact that I have an eighty-three year-old opera coach staying in my guesthouse, who I need to feed and water.

At this point, I am semi-rescued by Eva, who approaches us both. She looks hurt for some reason, glares at me accusingly. What have I done? She pulls her mother away and they enter an intense conversation that barely rises above a whisper. Occasionally, Eva glances across at me with an incredibly anxious look. In the end, I notice Petra very quietly reprimand her daughter, who walks off in a huff. Petra then returns to finish our conversation.

'What was all that about?' I ask.

Petra sighs. She seems reluctant to answer. But then she looks at me and says, 'She wanted to know if you are her father.'

CHAPTER 27

I feel like I've just been hit really hard in the face with a spade. I think back to the period where I was sleeping with Petra and Anke. Of course, I never used a condom. They both assured me they were on the pill. 'Well am I?' I ask, trying desperately not to raise my voice. 'Is that what this is all about? For me to be reunited with a daughter I didn't know I had for twenty-six, twenty-seven years? Christ, no wonder you wanted to get me involved, and no wonder you're looking after me. It's nothing to do with Anke, is it?'

Now Petra's getting upset. 'It's not true,' she pleads.

'What's not true?'

'About why I asked you to be involved.'

'What about Eva?'

There's a pause. 'I don't know, Solomon, I really don't know.'

'Well…is it at all a possibility?'

'It's possible,' she replies.

'Who else were you sleeping with at the time? There must have been others?'

'Yes, that's why I don't know.'

'And you never bothered to find out?'

'No. I met my husband when I was four months pregnant. As far as I'm concerned, he is Eva's father.'

'Why couldn't you have kept it a secret from her?'

Petra's face crumples into sadness. 'We did, but she always knew she was conceived out of wedlock, because of the birth certificate. I guess after talking to you today, she just looked in the mirror and worked out the maths.'

This is all too much, all too much. In one week, I have lost a wife and possibly gained a daughter, if not a divine child as well if Consuelo's vision turns out to be true. Fran must have got the numbers wrong. I don't know why I listened to him anyway, he was always hopeless at maths.

'I'd better go,' I say to Petra.

'I'm sorry,' she says.

'Yeah. Everyone says they're sorry, but it never changes anything.'

I walk out there and then. I pass Malachi who seems to want to talk to me, or at least say goodbye, but I can no longer speak. I get in the R8 and floor it out the car park, speeding off aggressively towards the M6. My phone keeps ringing, but I'm too angry to look at it. After one hundred and twenty miles of driving dangerously fast, the petrol gauge beeps at me. I need petrol. I'm also starving and thirsty. I pull into the next service station, fill the car up, fill myself up, and head off to the loo. It's only in the safety of the cubicle that I find the courage to look at my phone. There are several missed calls from Mili, my daughter – until today, my only daughter. I notice she's left a message. I listen to it. 'Hi Dad, Eric and I are bunking off a day early, can you pick us up from the station? We get in around six.'

I ring her back immediately. She answers. 'Mili, I'm driving back from Wales. You're gonna have to get a taxi.' I sound flustered.

'Chillax, Dad,' she replies, 'that's fine. What are doing in Wales, anyway?'

'A TV show...you know Malachi Jones?'

'Yeah, love his programmes.'

'Well, he's doing another one of these pop-opera shows and I've been asked to be involved.'

'Wow...sounds a lot cooler than the other one.'

'Yeah,' I reply, 'full of surprises.' I feel myself begin to well up. For a moment, I can't speak. 'I love you, Mili,' I say, eventually, and then realise how rarely I say it.

There's a pause. 'Love you too, Dad. What's wrong?'

'Lots of things,' I admit.

'I heard about Consuelo,' she says, 'I always said she was nuts.'

'Mili, please…'

'Raffy's really upset about it.'

'How does he know?'

'Mum called us both. He's desperate to come down and see her.'

'That's good of him,' I reply.

'Yeah. He wants to bring his girlfriend.'

This catches me by surprise. 'He's got a girlfriend? I always thought he was…'

'She's really good looking.'

'Oh, you've met her?'

'I'm friends with her on Facebook.'

'Of course.'

'What time do you think you'll be home?'

I look at my watch. 'Around eight?'

'OK, cos I was gonna take Eric to the Indian. Can I borrow the Porsche?'

'Sure, take the Porsche. Have fun.'

'Thanks, Dad.'

Problem is, it's Friday night and the traffic on the M5 south really starts to stack up. My estimation of getting home by eight is out by an hour and a half. Exhausted, I park the R8 in the garage, notice the Porsche is back in place, and head for the house to find Mili. I remove my coat and shout out her name once or twice, but the house is empty. She and Eric must be in the studio, hanging out with Dr Sparks. That didn't take long.

God, the smell when I eventually walk in – skunk, it's overwhelming. Mili, Eric and Sparks are sitting at the island, sharing a spliff. There's no attempt to hide it when I show up. Eric is spinning on his stool and acknowledges me on a half-turn. He's a big lad, wearing a thick Aran sweater, has a brown, foppish fringe and bad acne scars. Mili rushes over to hug me. It's a shock when I smell her breath.

'How was the Indian?' I ask as I waft away the smoke and settle on a stool.

'Excellent,' says Eric, in a thick Scottish brogue, 'I had the vindaloo, although it's not as spicy as it is in Aberdeen.'

I try not to laugh. I look at Dr Sparks and ask if he's eaten. He informs me that Rosa treated him and Tilda to some wonderful El Salvadorian food.

'How did it go in Wales?' he asks me, 'will I be buying tickets for the Royal Opera House?'

I can't help but picture the look on Eva's face. The more I think back, the more she resembles me. I wonder how Mili and Raffy would feel if they found out they had an older sister. I wonder how Jenny would take it. It would be the final nail in the coffin, I suspect.

'Good,' I reply, 'I sang well, you would have been proud, but I'm not sure if it's gonna work out.'

'Mili tells me you're quite a tennis player,' says Eric, changing the subject entirely. He then takes a big hit of spliff. Mili puts her hand over her mouth to feign extinguishing a laugh. I playfully scold her. 'I've brought my stuff if you want a game tomorrow,' he adds. 'I hear the court is blue. I've never played on a blue court before.'

I look at this stoned young man and wish I could play him right now. 'Yeah, well, hopefully it'll be a nice day,' I say.

'Can I put some music on, Dad?' asks Mili.

I pull a face that Mili knows well. It means, 'Please don't.' I then tilt my head in Dr Sparks' direction and say, 'I'm not sure Eugene's into hip-hop or dub-step or loud rock or whatever you want to play.'

'I don't mind,' says Sparks.

Damn you.

Mili grabs the Sonos controller. Clearly, she has her phone in the dock and is ready to go. I rue the day I taught my kids about technology. I ready myself for what's coming next – Eric's band's demos. I haven't forgotten my conversation with Mili from a week ago.

God, it really does sound like Big Country – ambient drums, stadium melodies. While the bagpipe guitars are swirling around the studio, I grab a glass of wine and go and sit on a sofa by the TV, just to get away from the smoke. A minute later, I am joined by Sparks.

'You have a lovely daughter,' he says.

Which one? I think to myself.

He notices me deep in thought. 'Tough day?' he asks.

'You wouldn't believe me if I told you.'

'Try me.'

I look back at Mili and say, 'Maybe some other time. Look, I was going to call Samantha,' I confess, 'just haven't found the right moment. Have you heard from her? Are you seeing her any time soon?'

Eric is tapping along on the island surface. I turn round to Mili and ask her if we can have the music a little quieter. She shoots me a look similar to the one I shot her earlier, but finally complies.

'She's popping in tomorrow,' says Sparks, 'with my grandson if you don't mind? I haven't seen him in a while.'

'I don't mind at all, I can't wait to see her.' And then I have a crazy thought. 'I don't suppose your grandson…er, Eugene junior…plays tennis does he?'

'Rugby, tennis, fencing, cross country running, he does them all with the fiercest determination.'

'Really? Tell him to bring his gear, just in case.'

Finally Eric's demos ramble to some kind of conclusion. Sparks and I return to the island.

'What do you think, Dad?' asks Mili.

'Nice drumming, Eric,' I say, trying my best to summon a compliment.

'Thanks,' he replies with a final paradiddle of raps on the wood.

'What's the name of the band, by the way?' I ask.

'The Crossing.'

'Right…isn't that the name of…'

'…Big Country's first album,' says Eric jumping in on the question.

'Of course,' I nod.

'We were gonna watch a movie,' says Mili, interrupting. 'Eric hasn't seen *Inception*. Have you seen *Inception*, Eugene?'

'No, I haven't been to the movies for a long time. I'll watch anything though, but don't be surprised if I fall asleep.'

'Do you mind, Dad?'

'I don't mind, but you might have to turn the subwoofer off or else Tilda will think that someone's dropping bombs on us.' Eric seems to find this funny, even if no one else does. And then I cringe. I probably shouldn't use the word 'bomb' in front of Sparks. 'By the way, Eugene,' I say, trying to change the subject, 'is there any chance we could get round the piano tomorrow with Samantha? Have a go at *Là ci darem la mano*?'

'Who's Samantha?' asks Mili.

'Eugene's daughter-in-law,' I reply, 'we're doing a duet…or, at least, I think we are.'

Sparks doesn't reply. Is he having second thoughts? Has Samantha lost her nerve? Does she hate me? The old man carefully rolls another spliff.

'Is this for the opera show?' asks Mili.

'No, Mili, it's just for the joy of singing, not for fame, not for glory, not for profit, just for the pure pleasure of it. Same reason Eric plays his drums. Isn't that right, Eric?'

'Absolutely,' says Eric, 'I'm hoping to become an astronaut.'

'There you go – well-grounded ambition. Anyway, I shall leave you three to your spliff and your film and bid you goodnight.'

'Oh, Dad,' says Mili, as I spin off my stool, 'Eric and I are gonna sleep up at the top tonight...so you don't hear us.'

'Oh...sure, no problem,' I reply, trying not to visualise Eric banging my precious daughter like she's a rack of toms.

'See you on the court tomorrow?' asks Eric.

'Actually,' I suggest, 'why don't we play doubles? Me and Eugene versus you and Mili.' Eric smirks at Mili, Mili smirks at Eric and they both look at the octogenarian Eugene whose wry smile tells me he knows exactly which Eugene I'm referring to. 'I'll put money on it,' I continue, 'all the change in your pocket. Deal?'

'Dad, you're going down. Deal.'

'Great. See you all in the morning.'

I'm just about to head out the door when Dr Sparks' voice drags me back. 'Solomon, I've left the *Là ci darem la mano* music on the piano in the conservatory. Perhaps you can make a copy of it and bring them both down with you tomorrow?'

That night, I don't just make a copy, I download the aria and listen to it until it's entrenched in my brain.

CHAPTER 28

'Nice legs,' says Samantha as I walk into the studio the next day. She's wearing a mustard-coloured woollen dress and sitting alone at the island, her hands wrapped around a coffee mug.

I look down at my thighs and shins, pink from running, as though they belong to someone else. 'Oh, thanks,' I reply. I'm still in my tennis gear, huffing and puffing from the exertion, racket in hand.

'How did you get on?' she asks.

'Amazing,' I reply, 'we thrashed them. Your son is so good, I barely touched the ball, except for a few easy putaways at the net. He's like a professional. Mili was furious. I left them playing singles and they're killing each other out there – the grunting, you should hear it. I think Eric's getting a bit jealous.'

Samantha is smiling at me and I'm not sure why. For a second I wonder if I'm poking out of my shorts or something. I glance down – all good.

'Look, she says, I'm sorry about the other night. I guess that song brought up so many emotions, I just got very defensive.'

'Let's make a deal,' I say, 'let's stop saying sorry, let's just relax and enjoy the music.'

'I'll try my best,' she replies.

'Where's the old man?'

'He's with Tilda…in the bathroom.'

'Everything alright?'

'I think so.'

'Look, do you mind if I take a quick shower? I'll be literally five minutes.'

Not quite five minutes, but about fifteen later I return to the studio looking a lot less like a big sweaty kid. Samantha is standing at the piano in conversation with Dr Sparks. It sounds intimate and troubled and I enter the room with caution.

'Ah, Solomon,' says Sparks as he spots me, 'you return victorious once more.'

'Oh, not a lot to do with me,' I reply, 'your grandson is a bit of a whizz. He hit everything as hard as he could to Eric's backhand.'

I glance at Samantha. She's not the happy, smiley woman she was before I left. She's also nervously clearing her throat.

'You OK to do this?' I ask.

'Yes,' she replies without sounding at all sure. 'I'm just worried about my son walking in. He's never heard me sing it.'

'Perhaps you'd like to warm up,' says Dr Sparks, who then strikes a low note on the piano to curtail any doubt. I slowly ease my way into an operatic tone, and at Sparks' instruction, Samantha sings along for a few scales as well. I'm encouraged. It's just like we did the other evening, we're blending well together. There's no clash of vibratos, no discrepancy over pitch. Once Sparks feels we've warmed up enough, he plays a few bars introduction and then I sing the first line, '*Là ci darem la mano…*'

It feels odd singing so sedately when fifteen minutes earlier I was hopping around the tennis court like a man possessed. I really have to force myself to get into character, to respect the music and everyone's memories. I'm still a little out of breath, but I manage to produce a tone, which is round and, to my ears at least, seemingly effortless. In fact, the first few exchanges sound very smooth. Samantha clearly knows the aria well, singing without sheet music in that soaring soprano I first heard in the centre of Bath. But it's after the phrase, '*non son più forte*,' that the nervous clearing of her throat starts to reappear. I can see she's choking up. I don't know what to do. Do I try and ignore it like Sparks does, or should I put my arms around her? Soon after, she stops singing.

'Sorry,' she says, wiping away a tear, 'this is harder than I thought it would be.'

'No more apologies, remember,' I say, 'you sound incredible. Don't worry about me, let's try it again and when you feel like you're going to lose it, lose the note, or dry up, cough or cry, just keep singing. It doesn't matter what it sounds like right now. This isn't a performance, it's an exercise.'

Sparks turns and raises an eyebrow at me. We start again and at exactly the same point, Samantha stumbles, but I encourage her to keep going and she does, singing through the tears, looking everywhere but at me, with those big, sorrowful eyes. At least this time we manage to get through it, but both Sparks and Samantha seem to have entered a black hole of grief. I don't understand, it's not a particularly emotional song, in my opinion, it's quaint. Don Giovanni is asking Zerlina for her hand in marriage, that's all. And yet, having been sung at Samantha's wedding, and at her husband's untimely funeral, the aria means more to her, more to Sparks, than I'll ever know.

The sound of the latch going on the studio door is a welcome distraction. I'm expecting the kids – the young adults – to come bouncing in, but it's not them, it's Rosa wearing that beaming smile again and carrying a bouquet of white lilies. I'm surprised when she hands them to me.

'Mr Solomon,' she says, 'I have good news, fantastic news... they tell me Consuelo come home tomorrow.'

'That *is* good news,' I reply, 'on your anniversary, as well.' Shit, I think, I haven't called Reverend Walker to confirm. 'This is Samantha, by the way, Eugene's daughter-in-law.'

'Pleased to meet you,' says Rosa.

'And you,' adds Samantha.

'Beautiful flowers,' I say, handing Rosa back the bouquet, 'you couldn't pop them in a vase for me, could you?'

While Rosa is doing just that, I offer to show Samantha the grounds. Maybe the air will blow away some of those blues? 'Grab your coat,' I suggest, 'and let me find you a pair of wellies. It's quite muddy in places.'

As we stroll up the drive, we see the Velasquez kids running and skipping back to the cottage. They're all looking so cheerful, so free, and I can see the uplifting effect it has on Samantha. We then catch sight of Mili, Eric and Eugene junior heading back from the court. Eugene is looking slightly humbled and Mili is pumping her fist. I did warn him that she does not give up.

'Thanks for letting Mili win,' I shout, once they're in earshot.

'Ha ha,' says Mili, 'fortune favours the brave!'

'Actually, when you've all showered, you strong lads…and lass…could you move a bit of furniture for me? All the stuff in the conservatory, except the piano, the large candleholders, and the rug, can go in the garage. Park the Mini outside and put the stuff in its space.'

'What's it worth?' asks Mili, showing off in front of the boys.

'The furniture?' I reply, 'It's just junk.'

'Very funny,' says Mili sarcastically. And then I hear her say to Eugene junior, 'your mum's so pretty, you must take after your dad.' She's never been a good loser or a good winner.

Before I go in search of a pair of wellies, I briefly show Samantha the conservatory, where, just like her father-in-law before her, she is drawn to the magnificent view, marred at the moment by a dormant bulldozer parked beside the hole. But when I tell her that this is where Dr Sparks wants to hold the recital, I sense her mood shift again.

'We can always do something else, you know, if it's that painful.'

'No, I should do it. I know I should do it.' She has her hands in her coat pockets. She's gone cold on me again. 'I hear you went up to Wales for the TV programme,' she says, turning to face me, putting the onus back on me, 'how did it go?'

I decide to bring Samantha into my confidence, at least to some degree. 'It went well, musically,' I say, 'but it's getting a little complicated, a little too personal.' To say the least.

'How do you mean?'

'The producer turns out to be an old acquaintance…an old groupie, to be honest with you, from back in the day.'

'And she still has the hots for you, is that it?'

'Something along those lines,' I reply.

Samantha shakes her head. 'What a life you lead,' she says, 'I can't even begin to imagine.'

I hear the sound of young adults descending. 'Come on,' I say, 'let's go for a walk.'

With Samantha squeezing her feet into a pair of Jenny's wellington boots, we walk through the garden, past the yet-to-flower rose bushes, down a gravel path lined by box hedges, past the allotment, the workshop and the greenhouse. I point out where the tennis court is – that fantastic swathe of blue poking through the skeletal winter foliage.

'Where do you live, by the way?' I ask, as we carry on down toward the vale.

'Daniel Street, in a two-bed flat at the top of a Georgian house. Not quite as grand as this.'

'Nice though. I'm sure it's as elegant as its owner,' I reply.

'Actually, I'm renting it,' she says.

Well done, Solomon.

We cut through an opening in a hedge of fir trees, where the formal gardens end. We trudge through the mud, circle the bulldozer and come to a stop a few feet away from the hole. 'This is what you could see from the window, our eco-pool,' I announce. 'A few days ago, it was an even bigger mess. They've only just put in the lining – organic seaweed something or other. It's taken months even to get this far. And over there,' I point at the next field, 'my wife wants to put a helipad. Can you fathom it, a helipad?'

'The marriage is in peril, but the building work goes on,' says Samantha. She doesn't seem particularly impressed by the opulence. She acts as though I'm trying to sell her a house she doesn't want, a lifestyle she can't afford. Maybe I am? I decide to lighten the topic. I tell her about the day that Ernesto slipped into the hole, about how I rescued him, about him losing his wedding ring, about me buying him and Rosa a new set. But I'm making myself sound like a bloody hero and I feel hypocritical because of Consuelo, because of Lexi, guilty because of how big this property is.

'I told Rosa we'd hold a little ceremony for her and Ernesto,' I explain, wishing now I hadn't made such a sentimental gesture, 'so I can present them with the rings, so they can renew their vows.'

'You like looking after people, don't you,' says Samantha. I'm not sure if she approves or disapproves.

'Yes, but at least I don't have to clean their teeth for them.'

Finally, I manage to make her truly laugh, but my optimism is short lived. 'I really should be getting back,' she says.

'Yep, it's turning cold,' I reply, but I really don't want her to leave. 'When will I see you again? Soon, I hope.' It sounds desperate, romantic, out of context.

Samantha looks at me questioningly. She sighs and I realise that it's not with any longing. 'You're in the middle of a lot of emotional upheaval, Solomon,' she says, 'I'm not sure I'm the answer. I lead an uncomplicated life. I certainly can't compete with all of this.'

'I wouldn't want you to,' I plead. 'Look, it's Rosa and Ernesto's anniversary tomorrow. I've spoken to Reverend Walker, the guy at the Indian. I just have to confirm everything. Consuelo's coming out of hospital; it's a big day for them. Why don't we sing together at the ceremony?'

'What, *Là ci darem la mano*?' She sounds horrified.

'Yes. There won't be many people; it would be like a dry run, none of the pressure.'

Samantha looks away and puffs out her cheeks. 'I'm not sure, Solomon, it's all a bit sudden.'

CHAPTER 29

Back in the studio, and at Dr Sparks' insistence, we run through the aria again. Samantha remains in control of herself, and her voice, but she's simply not investing any emotion or zest into the music. It's a little dead and Sparks knows it. I invite her to stay for lunch, but she explains she promised to take her son back to Bath so he can see some of his old school mates. I get the sense she finds me a little overbearing, a little too intense. There is a soft, refined quality to Samantha that perhaps doesn't sit so well with someone as crude and as bullish as me. I just hope I haven't blown it.

The moment Samantha and her son leave, I make a phone call to Reverend Walker. It's not the man himself that picks up the phone, but some well-spoken elderly lady. She explains that he is not there at the moment, but she has his diary in front of her. I assume she's his secretary.

'Great. Can you see if he's written anything down for tomorrow, four in the afternoon?'

I can hear her flicking a page. 'Yes,' she replies, 'renewal of vows, next to a question mark, is that it?'

Phew. 'Yes, that's it. Can you tell him Solomon Capri called to confirm.' I then give her my address and phone number, asking that she or the reverend call me if there's any problem. This, she promises to do.

Following that piece of good news, I take a walk out in the garden to make sure no one can hear what I'm about to say. I had an email from Petra that came in while I was with Samantha. It's from her non-business email and it reads, 'Please call me at your convenience.'

I settle on a bench down by the tennis court and brace myself. Truth is I don't know what I'm going to say, but I make a vow to stay calm, be polite, and above all, listen.

'Petra? It's Solomon.'

'Hi Solomon. I'm so sorry about yesterday. I mean it…very sorry. And I promise, swear on Eva's life, that I didn't contact you because of her.'

'It's OK,' I reply, 'I'm sorry too. I haven't been very candid with you…I'm having serious marital problems at the moment. It looks pretty terminal.'

'I'm sorry to hear that,' says Petra.

'Yeah…on top of that, the daughter of our housekeeper tried to commit suicide…you can imagine my stress levels right now are pretty high. I'm finding it very difficult to take things in my stride. I over-reacted yesterday. I hope I didn't offend you or Malachi.'

'No, he was worried he might have upset you.'

'Not at all. How is Eva?'

'Oh, she calmed down. She's very sorry as well, realises it was a crazy thing to do at that moment, and that she should forget about it altogether. After all, she has a father. She's just being greedy, she knows that. But, anyway, I have taken her off the project.'

'Why? Not for my benefit surely?'

'She was unprofessional, Solomon. She fully understands. She will work in the office. It's for the good of the show. I just hope this whole thing hasn't put you off…Malachi is really impressed. It would be a blow to lose you because of this.'

'I understand. Thing is I may not be Eva's father anyway, this might all be a storm in a teacup.'

'Exactly,' says Petra, 'we should draw a line under the whole episode.'

'Yep, yes we should.'

'Good. We're aiming to film next week at the Royal Opera House. I hope you can make it.'

'Drop me an email, I won't let you down.'

'Thank you, Solomon. See you next week.'

Well, that's taken the sting out of a potentially hazardous situation. I feel so much better now. I'd really given up hope, and was starting to believe the ITV show was the better option. That show, of course, is still not confirmed.

When I get back to the house, Mili is in the kitchen on her laptop, Eric is looking over her shoulder. I'm in a bloody good mood.

'How are you guys doing?' I ask.

'Starving,' says Mili, 'when's lunch?'

'Oh, it should be soon. I think we're eating in the studio because of Tilda.'

No one responds to my comment. They're both glued to the screen.

'Dad,' says Mili finally, 'I've had a friend request on Facebook from a girl who thinks we might be related.'

'Really? Who's that then?'

'Her name's Eva Cornellisen.'

There's that spade again, slap bang in my face. I can't fucking believe it. She's not going to let this lie. She's coming after me, coming after my family. She's going to hunt me down, hound me, stalk me until she discovers the truth. All that stuff Petra said was bullshit. Eva has lied to her mother, pretended she's going to drop it, and is doing it all behind her mother's back. I am furious. I bet she's been on the Internet looking at pictures of me when I was her age, looking at the similarities. I bet she believes there's no possible alternative to anyone being her real father – her sperm-donating father – than me.

'Oh,' I say to Mili, 'might be on your mother's side, second cousin or something. Or she might be a crazy fan trying to reach me through my kids?'

'She's too young to be a fan of yours, Dad, and too pretty.'

'Thanks Mili. Look, how easy is it to join Facebook?'

Mili looks at me like I'm still living in the Dark Ages. 'Duh! You just go on Facebook.com, give them your email and fill in the questions. Very easy.'

'I guess I can use a different name, other than my real name?'

'Why would you want to do that?' asks Eric.

'Well, there's already five imposters, no one's gonna believe it's me.'

'Of course you can use a false name,' says Mili, 'Mickey Mouse is on Facebook, do you think that's the real one?'

Fifteen minutes later, in the privacy of my study, Tom Bishop from Barnsley signs up to Facebook. He has no profile picture, there is no information about him other than his sex, and he has no friends. Mili shouts out that lunch is ready. I yell back that I'll be down in five. I find Eva Cornellisen immediately. There's only one such name in the London area. I look at her picture and it's definitely her. Facebook is telling me that Eva keeps her information private and if I wish to know more about her, I have to become her friend. How stupid, I might be her father. I can, however, send her a message. Whoop-de-do! I word it very carefully.

Hi Eva, it's me, Solomon. I'm sorry I rushed off like that the other day. It was completely the wrong response and I deeply regret it. I spoke to your mother earlier and she told me you've been taken off the project. I'm sorry about that too. Maybe I can convince her to reverse that decision? You see, I've just found out from my daughter that you've sent her a friend request, and that puts me in a very difficult position. So I'm going to make you a deal. I'll agree to a paternity test if you agree to leave my family alone, at least until the result is known. I am as anxious as you are. Solomon.

I push send and then join the others for lunch.

An hour and a half later, I'm back in the study. I log on to Facebook and check my messages. I have one and it's from Eva.

Please don't think I'm crazy cos I'm not!! When you walked out the other day, I thought it might have been for good. I'm so pissed off with Mum – she won't talk to me about it and has taken me off the project. If you could change her mind that would be great. And I'm sorry if I freaked you out by contacting Emilia. It took me a while to find her, because I didn't realise, until I looked at Wikipedia, that your real name is Capriati. I also sent messages to five Solomon Capri's. I realise now they're all fake. But, thanks. It's very kind of you to offer to have a paternity test. This whole thing is suddenly driving me mad and I don't know why other than I feel such a strong connection to you. I know Mum's filming next week at the royal opera house. Are you coming? If so, maybe we could meet up and get swabbed together? You'll need proof of identity, passport, driving license. I just found out online. Let me know, Eva xxx

Swabbed together? What the fuck does that mean? I google "paternity test" and "Harley Street" and discover that the Harley Street Health Centre provides discreet paternity tests and you do actually get swabbed – no blood involved. I message her back.

Let's meet up the day before filming. It takes about nine days to get the result. If it turns out positive, I would be proud to be your real father. Solomon xxx

You smarmy bastard, Solomon, you lying, manipulative bastard. I get a message back almost immediately.

You just made me cry.

CHAPTER 30

It's so good to see Raffy. Mili was right, his girlfriend, Amy, is a stunner. She's stick thin like a model, like a female version of him. Although, he's already a female version, so I don't know what I mean by that. I even asked him if he wanted to borrow the Porsche and show Amy around Wells, but he reminded me that, unlike his sister, he never actually passed his driving test. And it was great to see my son and daughter with their respective partners go out to the pub together, eat, and not come back drunk or too late. They've really grown up, my kids. I wish Jenny could see them right now.

I spoke to the hospital and they told me we could pick up Consuelo around three this afternoon, which is perfect. I'll bring Rosa and Ernesto with me leaving my lieutenants to usher everyone into place.

I had a very long conversation with Samantha this morning. She was really glad I called and, well, she seemed to find talking openly a lot easier on the phone than she did yesterday in the flesh. She told me that her son came in a little worse for wear last night, that they sat down and had a real heart to heart, went through some old photo albums, shed a lot of tears, and made a vow to each other that they would both try and move on. She also agreed to sing the duet with me this afternoon, and that, out of respect, her son wanted to be there too. She also confessed that she'd been in an on and off relationship with someone for the past two years – a woman, just as I suspected. With her son acting like a guard to the queen's fidelity, it seemed like the less complicated option. Who am I to resent her that?

I've told everyone to try and maintain an air of normality today, to not act weird around Rosa or give away any clues. She's busy preparing a brunch in the main kitchen – bacon, scrambled eggs, beans, toast, black pudding, fried tomatoes, left on a hot plate for anyone who fancies it, as and when they do. I've also asked her to prepare some sandwiches and canapés, a little later, for when we return from hospital this afternoon. She saw me put some champagne in the wine cooler and believes it's all because Consuelo is coming home.

After their crushing defeat in the doubles, Eric asked Mili to hit some balls to his backhand and I can hear them on the tennis court even from here. Mili's cruel laugh and Eric's Scottish roars of frustration. Raffy and Amy are sitting at the kitchen table sharing a glass of orange juice. Raffy is so polite to her, so calm. Conversation is cultured, opinions are expressed reasonably and I see now that he'll be an amazing husband and a great father. They're also chatting away to Rosa, who is as happy as she can possibly be. The atmosphere in Sunnymore is one of joy and optimism.

'How was the pub, last night?' I ask Raffy as I separate the supplements from the Sunday papers.

'Very busy, oh, and there was a bit of an altercation at the bar. That American friend of Mum's…'

'Lexi?'

'Yes, she was drunk and having a right go at the barman about something. They had to escort her out in the end.'

'Did you speak to her?'

'No, she didn't even recognise us. Spoke to Mum though. She rang when we were just about to leave.'

'How is she?'

'She said she felt…displaced.'

'That's odd, she sounded blissed out when I spoke to her the other night.'

'It's probably 'cos we're all here and she's not. Oh, and then Mili grabbed my phone and told her you were with a gorgeous woman yesterday, showing her around the house.'

'Good old Mili,' I reply, looking to the heavens. 'Does your Mum know that Consuelo's coming home today?'

'Yes.'

'Does she know about…?' I tilt my head in Rosa's direction and widen my eyes in faux alarm. Raffy nods. 'Did she say anything?' Raffy shakes his head. Oh well.

I'm cutting things a bit fine, I realise. I've arranged to run through the aria a couple more times with Samantha before I leave for the hospital. I've told her I'll be wearing a suit and she said she would wear something appropriate for the occasion, but not a wedding dress. That made me laugh. She also said she would stop by the barge and pick up her father-in-law's dinner suit, plus something sparkly to wrap around Tilda. This got me confused. I thought Almaviva was in dry dock. She then explained that Glen had parked it back at Hampton Wharf the day before yesterday. Kept that quiet, the cantankerous old bugger.

In the studio, I'm getting antsy. It's two o'clock and I've had a message from Samantha to say she might be late because of some charity half-marathon that's passing through the centre of Bath. I only hope she isn't making excuses. I run through the aria again with Dr Sparks, but with one eye on my watch. Finally, he assures me it cannot get any better and that I should just relax and enjoy the whole affair.

'So, you're OK to get Tilda up to the house?' I ask him, 'I mean, in her wheelchair. It's just the gravel might make it a bit tricky.'

'Don't worry Solomon, I have my grandson and several able-bodied people to help me, should I need it.'

'And you're OK to greet the vicar?'

'Yes, yes, yes, now get your arse out of here.'

I'm in the walk-in closet in my bedroom dusting off my best suit when my mobile rings. I glance at the screen to see who it is. Bizarrely, it's Simon, my agent; he's calling me on a Sunday. That's got to be a first.

'Solomon? It's Simon.' I can hear the urgency, the shakiness in his voice.

'Hi Simon, you sound worried. What's going on?'

'I think I'm in love,' he replies.

'Yeah, you're married, you should be in love.'

'No, I think I'm in love with someone else.'

'Who?'

'Marissa, the girl from ITV. We went out last night to the Savoy Grill, got on like a house on fire, drank cocktails in the American Bar, she had some blow, we ended up booking a room and, well, you can imagine the rest.'

'Simon,' I protest, 'you're married, you have kids. Remember how long it took to get pregnant, the IVF, the money it cost? You have such wonderful quadruplets, don't throw it all away because of one night of passion.'

'You're right,' he gasps. I can sense him slowly calming down.

'Anything else?' I enquire, keen to get back to what I was doing.

'Er…yes. This TV show, Popstar to Operastar.'

'Yeah?'

'Marissa let it slip that they've settled on a final eight.'

'Right. I can tell by your voice I'm not one of them.'

'Look, Solomon, people do drop out, y'know. And if they do, if two or three of them drop out, then you're in, my son.'

Disappointment can cut you like a dagger, but this feels more like a prod with a fish knife right now. 'Look, Simon, don't worry about it. I've got so many things on my plate at the moment, I'm not too concerned about the show.'

'Really?'

'Really.'

'Phew,' says Simon, 'I was a little worried about telling you. There's still plan B though, yeah. Malachi Jones? How's that going, by the way?'

I fall silent.

'Solomon?'

'I'll call you tomorrow,' I say, then hang up.

It's two-thirty. I park the Range Rover outside the cottage and knock on the door, but when Ernesto sees me wearing a suit and tie, he asks if he has time to smarten himself up too. 'Of course,' I reply, realising how appropriate that will be. Rosa is already dressed like she's going to church anyway and I can see she's a little anxious about bringing her daughter home.

Everything goes smoothly at the hospital. There are forms to fill in, of course, but Consuelo is awake, though in my eyes, lacking her usual spark. When I tell her that Raffy is down from London, however, that he was desperately worried about her, that he even has a girlfriend, a spark momentarily returns. It kind of disappears again when I tell her Mili is down too, but I thought she should at least be prepared.

In the car, on the way back, the three of them are chatting away in Spanish. It's almost like old times. Consuelo is becoming more personable with every passing mile, her mother slowly relaxing into her seat, even Ernesto losing some of his self-consciousness. But when we arrive at Sunnymore and the gates open, Consuelo falls ominously silent. It's like she's suddenly confronted with what she did, as though she can see the lights of the ambulance, hear the sirens, see her sisters all in tears. I'm not feeling too comfortable myself and I'm beginning to regret the fuss I've made. But it's too late to back out now. Consuelo wants to know why her sisters aren't there to greet her. She wants to go straight to her room, to change her clothes, to put on some make-up at least. I'm worried she might not want to come out, so I pull her to one side and explain exactly what is going on.

Five minutes past four, I get a text from Mili. 'Everything in place is there a problem?'

I text back: 'Waiting for Consuelo.'

I'm expecting a sarcastic reply but she simply writes, 'OK.'

I decide to test the water. 'Don't laugh when I'm singing opera!'
Again, the reply is simple. 'Promise.'

Five minutes later, Rosa goes up to Consuelo's room – she
still thinks it's some kind of homecoming for her daughter. I can
hear the muffled Spanish, and fear the worst, but after a creak of
bed springs, a shuffling of feet, they return together – Consuelo
looking a little more refreshed and dressed up, but her mood is
worryingly erratic.

It's a muted, almost formal walk up the drive. We go into the
house and Rosa immediately senses that something's going on. It's
quiet. No young adults lounging around, no music, just a visceral
buzz in the background. She heads into the kitchen, expecting
someone to be there. The food has been put out on plates, there
are empty champagne glasses lined up on the kitchen island, but
the kitchen itself is empty. Ernesto, too, is confused. There are no
chairs around the kitchen table.

Kipper looks up momentarily from his bed, but Smooch is
nowhere to be seen. 'Follow me,' I say, and then suddenly realise
I don't have the rings. 'Wait here!' I shout and hurtle up the stairs
where I hear Smooch scampering around on the floor above. I'm
back down in less than thirty seconds.

The only light that's been left on in the family room is a
Bakelite lamp that sits next to the sofa. The curtains are half closed
and the grey light from the windows is making the yellow and
rose furnishings look like they've been sprayed with grey paint.
We pass between the sofa and an old French bookcase and then it
becomes obvious to Rosa, Ernesto and Consuelo that everyone is
in the conservatory. I approach the doors, open one slightly, poke
my head through it, and give Dr Sparks the nod. The old man is
sitting at the piano looking dapper in his dinner suit. He beams
broadly at me and begins to play a song – *The Anniversary Waltz*. I
quickly scan the room, lit church-like by large candles. Samantha
is redolent in turquoise satin, her son, masterful in his military

uniform. Tilda could be ready for Christmas, a crimson sequined shawl wrapped around her upper body. The Velasquez children are sitting in a row on the kitchen chairs, and all but Olivia are swinging their legs. Raffy is standing behind them, next to Amy, Mili and Eric. The Reverend Walker has set himself in front of the piano, several sheets of paper in his hand, gold-framed bifocals perched on his nose. On the floor in front of him is a rectangular antique rug.

I turn to where Rosa, Ernesto and Consuelo should be, but they're not there. Consuelo has balked. She's sitting on the sofa, hair draped over her face, her mother and father pleading with her. This all will rapidly fall apart if I don't get Rosa and Ernesto into that room promptly. I approach them. 'It's OK, leave Consuelo for a while, let her adjust, she's just come out of hospital. Come with me, the pair of you. Oh…and happy anniversary.'

CHAPTER 31

Ernesto is a very proud man, he's also a very secretive man, but when Rosa places that ring on his finger, the frown, the tightly clenched jaw, all aspects of his proud exterior simply melt away. To think that only a few days ago, they sat stony faced in the gatehouse cottage, glaring at me as like I was the enemy. It's hard to believe: the love between the two of them shines brighter than the brightest candle in the room. I am secretly envious.

I hadn't contemplated how touching this would be. Even Mili is wiping away a tear. Tilda too is visibly moved by the sentiment. The only people who remain firmly in control are the two Eugenes – like grandfather, like grandson.

When the renewal of vows is over, Olivia stands up and hands her mother a small bouquet of purple flowers. She then directs Rosa and Ernesto to the two chairs left empty for them, directly between the piano and the conservatory doors. I glance at Samantha. She smiles at me. I think we both feel that singing *Là ci darem la mano* is absolutely perfect for the occasion, and that any pressure has been lifted. With the spotlight so firmly on Rosa and Ernesto, the candles, the half dome of the conservatory, Sparks looking so sharp at the piano – it feels like we've rehearsed this whole thing a thousand times. I never imagined it would turn out like this.

Referring to his sheet, Reverend Walker introduces us, and the aria, and then stands to one side as we approach the piano. There is gentle applause from the younger Velasquez girls. I briefly look at Mili in anticipation of a smirk, but she's wrapped up in a kiss with Eric. What's happened to her? What's happened to everyone? Sparks nods affirmatively at me, hands me my music, and begins the introduction. He looks so dapper, I can't help but have a brief flashback of when I first met him on the barge, wearing those giant tartan slippers and mistaking me for the Tesco deliveryman.

It brings a smirk to my face, which I know people will read as the confident smile of someone who has performed many times before. I turn to Samantha and sing the opening lines: '*Là ci darem la mano, là mi dirai di sì...*' I admit, it's not the most demanding of arias for me and it's well within my range. I feel comfortable, my voice is resonating well and there are no notes or phrases that are going to test me. In a sense, I'm more concerned about Samantha, whether she'll hold it together, but when she sings the lines, '*Vorrei e non vorrei, mi trema un poco il cor...*' any concern I may have had immediately disappears. We're growing in stature, the pair of us. We begin to act a little, something, which we hadn't rehearsed. She seems to have absolutely no problem pretending that I'm asking for her hand in marriage. I only hope her son isn't too horrified.

It's no surprise to me when the conservatory doors open. I'd anticipated Consuelo slinking in, drawn by the music, and I'd made a vow not to let it affect me like it did a few days ago in the studio. I'm not going to let Samantha or Dr Sparks down, and I don't. My next word '*Andiam!*' is rousing and loud, prompted by Samantha's perfect rendition of the line she struggled with so much yesterday. My singing partner has tears in her eyes, but she's staying firmly in the present, transforming a tragic memory into a glorious sound.

I glance for a split second at Samantha's son whose head is bowed – this must be tough for him – and then tell myself to focus on the middle distance. We finish majestically. Samantha is relieved and thrilled, and regardless of her son being there, I throw my arms around her and plant a kiss on her cheek. The applause is bountiful. 'Bravo!' I hear, 'Bravo!' Is that Tilda shouting? It bloody well is.

I feel so proud standing next to Samantha. During the performance, I caught a glimpse of that same mesmerising creature I first heard in the streets of Bath. I realise my feelings for her have fallen into sharp focus. We're good together, good for one another, I know it. I just wish she would give me a chance to get closer.

After the ceremony, we all head to the kitchen and within seconds there's a healthy amount of turmoil. The younger Velasquez girls are jumping around with half-eaten sandwiches, fussing over Consuelo, who, in turn, is fussing over Raffy despite the fact that a slightly protective Amy is clinging to his arm. Mili and Eric are talking tennis with Eugene junior, although he seems quite fascinated with Consuelo. I spot him looking across at her from time to time. Dr Sparks and Samantha are explaining to a very understanding, very contrite Reverend Walker why the aria we sang means so much to them, while in the corner, Tilda – I don't know how or why – is perched on Ernesto's lap, drinking a glass of champagne.

A radiant Rosa comes across and offers me a glass. 'Thank you, Mr Solomon,' she says, 'I am so happy, Ernesto is so happy!' She looks at her ring and then kisses me on the cheek.

A second later, Samantha walks up and informs me she has to take her son back to the train station, so might have to make a move pretty soon. 'Well done,' I say, 'you sounded like a pro.'

'Thank you,' she replies, 'you too, but then you already are.' There are kisses from Samantha and a handshake with Eugene Junior. Dr Sparks comes across and informs me he's going to walk them up the drive.

'We'll be out of your hair tomorrow, Solomon,' he says, 'Tilda and me, back to that freezing old barge.'

'You know,' I say, 'there's no hurry. Maybe you should wait until the weather warms up a bit.'

Sparks nods politely, but I can sense his resolve.

'I didn't get the TV show, by the way,' I confess, 'Popstar to Operastar.'

The old man seems vaguely amused. 'But you still have the other one, yes? Malachi Jones Goes To The Royal Opera House?'

All I can think of at that moment is someone taking a swab from the inside of my mouth. 'Don't hold your breath,' I reply.

'Well, there's always a series of recitals featuring the great Alberto Balsam. Then perhaps an audition for Bath Opera. I hear they're hoping to do *Don Giovanni* next.'

'Yep,' I nod, 'my life in opera has only just begun.'

It's approaching ten o'clock. I'm alone in the house. I've just left Mili, Eric, Raffy, Amy and the Velasquez girls, in the studio with Dr Sparks, watching Tim Burton's *Alice in Wonderland* on the big screen. Mili's being super nice to Consuelo. Sparks, thankfully, is yet to light up a spliff.

It's weird. Earlier on, I sent a friend request from Tom Bishop of Barnsley to my wife, Jenny, and even though there is absolutely no information about him, she accepted. Tom is now Jenny's friend. I've seen all the pictures of her skiing, read a lot of her updates, some of which are a little too revealing about the state of our marriage with sideswipes at me. But the latest update is even more alarming. There's a picture of her – you can't see the top half of her face, just the lower half. She's pushing her boobs together, into as big a cleavage as she can muster. The comment attached is, 'About to do something I've always wanted to do. Watch this space!'

There are nine 'likes' or thumbs up, and a comment from Lexi. 'Go for it girl!' I always told Jenny that if she ever had a boob job, I'd divorce her. I guess that threat means nothing now.

I know it's late, and I know that maybe I shouldn't, but I call Samantha. After one ring, she answers.

'Hiya,' I say.

'Hiya,' she replies.

'Not in bed are you?' I ask.

'No, just having a cup of tea and reading my book.'

'What are you reading?'

'*Wolf Hall* by Hilary Mantell.'

'Oh, yeah. Didn't she win the Man Booker prize?'

'That's what it says on the cover.'

There's a pause as I try and summon the courage to speak honestly. 'I thought we sounded great together today,' I suggest.

'We did,' she replies, 'yet again. Thanks for asking me to do it.'

'Your son wasn't too horrified then?'

'No, he's beginning to understand.'

Again I fall silent. There's so much I want to say. I feel that stupid lump in my throat again. 'You know, a long time ago I had a musical partner. He was the guitarist in our band, I don't know if you remember. His name was Fran. He died, unfortunately, when he was still a young man. He was my best friend and we had this remarkable connection. My wife said something the day before she left, she said that when Fran died it felt like the sun had disappeared from our lives. She was right.' I feel a tear roll down my left cheek and have to catch my breath. 'But when I was singing with you today, it felt like that sun had finally returned.'

Samantha says nothing. She can hear I'm emotional. I hear an occasional sniff – maybe she's crying too?

'I'm not who you think I am,' I continue, 'this house…it's not me, it's not who I am. I don't care where I live. I don't need all this, I need to feel the connection I felt today…I need to be with you…'

There's another pause. 'Maybe we can meet up for lunch sometime next week,' she says meekly. It's not what I want to hear.

'I mean now.'

'Solomon, it's late.'

'Don't tell me you've got a scaling and root planing to do at nine?'

'No, I need to resolve something, just like you do.'

'OK, one last request…let me hear you sing over the phone.'

'Solomon, there's an elderly couple living downstairs, they're probably in bed.'

'Not loud, not opera. Sing some Joan Baez for me, make me go to bed with a smile on my face. Fetch your guitar, put the phone down and sing for me.'

'You're so silly,' she replies. But, thankfully, I hear her comply. I hear the clunk of a guitar, a quick attempt to tune it. She picks up the phone again. 'Are you still there?'

'Yes.'

'Here goes…' she places the phone somewhere close enough for me to hear her, and starts to finger-pick the nylon strings, then she sings, 'Virgil Caine is my name and I served on the Danville train, till Stoneman's cavalry came and tore up the tracks again…'

It's hard to believe, hard to admit, I've seen U2 play the LA Sports Arena in 1992 during their Zoo Station tour, I saw Aretha Franklin not long after in Detroit, playing in front of her home crowd. I saw Talking Heads in London on their Stop Making Sense tour, Nina Simone at Ronnie Scott's, and in 1980, I watched Joy Division at the Moonlight Club in West Hampstead. But right now, at the age of forty-nine, with all that has been going on lately, *The Night They Drove Old Dixie Down* sung by Samantha and coming out my phone's tiny speaker seems like the most incredible thing I've ever heard. I think I may have resolved something. Before the song is even finished, I'm in my car heading for Bath.

CHAPTER 32

'I wasn't sure you were gonna let me in,' I admit. I'm sitting in an armchair in the living room of Samantha's warm and cosy flat in Bath. There's a small television to the right of the fireplace, a stack of CDs to the left, and shelves either side of the alcove stuffed full of paperback and hardback books. The walls are covered in a cream wallpaper with faint gold stripes, and, on a semi-circular, foldaway dining table pushed against one wall, are framed photographs of various family members, and of Samantha performing in numerous operas. Samantha is sitting on her yellow sofa in a pair of jeans and an ivory cashmere sweater with her feet tucked up beside her. In front of the sofa is a low cherry wood coffee table. Propped up against the sofa is Samantha's Spanish guitar.

'Well, it's always good to see how the other half lives,' she jokes.

'So you're my other half, are you?'

'I'm beginning to feel like it, can't get rid of you,' she replies, 'besides any man who'll listen to my Joan Baez impersonation can't be all that bad.'

I think that's the first time she's given me any romantic encouragement.

'Actually, I'm glad you came over,' she continues, 'that was fun today. A little hurdle cleared. Sorry I don't have any wine to celebrate.'

'That's OK, I have to drive back,' I say, hoping she'll say I can stay the night.

Samantha simpers at me like I'm a newborn kitten behind glass in a pet shop. 'So,' she says, 'busy week ahead?'

'Yeah,' I reply, imagining just how strange it will be seeing Eva again, 'you could say that.'

'Care to elaborate?'

I'm not convinced my piece of news is going to endear me any more to Samantha, but I realise I'm going to have to confess to a lot of things if I really want her to see the real me.

'Remember I mentioned yesterday about that Malachi Jones show getting a little personal, a little complicated?'

'Yes, I remember: the groupie that still has the hots for you.'

'Yeah, well, that was a bit of white lie.' I hesitate and nervously brush my hand over the chair's arm. 'I'm going for a paternity test on Tuesday,' I admit, 'with that groupie's oldest daughter.'

Samantha gawps. 'Am I the first person, you've told?' she asks.

'Yes.'

'Oh my. What are the chances, do you think?'

'The same as Russian Roulette?'

'I mean, does she look like you?'

'A little like my grandmother, I guess.'

'So is this just coincidence? Is this entrapment? Is this why this groupie got in touch with you after all these years?'

'Petra, her name's Petra, and I'm inclined to believe her when she says not. She's actually a lovely lady, just recovering from the big C.'

'How do you think your kids will react if it turns out to be positive?'

'I've no idea. To be honest, they keep surprising me, so maybe they'll be forgiving, maybe it'll give me a little kudos even?'

'What about your wife?'

My grimace says it all.

'We haven't talked about your wife, have we?' Samantha continues, 'Do you want to?'

'Not really. What about your…friend? Do you want to talk about her?'

'Not really,' she says, swinging her feet onto the carpet and looking at me like she hasn't been entirely honest herself. 'I was lying about the wine,' she adds. 'I've got some red in the cupboard. It's just a screw-top, would you like a small glass?'

'That would round off a lovely evening, thank you.'

Samantha returns with two glasses, places them on the coffee table and beckons me to sit on the sofa beside her.

'So, when will you find out the result?' she asks, taking a sip.

'Nine days after the test. Nine days that could seal my fate.' I too take a sip. 'Look, while I'm being honest,' I add, 'I have to tell you that things aren't quite what they seem with me…the big house, the staff, the cars, this lavish lifestyle I lead, it's funded to a large degree by my wife. She's the one with the money, really, and I believe she's about to cash in her chips. There's a pre-nup, from the days when my career was on the up and up – my fault. If things got nasty, I don't know what my financial situation would be.'

'So you might end up destitute then?' says Samantha, teasing me, 'I'm not sure if I'd fancy you if you did.'

'Does that mean you do now?'

She doesn't answer me.

'Do you mind if I put some music on?' she says.

'Of course not. What did you have in mind?'

'Wait and see,' says Samantha, putting down her glass and getting up off the sofa. I watch her as she browses her selection, making a bit of a mess in the process.

'You have a lot of CDs,' I say. 'Have you not thought of getting an iPod and just copying them all across? Save a lot of space.'

'That's what my son keeps saying. I've just never got round to doing it.'

'I could do it for you. I'd love to. I could buy an iPod, get it engraved. "Samantha and Solomon forever."'

Samantha chuckles. 'You are irrepressible,' she replies, as she locates the CD she's been looking for, then kneels and places it in the pop-up lid of that old ghetto blaster she has. The music begins to play. 'You make me want to sing about love, every time

I raise my head…' It's *Slow* by Rumer, the song I played the other evening when Samantha broke down.

'You bought the CD,' I say.

'The very next day,' she replies.

For a moment, she seems lost in the music. She hasn't moved, still on her knees by the old, plastic ghetto blaster. I can see her eyes watering and I wonder if I'm going to lose her once again to the memory of her husband. But then she stands, moves the coffee table carefully out of the way, and holds out her hand.

'Shall we dance?' she asks.

'If you insist,' I reply, standing up and feeling like I've just walked out from a cold kitchen into the hot morning sun.

The song's chorus drifts in as Samantha puts her arms around my waist, her head on my shoulder.

'Slow, slow this right down, don't burn it out, don't let it show. Slow, oh how my heart is racing, to hold your gaze and let it go…'

I don't know what it looks like from the outside, but inside I feel like a teenager smooching with the hottest girl at the disco. I just hope she's not using me as some exercise in grief, dipping her toe in the water to see if it's OK to dive in, because my heart really is racing.

But then she puts her face up to mine and we kiss, gently at first and then so passionately, I almost don't recognise her. She has so much unexpressed desire, so much longing. I don't know why I'm surprised. I've heard her sing with such spirit, but to feel it now with her lips against mine? It's overwhelming. I just hope to God this song segues into Marvin Gaye's *Let's get it on*, because I'm finding it hard to restrain myself. We hold each other and sway, turning in a small circle.

'You never know until you kiss someone, do you?' she says, putting her head back on my chest, 'You can talk, flirt, joke, sing, but you're never really sure until that first kiss.'

'And now you are?' I ask.

She doesn't answer me directly. She closes her eyes. 'Shit, I'm so turned on,' she admits, somewhat out of character, pulling a face of absolute frustration, 'I could drag you into the bedroom right now.'

'But you won't...because?' I reply.

'Because I want to remember this as it is right now. I want this to be a new memory. Over the next few days, until I see you again, whenever I'm scraping away at someone's teeth, or poking at their gums, I want to think back to this moment and feel as warm inside as I do now.'

She sounds horribly reasonable. 'I think I'm falling in love with you,' I say. And I mean it.

She looks away briefly. 'You're a married man, Solomon,' she says, 'I really don't want to be the other woman.'

'No, I don't want you to be either.'

It's nine days after the paternity test. I'm sitting in the kitchen staring at the letter that arrived this morning from Harley Street Health Centre. It's eleven a.m. and I'm on my fifth cup of coffee. I'm not at all surprised when my phone rings. It's Eva. I'm more surprised she didn't ring earlier.

'Solomon, have you received the letter yet?'

'Yes, I have.'

I hear an intake of breath. 'How do you feel?' she asks.

I'm not quite sure how I feel. A part of me really is proud, another part feels cheated.

'Well...to be honest,' I admit, 'it's what I expected. I was looking at old photographs of my grandmother, on my father's side, last night – your great-grandmother, I guess, and well, you should come down some time. I'll show you all the old family albums. Congratulations, you have a little Italian Jewish in you.' I hear her laugh. 'More importantly, how do you feel?'

'Confused,' she admits, 'on the one hand it answers a burning question that has been eating away at me, but on the other hand it doesn't really change anything. I haven't told Mum. She doesn't know about the paternity test or the result. I haven't put it on Facebook either.'

Now I'm laughing.

'You know,' she continues, 'I don't have to tell anyone, I just needed to know. What do you think, how would your kids take it?'

'I don't know…maybe they won't mind. It's not like they're five year-olds and you've just stolen their toys or moved into one of their bedrooms. They're great kids. You'd get on really well with them.'

'What about your wife?'

'That could be more problematic. I should probably call her right now.'

'OK,' says Eva, 'great news about you singing before the Royal Opera House panel. You must be really chuffed.'

'Yeah, Malachi has been really inspirational.'

'I guess I'll see you then…promise I won't call you Dad.'

That makes me chuckle. 'You're not too old to be put across my knee, young lady,' I jest.

'You could try,' she replies, 'but just to warn you, I'm a black belt in karate. See you next week.'

As soon as I get off the phone to Eva, I call Jenny. I know she won't answer but I intend to leave a message in such a tone that curiosity might well get the better of her.

'Jenny,' I say, calmly and quietly, 'I've just had some news, some family news, and I think you might want to hear it. If you could call me back, I'd greatly appreciate it.'

It takes twenty minutes but finally she does.

'What's wrong Solomon,' she says, 'is Mili pregnant? Is it your mum?'

'No,' I reply, 'but you might want to sit down…'

CHAPTER 33

It's Sunday, June the 5th, an unusually clear, hot day. Samantha and I have been lounging by the pool all afternoon. You should see it now – once the council signed off on the project, I got rid of the reeds and the lilies, and put in some chlorine filters and some heating. There's a bar down there as well, with a small refrigerator. It's looking less and less eco as the summer progresses.

I've been seeing Samantha regularly over the past few months. I guess you could say we're an item. She convinced me to join Bath Opera – I couldn't really say no, she was naked and pinning me down at the time. The director came to a recital in our conservatoire and pretty much offered me the lead part in *Don Giovanni* there and then. I played opposite Samantha, and every night when we got to sing *Là ci darem la mano*, she had a little tear in her eye and would silently mouth the words, 'Thank you.' The reviews were excellent too, although it didn't take long for the local press to work out just who Alberto Balsam really was. *Don Giovanni* only ran for a week, and then it was back to filming with Malachi. Oh, I forgot to mention, I sang before the Royal Opera House panel and landed the lead part in *Jerusalem: The Opera*.

And yet I'm still anxious about this evening. They're airing the first instalment of Popstar to Operastar tonight. I've seen the line up and still can't believe they didn't want Solomon Capri. Perhaps, once I hear all the contestants sing, I'll realise why. We're having a small gathering in the studio to celebrate – or commiserate – and we'll put it on the big screen. Dr Sparks is coming down with Tilda, who is now walking with a stick and speaking, albeit with a slight slur. The Velasquez family will join us too, but not Consuelo. She has returned to El Salvador where she is working for Pastors, Francisco and Celia Pablo at their Mercy of God mission. She sends the occasional letter to her parents, but, as of yet, there has been no mention of a divine child. It seems it was, in fact, more of a fantasy than the one of me singing opera in front of thousands, and that Fran's numbers, at least, were correct.

Far from being angry, and much to my relief, Mili and Raffy were delighted to have an older half-sister. Raffy often gets together with Eva in London and, of course, they're all friends on Facebook. Jenny, though, didn't take kindly to the news. That's when she started divorce proceedings. In all fairness to her, she's offered me the house and, what most people would consider, a large amount of money. The helipad project, however, has not gone ahead.

Around seven-thirty, Rosa puts out a few plates of *amuse-bouche* on the kitchen island. She's made these lovely little blini with toppings of sour cream, chopped egg yolk, chives and caviar. They're so delicate and scrumptious and go so well with the champagne. The television is already on and during the advert breaks they're running trailers for the show – very well shot trailers, in my opinion – I get such butterflies in my stomach when I see them. I look around me, at Samantha, and Dr Sparks. They're so relaxed, not really looking at the screen. Rosa is busy preparing duck à l'orange, Ernesto is deep in conversation with Tilda. It really seems like a miracle recovery from when I first saw her at the barge. The two younger Velasquez girls are sliding around the floor in their socks, but Olivia is sitting alone, deep in concentration. She's now sleeping in Consuelo's old bedroom. I've redecorated the entire gatehouse cottage so, thankfully, she doesn't have to look at old pictures of me.

The show unfolds. They have two new judges, which is an immediate improvement, but I feel so bad for the contestants. I can see the fear in their eyes, each person desperate not to fuck up, not to be the first one booted out. I remember Dr Sparks' words, the first day I met him on the barge. 'Your heart will be beating fast, you will be sweating, your mouth will be dry.' He was so right.

The singing is really shaky and no one is managing to adopt a truly operatic tone. There are far better singers in the chorus of Bath Opera. The more I watch, the more uncomfortable it becomes, and the more I feel like I've escaped the jaws of death. Samantha pulls a face that says, 'Thank God that's not you up there.' I expect Perry Lighthouse is sat at home watching it too, thinking the same thing about himself…unless of course he's back in Africa saving the world. At one point, Olivia turns to me and says, 'You sing much better than these people, Mr Solomon.'

'Thanks Olivia,' I reply.

And then the texts start coming in, all basically saying the same thing. 'Watching PS 2 OS lucky escape, Solomon.' Funnily enough, I remember so clearly why I was so keen on it in the first place, so obsessed – something to do with rescuing my marriage? Well that worked, didn't it? And yet, the crazy thing is, it set me on a path and in a month's time I'll be singing at the Royal Opera House. What a journey. It reminds me of something else Dr Sparks said on that first day. 'The question you need to ask is whether the journey is more important than the destination. Will these efforts make you a better man? Will you have learned something about yourself?'

Who am I to judge? I look back at the room and see Samantha chatting away to Rosa. I accept I've played a part in Samantha's rejuvenation, a rather selfish one at times, and having her as a partner, and a musical partner, has filled the void left by both Jenny and Fran. Perhaps taking Tilda off that freezing barge for a few days, surrounding her with life, running her around the garden in a wheelbarrow has hastened her recovery? But what about Consuelo? Did I help her, or was she violently forced to change, to swap one obsession for another, to become a force for good in the world as though that was her destiny all along? I don't know. My champagne glass is empty and I've got a terrible feeling that Midge Ure, another friend of a friend, another fully paid up member of the West Country Semi-Retired Pop Stars' Club, who, just as Fran had predicted, did make it onto the show, will be voted out first tonight. I hope the journey was worth his while.

Six weeks later, I'm back at the Savoy, in the same river view room 720. I had slight concerns about bringing Samantha here, because of what happened to me and Jenny following both our stays in this hotel. But I set them aside, treated them as superstitions, simply because I wanted Samantha to see this remarkable view. We're both standing at the window, watching the London Eye revolve incrementally.

'Nervous about tonight?' she asks.

'Not as nervous as I was before the first performance of Don Giovanni,' I reply.

'The dress rehearsal sounded amazing,' she adds, 'how's the throat?'

'Holding up. I just need a bit of steam and to keep sucking these sweets. Sorry about the smell. Promise I'll brush my teeth before I kiss you.'

'You can kiss me any time,' she says. So I do. I swallow the sweet and put my lips to Samantha's, my arms around her, my menthol-liquorice tongue in her mouth. I wonder if the people in the Eye can see us?

'I still can't get used to that moustache,' she says, when we both pull away. 'I like your hair shorter though.'

'I promise to shave it off once this is done, the moustache, I mean. How are Eugene and Tilda doing?'

'They're so excited. They can't believe their room. So sweet of you to invite them.'

'Yeah, well, I didn't know they'd put them next door. We're gonna have to keep the noise down.'

Samantha chuckles. 'What time's the car?'

'Six. Malachi wants us all to be there early.'

'OK, I'm gonna take a quick shower.'

'Mind if I join you?'

'I insist.'

The big moment has arrived. The cast is gathered backstage and Malachi is really geeing us up. We're all in costume – me in a Prussian brass-spiked helmet, World War II goggles around my neck, Silky Swann in her fairy wings and Richard Crawley is wearing round specs, a boater and a white jacket. Peter Duffy looks nutty and natty as a Morris dancer, and all the other cast members are dressed like the cool, young dudes they really are. We can hear the audience gathering, members of the orchestra picking at or tooting away on their various instruments. Petra, whose hair has grown back like a feral mane, comes up and gives me a big hug, as does Eva. They'll be sitting in the audience in one of the boxes along with Samantha, Mili, Raffy, Dr Sparks and Tilda. Jenny has chosen to sit elsewhere.

I realise after Silky goes on and sings *Jerusalem*, and I look out at the audience in this stunning theatre, just how special this moment is. This beats hands down the first time I appeared on Top of the Pops or our first number one or the time Fortune Favours The Brave played to more than one hundred thousand people in Rio. The opera is so well constructed, so well directed, it performs itself. It's like a brain and a heart totally in sync. I am carried along and away by the music, the lyrics travelling unconsciously from my mind to my mouth, swear words and all – the actions and movement drilled into me, already practised a thousand times. There is a slight malfunction with my loudhailer at one point, and the scene where I get beaten up feels a little unreal. I struggle with one of the high notes, but it matters very little. The show goes by in a flash and before we know it, we are being slapped on the back and applauded by Malachi and the crew backstage. If I could, I would go back on stage and do it all again. I will tomorrow, so I really better save my voice.

I know I shouldn't drink, but back in the dressing room I can't resist the celebratory glass of champagne. I'm still in my make-up, wearing my wife-beater vest, when there's a knock on the dressing room door. It's Simon, my agent.

'Fucking hell, Solomon, I didn't recognise you out there, you can really fucking sing,' he says. 'Arms are looking good as well,' he adds, 'you been doin' weights?'

'Yeah,' I admit, 'just for the part really.'

'Mate,' he continues, 'I'm really impressed. Did you hear the audience? He's done it again, Malachi Jones, I can't believe he's pulled this off. Er…I've got Marissa outside, do you mind if I bring her in?'

'I don't mind.'

Two minutes later and we're joined by Petra, Eva, Raffy, Mili, Dr Sparks, Tilda and Samantha. And it's not a big dressing room. I have two bottles of champagne on ice and I start pouring a little into the glasses provided, trying to make sure everyone has a drink. Sparks comes across at one point, nudges me and says, 'I don't suppose you have any Hobnobs do you?'

I quickly scan the crudités, the nuts, the crisps, the large bowl of fruit. 'I could ask one of the runners…maybe someone in the next dressing room…'

He peers at me through his thick glasses and says, 'I'm joking, for God's sake. Great job. A little shaky on the top F, but I'm sure no one noticed.'

'Thanks. I knew you bloody would.'

'Pull your chin back tomorrow when you hit that note. Pull the stomach in, clench those buttocks. It's not far off.'

It's like a scene from a dream, that old cliché about all the events of your life leading up to this one peak moment. I think I'm truly happy. And then I remember that Jenny was in the audience.

'Have you seen your mum?' I whisper to Mili.

'Yes. She thought you sounded great.'

'Is she still here?'

'She was waiting outside in the corridor...she didn't want to come in. She might still be there.'

Everyone is chatting and laughing, introducing themselves to each other, explaining how they're connected to me. Thoroughly on a high from the show, no one, except maybe Mili, notices me slip out of the dressing room. The corridor outside is empty of people save for two ageing security guards who for some reason are dressed in gleaming white suits. They both smile at me with immaculate teeth. There's no sign of Jenny, but I notice a glow at the far end of the hall – a golden glow. And then I catch sight of a Cuban-heeled figure standing with his back against the wall, eyes firmly on the phone in his hand, occasionally puffing from a cigarette in the other. It's Fran. I'm still in this vest with a ridiculous blacked-in moustache, hair, shorter than it's been for years, face, caked in make-up. He doesn't look up, doesn't speak until I'm a few feet away.

'I see you didn't take my advice then,' he says.

'No, Fran, just went with the flow.'

'Probably wise.' A pause. 'Damn!' he suddenly yelps.

'What's wrong?'

'I'm playing Super Mario and I just fell off a bridge.' Finally he turns to face me. 'Whoa, Solomon, you look scary. Not sure about the 'tache.'

'It's just for the show,' I reply.

'Or the arms, or the pecs. You look like that Schwarzenegger bloke.'

'Hardly. Anyway, why do you need a phone all of a sudden?'

'Got a bit bored, borrowed it from one of the dressing rooms. Don't worry I'll give it back. I just came to say goodbye.'

'Really...where are you going?'

'Moving on, Solomon. Fran's just a name, just a memory. I'm moving up in the world.'

'Where? What are you gonna become?'

'A ball of pure spiritual energy.'

'What…like a soul?'

'Soul, spirit, call it what you like. I'm gonna become a part of something greater than myself. Have you not read Deepak Chopra?'

'No. You mean I won't see you again?'

'No, mate, you found a new muse.'

'Where?'

'In there, in your dressing room, the opera woman.'

'So you're saying you were my muse up until the day you died.'

'And after. I was there, hovering around you when you were trying to write a new song, waiting for you to hit that patch of frustration, the brick wall where I could jump in and provide a divine spark. But you always gave up too easily, didn't give me a chance.'

'Wow, now it all makes sense.'

'Anyway, I'd better give this guy his phone back then climb that silver ladder back upstairs. Bye Solomon.'

'Just like that? Aren't you gonna wish me luck?'

'You don't need luck, mate, you've got Samantha. Treat her well.'

THE END

Lightning Source UK Ltd.
Milton Keynes UK
UKOW03f1908290117

293149UK00004B/100/P

6285734R00201

Printed in Great Britain
by Amazon.co.uk, Ltd.,
Marston Gate.